AFTER TODAY

JACQUELINE HAYLEY

Editing by Sarah Proulx Calfee www.threelittlewordsediting.com

JacquelineHayley
Romance ♥

Dedicated to Kylie Scott, who wrote the greatest ever zombie romance novel.

ACKNOWLEDGMENT

This novel was written on Wiradjuri Country in Central West NSW, Australia. I would like to acknowledge the Wiradjuri people who are the Traditional Custodians of the Land, and pay my respects to the Elders both past and present.

CHAPTER ONE

Fuck. Fuck-fuck-fuckity-fuck.

Mackenzie Lyons fell back against the sofa cushions, letting papers from her current case fall haphazardly onto her crossed legs.

What did it matter if some pages dipped into her wonton soup? What did anything matter now?

If what she'd just read was true...

God*damn* Peter for throwing this case into her lap. Shaking herself, she reached for her cell—knocking more papers into her Chinese takeaway—and dialed his number. Her knee jittered when his familiar voice mail picked up. The man couldn't keep his phone battery charged if his life depended on it.

And it just might.

"Peter, you need to call me back. This Northern Memorial Hospital case you handed me, it's—" She paused. "Just call me back. Unless you're still coming over tonight..." She trailed off. He could be such a dick boyfriend sometimes. Case in point, canceling their dinner reservation at the last minute and leaving her to drown her feelings in wonton soup. Alone. "Look, I'm not mad about tonight. But this is urgent. Call me as soon as you get this message."

Was this actually happening?

Anxiety bloomed in Mackenzie's chest, hot and heavy.

Standing, she turned on the television, flicking channels to find a live newsfeed.

Just more right-wing male politicians, claiming they had a right to determine what a woman did with her uterus.

Nothing on Sy-V.

For several days now, reports had been popping up all over social media on Sy-V—a virus that had originated in the Syrian refugee camps. A virus that was having unprecedented mortality rates. A virus that apparently didn't rate any sort of mention on tonight's news.

Most media outlets were taking their cue from the president of the United States, who was casually dismissing the suspected pandemic as a fake-news media conspiracy.

Never mind the multiple accounts that hospitals in the UK, Germany, and France were overflowing with people suffering severe headaches, coughing, and nosebleeds.

Only today the president had blatantly disregarded recommendations from the World Health Organization—his trumped-up media briefing sitting uneasily with Mackenzie. And now...

Now, Northern Memorial needed Baker & Baker's legal service to confirm there were no environmental factors that had led to the sudden death of thirty-six patients. Patients who'd all recently returned from overseas and had all suffered severe flu-like symptoms.

With nose bleeds.

Nope, Mackenzie wasn't nearly experienced enough to deal with this situation, and she sure as hell wasn't prepared for the knowledge that Sy-V was, in fact, in North America.

Because if Sy-V was in the US—in Chicago—surely *she*, Mackenzie Lyons, slightly incompetent and definitely inexperienced, shouldn't be the person to figure it out?

She wasn't a heroine in some Hollywood blockbuster. She was a twenty-six-year-old environmental lawyer, living in Lincoln Park and trying to forget Sanford, the hometown she knew had forgotten her the moment she'd skipped out.

Feeling somewhat suspended from reality, she muted the television and stared blankly at the wall. If it was Sy-V that had caused the deaths at Northern Memorial, shouldn't she call someone? The mayor? The governor? *The Chicago Review?*

Instead, she called Chloe.

"Mac, what are you doing calling so late?" her best friend asked, sounding wide awake from Sanford. Chloe's husband, Ash, must be traveling for work. She never slept well when he was away.

"I need you to tell me I'm not crazy."

"Okay. What are you being not crazy about? Is Peter being a jerk?"

"You've heard about Sy-V, right?"

"That super-flu?"

"What if I told you it could be in Chicago?"

"What? I was just on Twitter, the only thing trending was Lady Gaga's new release."

"I'm serious, Chlo."

"Hang on, let me turn on the television."

"I don't think anyone else knows about it yet," Mackenzie said.

There was a pause, and she could hear Chloe switching through news channels.

"Honey, how many coffees have you had today?" Chloe gently asked.

3

"Three. Okay, five. But this isn't a caffeine-induced paranoia. Peter gave me this new case, and Northern Memorial has these unexplained deaths..." She stopped.

She was breaking all sorts of confidentiality clauses, and she *did not* want to get fired. She wouldn't be able to afford this overpriced apartment, and she'd have to move back to— oh god. Sanford. Mac shuddered.

Did she seriously think that she'd know something of this magnitude before anyone else? Maybe that fifth coffee hadn't been a great idea.

"Mac, I want you to drink a big glass of water and go to bed. Straight to bed. *Do not* get on the internet and start doomsday scrolling. Do you hear me? Straight to sleep."

"Okay," she said meekly. "Sorry for calling so late."

"Call whenever. You know that."

WAS IT JUST HER IMAGINATION, or was the L significantly less crowded this morning? Mackenzie easily found a seat as the automatic doors slid shut, breathing a relieved sigh as she dumped her work files onto the free seat beside her.

Although unrepentant about wearing heels on public transport, she was grateful for the rare opportunity to sit on the commute to her office downtown.

"This is a complete shit show," muttered the passenger to her right.

Mackenzie glanced over, realizing the man had been talking to himself, his bespectacled eyes glued to the screen of his smartphone. It appeared the White House was holding yet another press conference and, in what was becoming an increasingly common scenario, it had quickly deteriorated into chaos.

"And it will go away," said the president as he gestured wildly, distinctly lacking any calm himself. "Just stay calm. It will go away."

The same anxiety that sat heavily in her chest last night threatened to creep up her throat. Forcing herself to look away from the media briefing, Mackenzie brought the heel of her hand to her chest and rubbed. She swallowed as her eyes came to rest on the work files.

"Is it unpatriotic to admit our president is a dickhead?" Bespectacled said, putting his phone away.

"What'd you say?"

Mackenzie jumped in her seat. Another passenger turned to confront Bespectacled, spittle flying from his fleshy mouth. "You're damn right it's unpatriotic. This whole Syrian Virus is a hoax—it's a conspiracy to control us."

Relieved the L was pulling in at her stop, Mackenzie stood and made eye contact with the bespectacled man. Shaking her head slightly, she tried to warn him against any further engagement with the enraged passenger.

She and Bespectacled made a hasty exit, both of them wincing at the booming voice that followed them.

"It's a plan-demic! Big pharma is behind it!"

Shifting the heavy files in her grasp, Mackenzie gritted her teeth against the irony. Environmental law wasn't the least bit environmentally friendly when it came to paper consumption.

It was only a short walk to her office building, and usually she'd heed her body's craving for caffeine and stop for a tall, nonfat latte. With caramel drizzle.

This morning, however, she bypassed Starbucks, ducking instead into the drugstore next door. She tried to shrug off her self-consciousness at buying hand sanitizer and a few disposable face masks, momentarily wondering if she was completely offtrack with this case.

But her gut told her she wasn't wrong.

Mackenzie had awoken this morning convinced she'd been correct about Sy-V causing the deaths at Northern Memorial. With international travel a way of life, it was insane to think the US would be immune. Stashing her purchases at the bottom of her purse, she resolved to message Chloe as soon as she got to her desk. They all needed to be careful.

But first, she had to talk to Peter.

The lobby of her office building was unusually subdued, and Mackenzie noted a stressed receptionist reporting sick calls to HR. After taking the elevator up, she headed straight for Peter's corner office and found it empty save for a ringing telephone.

It rang out and then started again. She sighed, regretting the decision to skip coffee. "Hello, Peter Johns' office."

"I need to speak to Peter right now!"

"I'm sorry, Mr. Johns isn't available right now. Can I take a message?" Mackenzie raised her eyes to the ceiling, wondering where Peter's secretary had got to.

"Yes, Hilary needs to be picked up from school. She's got a nosebleed."

"I'm sorry, who is Hilary?"

"His daughter. Who is this? Where's Mary Beth?"

Mackenzie's first thought was that all this time she'd been calling Peter's secretary Mary Ann, which would explain why the woman was distinctly unfriendly.

"His *daughter*? Are you sure you've got the right extension?"

"If this is the office of Peter Johns, then yes, I have the right extension. I'm Julie, his wife, and I'm currently out of state. I need him to collect Hilary. The school nurse has already called twice. Apparently, there's some kind of virus going around. Now, can you get him for me or not? He's not picking up his cell phone."

Her boyfriend's *wife* sounded harried, and Mackenzie could hear the background noises of an airport with repeated canceled flight announcements.

"Hello? Are you still there?" Julie asked.

Ringing ears and rising nausea had Mackenzie sliding off the desk and onto the floor, her head hanging between her knees. She didn't know if she could answer.

"Hello? I'm trying to board a flight before they're all canceled. I need to know that Peter is going to get Hilary." It was Julie's mounting hysteria that snapped Mackenzie from her shock.

This woman needed to know her child was being taken care of.

"Yes, I'm here," she replied, raising her head. "Does Peter know what school she's at?"

"Are you on crack? Of course he knows her school. Is he there? I don't care how busy he is. He needs to pick her up. Right now."

Mackenzie smiled at the crack comment. It was something her friend Kat would say. Not that she was going to be making friends with Julie any time soon.

"Yes, sorry. Of course he does."

"Okay, well, I'm putting my faith in you. What's your name?"

"Mackenzie."

"Mackenzie, make sure Pete gets this message and picks up our daughter. Do you understand?"

Her boyfriend of seven months was a father. A husband. To a wife who called him Pete. *Well, fuck.*

The clammy dizziness dissipated in a flash of acknowledgment. Yes, he was a lying piece of shit. But wasn't she the stupid one who'd fallen for him?

"Mackenzie? Are you there?"

Mackenzie realized she wasn't inspiring confidence in her ability to pass this message along. Suddenly, she couldn't wait to tell her boyfriend that his wife wanted him to pick up their daughter.

"Yes, I'm here. I'll personally make sure he gets the message."

"Thank you." Julie's relief was palpable. "Ask him to call me when he's got her, okay?"

"Uh-huh. Sure, no problem."

With a cultivated air of mystery, Peter was an enigma. Mackenzie had been beside herself when he'd shown interest. *No one* noticed her. Anonymity was one perk of having left Sanford.

They'd developed a comfortable and steady relationship that, Mackenzie now realized, had made her stupid. All those weekends he had to "visit his mother in the country," his unwillingness for her to meet the brother she knew also lived in Chicago, the phone calls he had to take in private—she bet they covered those topics in Having an Affair 101.

"Holy shit. I'm the other woman," she muttered, rubbing sweaty hands against the front of her pencil skirt. Lost in thought, Mackenzie startled when Mary Ann—sorry, Mary *Beth*—appeared in the doorway.

"What are you still doing here? Everyone's leaving, they're evacuating the building," she said, her words rushed as she gathered up her belongings.

"Why?" Mackenzie scrambled to her feet.

"It's that super-flu. They've closed Disneyland. And

there's rioting at O'Hare International," Mary Beth said, picking up her purse.

"The airport? Wait! Where did you hear this?"

But Mary Beth had left, and Mackenzie could see a stream of her colleagues heading for the elevator.

"They're trying to contain it—"

"Quarantine—"

No one appeared overly panicked, but there was a definite buzz of confusion.

Undecided, Mackenzie glanced out the impressively large windows onto Roosevelt Road five floors below. The sidewalk was uncommonly crowded for this time of day and traffic was choked to a standstill. The wail of an approaching ambulance had vehicles attempting to pull to the side, which only added to the turmoil.

She needed to tell Peter about his daughter, and then— what? Get some groceries and hole up in her apartment until they got everything under control?

Her cell chimed with a text message.

Chloe: Shit is getting crazy, get out of the city. Come home.

Mackenzie grinned wryly. It was no surprise that at the first hint of trouble, Chloe would urge her to come home. Her phone would blow up with messages from Kat and Rachel soon.

The four girls had grown up together in the small rural town of Sanford, two hours from Chicago. While Chloe, Kat and Rachel constantly begged her to come back, Mackenzie had no intention of subjecting herself to that judgmental community ever again. Having escaped for college, she could count on one hand the number of times she'd been back.

Sure enough, before she could respond to Chloe, another message came through.

Rachel: Chloe thinks we should send Jake to come and get you.

Mackenzie: I don't need anyone to come and get me.

Rachel: You don't have a car, how are you going to get home?

Mackenzie: I am home.

That would definitely piss Rach off.

Her face fell when she spied Peter from the window, exiting beneath the building's awning and bolting into the foot traffic. Her stomach sank at the confirmation that she meant so little to him he could leave without finding her first.

Recalling her conversation with Julie, Mackenzie tried to call his cell. Regardless of how hurt she was, there was a little girl waiting to be collected.

When he didn't answer, she swore under her breath, sending him a text and hoping like hell he was on his way to the school now.

Slowly, she walked back to her own desk, collected her belongings in a daze. She'd been right. Sy-V was in Chicago, only she wasn't sure what the hell that meant.

Rioting at the airport? That was batshit crazy.

It wasn't until Mac was heading to the elevator that she clocked the eeriness of the silent, deserted office. She was the only one left on the floor, and as the hairs on the back of her neck prickled, she quickened her pace.

When the elevator door slid open, it was crammed to capacity. Her movement forward was halted by a brusque, "No room, catch the next one."

Stepping back, she answered her ringing phone. "Hey, Jake, let me guess. Chloe wants you to come and get me?"

Today was crazy enough without adding pointless drama involving her best friends. Jake was Chloe's younger brother, and at twenty-three he was three years her junior. It was a running joke between them that although she referred to him as Chloe's 'little' brother, he'd been towering over all of them since he turned seventeen.

Mackenzie jabbed at the down button of the elevator again.

"I've already left. I'll meet you at your apartment."

"What! You're not serious?"

He was silent.

"You aren't really coming here, are you?"

"I don't know what's going on, but it's not good."

"So, I can just wait it out. There's no need to come and rescue me," she protested. "And if it gets serious, then you shouldn't be out driving in it. Stay home, Jake."

"Two hours, Mac. Be ready."

The elevator door slid open again, and Mackenzie disconnected the call.

She wasn't a damsel in distress who needed rescuing.

This time, the only occupant of the elevator was Richard Drammel, a paunch-bellied senior partner at the firm who Mackenzie had never actually spoken to.

He grunted an acknowledgment as the doors slid closed.

"Do you know what's going on?" she asked, forcing herself not to bite her bottom lip.

"Haven't you heard? That virus from overseas is here and is worse than anyone could've imagined. There was rioting at the airport and they just fucking bombed it."

"What?" A buzzing started in her head. "Like, bombed it with an actual bomb?"

Richard looked at her as though she were stupid. Which, she had to admit, she'd accused herself of only twenty minutes ago.

"Yes, like an actual bomb," he said. "They were trying to quarantine it when riots broke out and the military came in and bombed the hell out of it."

"When?" she breathed.

The elevator dinged as it reached the foyer.

"It's happening right now. It's streaming live across pretty much every feed. Apparently, most of Europe declared martial law early this morning, but communication is getting sketchy from overseas." He placed his arm over the closing doors. "Are you getting out? I'm going down to the garage."

Looking out at the shiny tile foyer, Mackenzie felt the first grab of genuine fear in her gut. She didn't think she could face what was out there.

"Do you have a car? Maybe you could—"

"Nope, not taking you anywhere. I've got to get to my wife on the other side of the city." He softened marginally. "Look, if I were you, I'd stock up on supplies and get yourself home real quick. Good luck." Then he pushed her gently from the elevator.

"Supplies? What kind of supplies?!"

But the door slid smoothly shut, her frantic question unanswered.

Fuck. Fuck-fuck-fuckity-fuck.

———

JAKE SLAMMED his fist down on the steering wheel. Frustration rode him hard, and his jaw ached from the constant clench of his teeth.

For the last hour of his trip to Chicago, he'd been barely inching forward, choked by frantic traffic. The I-88 had been relatively free flowing until he took the exit onto I-290, where the exodus from the city was attempting to take over all eight lanes of the highway.

Every radio station was staticky white noise or on a prerecorded loop advising listeners they were in a state of emergency and to remain indoors. But Jake didn't need a news anchor to tell him things were bad. Really bad.

As he got closer to the city, nothing looked amiss. Until you noticed the enormous plumes of black smoke clouding the sky to the north. And once you saw that, you couldn't unsee it.

Whatever the fuck it was, it wasn't good.

Jake had been in his mechanic shop that morning, fitting a throttle valve into a carburetor when his sister Chloe arrived, the rear tires on her car kicking up gravel.

"The way you drive, I'm going to need to change the brake pads on that vehicle soon," he said, wiping grease-stained hands on his jeans.

"Are you not listening to the radio?" she screeched.

"Whoa. What's going on? Calm down."

"Calm down? Don't tell me to calm down. The world is freakin' ending. I'm not going to calm down!"

"Did you have a fight with Ash? I thought he was out of town?"

"Yes, he's out of town, and the jerk wouldn't listen to me this morning when I begged him to come back." Chloe was literally wringing her hands in distress.

"How exactly is the world ending, Chlo?"

"The WHO has declared a pandemic—Sy-V is in the States."

"The WH-who?"

13

"World Health Organization," Chloe almost yelled. "They're saying the rate of community transmission is so fast that containment is basically impossible. Schools are closing and Twitter is exploding with reports of the military mobilizing." She was breathless with agitation. "You need to get Mac."

Jake was already moving toward his SUV before Chloe finished speaking. His mind set on one thing—to rescue Mackenzie. Hell, she was one of the few things he'd thought about since he was fourteen.

"I'll call Mac and tell her I'm on my way. You call that damn husband of yours and tell him to get home."

"I can't get through to Ash, I just keep getting a busy signal."

"Keep trying. I'll message you when I get to Mac."

Since then, he'd tried several times to send messages to both Chloe and Mackenzie, letting them know he was delayed. Each time, the messages bounced back unsent, and his calls wouldn't connect. He was now almost two hours late to meet with Mackenzie.

Worry gnawed at his stomach, causing bile to rise in his throat.

Jake's unrequited love for his sister's best friend meant he knew Mackenzie probably even better than Chloe did. He absorbed every gesture and nuance when he was with her. Hell, he remembered details she'd probably forgotten about herself.

He knew she secretly loved One Direction and that she couldn't stand cooked tomatoes. That she bit her bottom lip when she was nervous, and it was her deadbeat father—and the fact he owed money to half the town—that had driven her from Sanford.

He also knew, with dreadful clarity, she would not be

prepared for whatever was coming. Grams had always said Mackenzie was book smart, not street smart. It didn't matter how many hundreds of hours that girl had spent studying to be a lawyer; she needed protecting.

The urge to get to her *now* had his foot pressing on the accelerator. The front corner of his vehicle nudged the car blocking him; heading in the opposite direction, he could see the despair in the heavy frown lines of the man driving it.

"Move over!" Jake gestured to him.

They locked eyes, and Jake saw when the man decided to help. With no acknowledgment, his beefy arm went over the headrest of the passenger seat as he turned to look backward, looking for a gap in the next lane to move into.

In this manner, appealing to each oncoming driver's humanity, Jake moved forward until suddenly he was behind a garbage truck that was forging ahead, heedless of the oncoming vehicles. Sitting on the truck's tail, Jake was light-headed with relief that he was finally making progress.

In the end, he had to park several streets from Mackenzie's Lincoln Park apartment because the roads were clogged with stalled or abandoned cars. There were fewer people on the sidewalk than he would've expected, and those he saw were covering their mouths and noses with articles of clothing.

Smart.

Shrugging out of his shirt, he held it over his face and started a steady jog to Mackenzie. After hours of sitting tensely in his vehicle, it was liberating to stretch and morph his worry into physical action.

The entrance to the apartment building was open and Jake bounded the steps to the second floor, stopping short of crashing into Mackenzie's door. Knocking sharply, he breathed deeply to calm his racing heart.

"Mac?" he called, knocking harder.

No response.

"Damn it, Mackenzie! Are you there?"

Dread threatened to swallow him. Without stopping to think, he rammed the door with his shoulder, attempting to force his way through.

Standing back, he rubbed at his now throbbing shoulder. Too bad he'd never learned how to pick a lock.

"Damn it, Mac! Are you there?" Bracing his bent elbows against the wall, he rested his bowed head. The unfamiliar creep of defeat was bitter.

Jake hadn't allowed himself to think beyond getting to Mackenzie, and now he was here, and she wasn't. He had no idea what route she'd take to get home from her office, whether she'd take a bus or the L. If he went out looking for her, he may miss her.

"Jake?"

The small voice came from behind, and before he could turn, Mackenzie had thrown herself at his back, wrapping her arms tight around his waist.

Grinning stupidly, he turned and pulled her into his arms, relief exploding in his chest. His smile widened as she burrowed against his bare chest, her voice muffled. "Gross, Jake, you smell."

"Where have you been? I thought you'd be here waiting for me."

She pulled back, and he looked at her properly. Her blouse was untucked, her hair a mess, and her bare feet were grubby and bloody with blisters.

"Jesus, Mac! What happened? What happened out there?" he asked, worry lacing his tone.

"I ended up having to walk and ditched the heels about halfway. It's crazy, Jake. I saw a bunch of police officers trying to reason with a group of people and then out of nowhere the army was there and started *shooting*." She paused, stifling a sob. "They just pulled out guns and opened fire into the crowd."

"*Fuck*," he said. "Come on, open up and let's get you packed. We need to get out of here."

"No judgment from you, okay? I didn't know I was going to have visitors, and the place is a mess." She jiggled her key in the lock.

"I'm not going to be checking your kitchen sink for dirty dishes, Mac."

Turns out that wasn't exactly what Mackenzie was referring to. Living in an apartment with no clothesline or dryer, she'd rigged up several strings along which lacy lingerie was drying.

Jake would've paid money, *a lot* of money, to peruse each delicate piece. Instead, he cleared his throat and forced his gaze away.

Now was not the time.

"Pack enough for a couple of weeks. We don't know how long this is going to go on for. Do you have spare asthma inhalers?"

"Damn! I should've picked up extras at the drugstore this morning. I'll have to do that before we get going—I emptied mine on the way home."

Striding to the kitchen, Jake opened the refrigerator and grabbed two bottles of water.

"Pack cold weather gear," he called out.

"You're not my dad," she said, coming into the room as she slung a backpack over her shoulder. She'd changed into sneakers, leggings and a sweater.

17

"That's all you're taking?" He raised a skeptical eyebrow, ignoring her comment.

"I don't know what's going on out there, but when it all blows over, I'm coming back here. It's not like I'll be in Sanford when winter comes—there'll be a vaccine before we know it."

"I wouldn't bet on it. Are you sure you've got everything you need?" he asked, passing her the water to put in her backpack.

"Yes, *Dad.*"

That rankled, knowing Mackenzie's feelings toward her father. Having pulled his shirt back on, he grabbed two dish towels from the drawer, telling her they were to use as face masks.

"How did you know which drawer they were in?"

"Dish towels go in the third drawer down. Everyone knows that."

"You're such a know-it-all," she said.

"A know-it-all who's here to save your ass. Let's go."

"I don't *need* saving."

"Sure, Mac."

"Save the towels. I've got proper face masks." She handed him one. "And I'm glad you're here," she admitted quietly, pulling the front door closed behind them.

He hid a smile, but it slipped as they started down the stairs.

If the military was massacring in the streets, he didn't think the situation was going to be blowing over soon.

CHAPTER TWO

In the short time Mac had been in her apartment, the air outside had grown thicker with a choking smoke, and her lungs tightened. The intensity of noise had amplified too. Wailing sirens competed with blaring car alarms. People were no longer hushed and frantic, but loud and belligerent.

"Can you believe they bombed O'Hare?" Mackenzie said.

"They *what*?" Jake's eyes widened above his face mask.

The red-and-blue flashing lights of a police vehicle parked on the block over caught their attention—an officer was shouting from a loudspeaker for civilians to stay indoors.

"When did they start calling us civilians?" Mackenzie glared at the cop. "It sounds like we're in a war zone."

"Look around, Mac. We *are*."

"Why aren't we seeing anyone who's sick?"

"I don't know." Jake pulled her backpack from her and shouldered it himself. "Which way to the drugstore?"

It was only a short walk to the nearest shopping strip, but they'd barely started out before Mackenzie was limping.

She'd washed her feet and applied Band-Aids, but the blisters from trekking half the way home in her three-inch Fendi slingbacks were worse than the time she'd worn new heels clubbing until dawn.

The friction as she walked was excruciating.

Jake noticed and shortened his strides to accommodate her slower pace. "I'm guessing you won't be wearing those heels again?"

"Nope. Couldn't even if I wanted to. I dropped them and ran when the shooting started. Those people just started falling over, like it was some kind of game. And the sound of a gun is so much *louder* than it is in the movies. And then people started screaming—" She choked. "I just can't believe it was real. That it *happened*."

Jake pulled her tighter against his side as she fought back the tears burning in her throat.

"I'm glad Chloe sent you," she admitted.

"I would've come for you even without Chloe," he said roughly. "I'll always come for you, Mac."

Unlike my jerk of a boyfriend.

There was something in the way Jake was looking at her, eyes serious over the top of his mask, that had Mackenzie's stomach doing a funny little twist.

There was no time to think as they came abreast of the small supermarket and Jake tugged her against the wall to avoid being rammed by an exiting shopping cart, piled high and steered by a wild-eyed man in a business suit. A woman with a red-faced screaming baby strapped to her front, her cart also loaded to the brim, followed him.

Jake caught her eye. "Think they know something we don't?"

"They're just panic buying. Remember whenever there's a severe storm warning in Sanford? The whole town mobs the grocery store, thinking they'll never get the chance to buy food again," she said. "We'll probably have to stay inside for a week, two at the most, until they contain the virus."

"Still, it can't hurt to grab some supplies. With the way traffic is, it's going to take a lot longer to get home. We'll need food."

It was on the tip of her tongue to reply that while Sanford may be *his* home, it sure as hell wasn't *hers*. But his mention of supplies stopped her. Hadn't that been what Richard Drammel told her to do?

"Yeah, okay. And the drugstore is two down. It shouldn't take long."

"Holy *shit*," Jake breathed as they walked through the automatic front doors of the supermarket, reflexively pulling Mackenzie closer.

Recoiling from the utter pandemonium, Mackenzie stepped backwards. It was like they'd entered an alternate universe, where instead of neat shelves and orderly lines, people were arguing and jostling in lines that snaked back into ravaged aisles. Customers were actually running, sweeping products indiscriminately into their carts. Two harried women staffed the checkouts where a fight had just broken out.

"What do you mean, cash only? I don't have any cash!" yelled an elderly man brandishing a bank card at the cashier, whose bangs were matted to her forehead with sweat.

"I'm sorry, sir, really I am. But our system just went down. I can only accept cash payment," she said, holding up beseeching hands. As she spoke, the overhead lights flickered and several people screamed in fright.

"Cynthia, it's time to get the hell out of here,"

Mackenzie heard the other cashier say. "We don't get paid enough to deal with this."

In the space of a second, the tense atmosphere flashed from frantic uncertainty to dangerous hostility. Another flicker of the lights and chaos reigned.

Abandoning the semi-organized lines, shoppers—fiercely protective of their carts—charged for the exit. Two men were trading blows, a box of bottled water on the ground at their feet, and a teenage boy who'd just entered the store was knocked to the ground and trampled.

"Jesus *Christ!*" Jake lunged forward to help the boy to his feet, dragging him to where Mackenzie was cowering against a display of fresh flowers. "Are you okay?"

"Fuck you! Get your hands off me!" said the boy, snatching his arm from Jake's grip and dashing away.

Dry mouthed, Mackenzie couldn't get her body to move. She knew the longer she stayed frozen, the less likely they were to find anything worth salvaging on the shelves.

The need for haste pulsed through the air, and everyone was breathing it and reacting accordingly.

But her? Nope. The utter unreality of people being shot in front of her earlier in the day had been so surreal, she still couldn't quite grasp that her world had altered irrevocably. And now people were literally going mad, grabbing anything and everything from the supermarket shelves before barreling out without paying.

"Oh god," she blurted. "I've just thought about the airport. Before, I was thinking about the structure of the buildings getting bombed. But the *people*. Imagine how many people were trapped there. It makes me feel sick."

"You can't think about it now. We need to get some food and get the hell out of here," Jake said with grim determination.

He grabbed a shopping basket and thrust it at her, taking one for himself.

"We stick together, okay? Let's take it one aisle at a time; you look at the shelves on the right, I'll look at the left. We want fresh food because most people are bypassing that in favor of the packaged, long-lasting stuff. And we can get that back in Sanford."

Mackenzie stuck a hand in the back pocket of Jake's jeans, staying close behind his broad back as they jogged to the fresh produce section. The safety she felt being shielded by him was comforting, and she had a moment of marveling at how Chloe's little brother suddenly seemed years older and more grown up than she was.

There was no sign of the freckle-faced, scrappy kid who used to torment her with frogs.

Taking a handful of carrots, she had a brief, bizarre moment of imagining she was on one of those reality television shows where you had sixty seconds to grab as much as you could from the supermarket shelves, and whoever had the most expensive cart at the end won. And then a woman shoulder-checked her, reaching for the last loaf of fresh bread.

This was more *The Walking Dead* than *Supermarket Sweep*.

Mackenzie gave herself a mental shake. She needed to get her head in the game, or they were going hungry. With renewed focus, she darted and dodged between the other shoppers, blistered feet forgotten, snatching at products until her basket was full.

"Good job, let's get out of here," Jake said, his own basket overflowing.

"Should we at least leave some money?" she asked, feeling an ingrained guilt at leaving without paying.

"I love that you're worried about that, but no. We need to get your asthma inhalers and go."

Exiting the store, Mackenzie immediately turned right, heading for the drugstore, only to have pain rocket up her arm as the basket was wrenched from the crook of her elbow. Stumbling, she shrieked, apples spilling onto the ground from the impact. The man in the hoodie didn't even pause. Just took off running with her hard-won basket of food.

"What the *fuck*?" yelled Jake, pushing his own basket at Mackenzie and taking off after the thief.

"Jake! Stop!"

Don't leave me.

If he heard her, he didn't stop. Clutching Jake's shopping basket to her chest, she watched helplessly as he charged away. Not taking her eyes from his retreating figure, she backed slowly against the front wall of the supermarket, suddenly very conscious of the fact she was holding a precious commodity in a volatile environment.

A woman scooped up the fallen apples and didn't even glance her way.

Mac had the distinct, sudden knowledge she was not safe. The intense instinct to run away as fast as she could had her heart beating double time.

What if the guy had a gun? What if he'd snatched her backpack instead? Not that he'd have much use for the designer ballet flats she'd packed.

God, what *had* she packed?

Even with her advance knowledge, she hadn't been taking the situation seriously enough. She really should've spent the extra ten minutes searching for her passport. And tampons took up hardly any space—why hadn't she packed more of those?

If the world really was going to shit, and she was now realizing that was more than a distinct possibility, then shouldn't she have packed practical, helpful things? A tent? Matches? What the hell else did those apocalypse preppers have in their bug-out bags? And where did one purchase a tent, anyway?

And where the hell was Jake?

Nearby, a mob of young men—boys, really—used a trash can to smash the front windows of an electrical store, hooting and hollering as they forced their way inside.

Really? Upgrading their television was a priority?

The speed with which civilization was disintegrating was terrifying.

A splinter group of the original mob turn to approach the supermarket, and Mackenzie's legs started moving of their own accord. There was no way she was staying there like a sitting duck.

Walking quickly, she headed for the drugstore, hoping that Mr. Zhang was still open amid all this madness.

Turned out she should've added "gun" to the mental list of things she wished she'd packed.

———

JAKE WAS PUFFING HEAVILY as he lugged the rescued groceries back to where he'd left Mackenzie. Anxiety tightened its hold on his throat when he realized how long he'd left her alone. Anxiety that rocketed to unadulterated terror when he didn't see her.

Jesus, was a bag of carrots and potatoes worth leaving her over?

Scanning the area a second time, he again saw no sign of

her. Surely Mackenzie hadn't gone back into the supermarket?

At a run, he headed in the direction she'd said the drugstore was and skidded to a halt when he saw the shop. It was dark inside and the metal rolling gate was pulled halfway down. Ducking under, he blinked, his eyes adjusting to the dimness. There was a light at the back of the store where the dispensary was, and he could see movement in a small room beyond that.

"Mac? Are you there?" Stress made his voice hoarse. He cautiously made his way farther into the space.

There didn't appear to be any customers, and the shelves hadn't been looted. Caution didn't stop him from calling out again, and he could've kicked himself for this carelessness when, alerted to his presence, a man wearing a grey hoodie emerged from the back room.

With a Remington 870 pointed at Jake's head.

Well, fuck.

"Whoa! I'm just looking for a friend, I'm not looking for trouble." There was nothing like having a firearm leveled at you to make you feel alive. "I'm looking for a brunette, about yay high." He waved his hand to indicate five feet four. "Have you seen her?"

"Keep your hands out in front of you and walk toward me slowly," the man said, the pitch of his voice betraying his nervousness. His shotgun shook.

"Are you the owner? Maybe you know Mackenzie?"

"Shut up!" The man waved the gun to show Jake should keep coming forward.

Jake complied, his eyes tracking the movement of the weapon.

The man backed into the small room and Jake followed, rushing the last steps when he saw Mackenzie huddled against the wall with a small Chinese-American man wearing a white lab coat.

"I said slowly!" yelled Grey Hoodie, brandishing the shotgun. Sweat was beading on his forehead and his eyes were frantic.

"Easy now." Jake turned to face him, his back shielding Mackenzie. "We just need to grab some medicine and we're out of here. We aren't a threat to you."

"Mr. Peters, please. I have your son's medication. Take it all," pleaded the Chinese man. "Just take it, don't worry about money."

Jake could hear Mackenzie's panting breaths behind him, and his heart squeezed.

"Come on, man, please. Put the weapon down. Take what you need and we can forget we ever saw each other." Jake spread his arms out, palms up.

The shotgun barrel wavered.

"I have what I need," came Mackenzie's small voice as her arm rose from behind Jake, holding a paper bag. "Please, just let us go."

The urge to remove Mackenzie—and himself—from the situation was a visceral thing, but Jake couldn't just walk away. "Why don't you lower the weapon, and this guy—"

"Mr. Zhang," Mackenzie supplied.

"—can get you what you need and you can be on your way," Jake said.

The shotgun lowered, inch by inch, until it was hanging loosely and Grey Hoodie's shoulders sagged. "I'm sorry. This isn't me, but I ain't getting paid 'til Thursday and I need to get my son's meds. He needs them, and I can't leave without them."

"No problem, no problem!" Mr. Zhang gesticulated with his hands. "I'll get them now, and then you can go." He edged toward the dispensary warily and Grey Hoodie followed, having tucked the weapon into the back of his belt.

A minute later, they turned as Mr. Zhang reentered, holding out another bag to Mackenzie.

"He's gone. Miss Lyons, take more asthma inhalers, okay?"

"Okay?" Mackenzie accepted the shopping bag, which was bulging. "This is a lot of medication, Mr. Zhang."

"Yes, and you'll probably need them. I'm going to my daughter's. I don't know when I'll come back. If ever. Go, and take good care of yourself, okay?"

"You too," Mackenzie said, giving the old man a quick hug. "I'll see you later."

He gave her a doubtful look but said nothing, instead shooing them out.

Making their way back through the semi-dark store, Jake turned to Mackenzie and she launched herself at his chest, hugging him tight. He couldn't help the flash of lust that drove through him, as inappropriate as it may have been. He'd been waiting seven years to feel Mackenzie's body against his and, god*damn,* it felt good.

She was tiny, the messy bun on top of her head brushing the underside of his chin, but the woman had curves for days. Tucked against him with her arms wrapped tight around his torso, he had an agonizing view of her ass, which was *so close* his palms itched.

The peachy scent of her hair invaded his senses and her tits, Jesus fucking Christ, her *tits,* were pressed against his chest, and thank god she stepped back before she felt just how much he was enjoying her proximity. His cock was painful behind the zipper of his jeans.

"You *left* me!" She slapped at his chest, the color high

on her cheeks. "It's scary out there and you took off and abandoned me."

Her trembling bottom lip gutted him. "Fuck. I'm sorry, Mac."

"It was a dick move, Jake."

He cupped her cheek, his big thumb rubbing at a stray tear that was tracking down her face. "Don't cry, babe."

"Since when have you called me *babe*?" Her brow furrowed. "I'm the one breaking down here. We don't have time for you to lose your mind, too. Hold it together and get us out of here."

His face heated. Right. He was her best friend's younger brother, and they were in the middle of a societal meltdown.

Stepping onto the sidewalk, they tugged their face masks back over their mouths and, in the encroaching darkness, made their way to Jake's vehicle.

"HOW ARE YOU FEELING?" Jake asked.

They were in his SUV, inching forward in the glut of traffic that was evacuating Chicago. Taking his eyes off the endless stream of red taillights ahead, he glanced at Mackenzie, who was chewing on a protein bar.

"I'm okay. Look, I know I had a slight meltdown back there, but you don't need to parent me. Even my actual father is too useless to try that."

"I'm not trying to parent you, Mac. I'm just worried."

"So it's back to Mac now, huh? No more *babe*?" She raised an eyebrow, smirking.

He looked back at the road. "Would it be so bad if I called you babe?" he asked evenly.

"Uh, yes?"

29

Without looking, he knew her nose was crinkling in confusion. Fuck, she was adorable. "Why?"

"Why? Because I'm not your *babe*. That's something you call a girlfriend, not... *me*."

"What if it was something I wanted to call you?" Jake's tone was mild, but his heart was jack-hammering.

Over the years, he'd imagined a million different scenarios where he'd declare himself to Mackenzie. Strangely enough, fleeing a city at the beginning of an apocalypse hadn't featured in any of them.

Mackenzie shifted in her seat to face him squarely and, as they were currently stationary, he didn't have the excuse of looking out through the windscreen. It was time to man up and tell the woman he was mad about her.

"Why... why would you want to?" She was biting her lip. Good. She wasn't trying to tease him anymore. She was taking this seriously.

In none of his imagined scenarios had Jake been stuck in a vehicle as this played out. There would be no suave, pulling-her-closer moves here. Awkwardly, he stretched out a hand and placed it on her thigh, squeezing gently.

"Jake?" Mackenzie's leg tensed and her eyes locked on his hand. "What are you doing?"

"Mac, look at me," he said, his voice taking on a deeper timbre.

That luscious lower lip of hers was caught between her teeth, but she raised her gaze and held his stare.

"I've been in love with you since that day you sprained your ankle at the lake. Remember? I carried you to the car so you could go get it x-rayed."

"You... love me?"

"Yes."

"I was like, nineteen, when I sprained my ankle."

"Yes."

"That's seven years ago, Jake."

"Uh-huh."

There was silence as they looked at each other.

"Stop gnawing on that bottom lip," Jake said, "you're going to draw blood."

She swallowed and looked away. "But, you're Chlo's little brother."

"I am," he agreed. "But I'm also twenty-three and know what I want. I want you."

A mix of dizzying relief and hot terror was swirling in Jake's chest and his mouth was dry. He swallowed.

"Why now? Why are you telling me this now?" she whispered.

"Because you need to know. Because life is short and I've already wasted so much time. On my way to get you today, I thought that if I never got the chance to tell you— well, I can't think of anything worse," he finished softly, removing his hand from her leg. "You don't need to say anything. I just needed you to know. Think about it, and when you're ready to talk about it, I'm here."

Facing him again, she raised both eyebrows. "That's a hell of a conversational bomb to drop, Jake. I don't... I don't know what to say."

"Don't say anything. Just think about it."

A chorus of car horns started blaring ahead of them. Several people were getting out of their cars, illuminated by the multitude of headlights snaking behind them.

Putting the gear stick into park, Jake switched off the ignition. "I'm going to get out and see if I can see what's happening. Sit tight, okay?"

"Should I come?"

Her bottom lip was back between her teeth, and Jake

realized she was nervous about being left alone. "Lock the doors behind me. I won't be long, promise."

The night air was cool as Jake approached a group of people standing between cars in the middle of the highway, waving his hand in greeting.

"Anyone know what's happening up there?" he asked.

"There's been an accident. A bad one," said a middle-aged man.

"Looks like traffic is totally locked up," said another. "And cells aren't working, so there's no help coming. We're not going anywhere."

Jake surveyed the scene. With a sharp embankment dropping away on one side, and a concrete wall on the other, there was no hope of bypassing the accident ahead or turning around. Not that going back into Chicago was really an option.

"We wait it out or walk," said the first man, coughing violently as he turned to get back in his sedan.

Mackenzie popped the locks as he came back, watching nervously as he slid into the driver's seat and rolled his shoulders, attempting to release tension.

"So?" Mackenzie prompted. "What's going on out there?"

"We're stuck," he replied heavily. "There's an accident up ahead. We can try to wait it out, but it's going to get cold in here because we'll need to keep the engine off to conserve fuel. And we have no way of knowing how long we'll be stuck. Or—" He paused.

"Or?"

"We walk."

"Walk! Walk where?"

"Just until we get past the roadblock."

"And then what? We won't have a car to keep driving." Mackenzie was shaking her head.

"We keep going until we find a car I can jack," he answered.

"Really? Like, you know how to steal a car?"

Mackenzie's skepticism was wounding. "Yes, Mac. I have a lot of skills you don't know about."

It was beyond grating that she saw only the teenage version of him. And he thanked a god he didn't really believe in that she hadn't witnessed his earlier attempt to break through her front door.

"So, we're just going to get out of this nice safe vehicle and go wandering around outside in the dark?" Mackenzie said.

"It's not wandering when you're following a road, Mac."

"You know that my version of being outdoorsy is getting drunk on the patio?"

"I'm well aware of that."

CHAPTER THREE

Jake had found a flashlight and an old sports bag under his seat, which he loaded with the groceries they'd stolen. Mackenzie was still feeling guilty about taking the food—she'd never so much as stolen a pack of gum in her life.

Considering the magnitude of shit that was currently going down, she wasn't sure why that was bothering her so much. And then Jake had to go and say the L-word.

Talk about being blindsided.

"Ready?" he asked.

"I can't believe we're really doing this," she grumbled, shouldering her backpack. "You know I've been hiding from exercise. I'm in the Fitness Protection Program."

He huffed out a laugh. "That was a lame joke, Mac."

"It wasn't a joke. And the blisters on my feet are killing me."

She knew she sounded like a whiny brat, but the rubbed-raw skin on her heels was excruciating.

"We'll take it easy. It shouldn't be too far," he reassured her.

Walking in single file between the snarl of vehicles,

Mackenzie stayed only a step behind Jake. More and more people were exiting their cars, most milling around aimlessly, but some were loaded with bags and walking determinedly forward. She couldn't help noticing how many of them were coughing and readjusted her own face covering.

A keening wail broke out, its intensity heard over the general cacophony of car horns. Jake halted and reached back, feeling for her hand.

An involuntary shudder raced down her back as the cry continued.

"There's a woman up ahead, holding a baby in her arms," Jake said grimly. "I think it might be... I don't think it's alive."

Mackenzie's stomach dropped as she spotted the woman, who'd fallen to her knees and was rocking backward and forward, the devastation in her moans heart-wrenching. Obviously not thinking, Jake took a step toward her.

"Jake! Don't you dare. She could be carrying the virus," Mackenzie cried, grabbing onto his arm and holding firm.

"So we just leave her?" Jake twisted his arm in her hold.

Tears blurred her vision and ran unchecked down her cheeks. She was a wretched human, and there was probably a spot reserved in hell for people who turned away like this. "We can't help her. There's nothing we can do."

Resigned, Jake nodded, and they walked silently away from the sobbing woman until they were edging between the concrete retaining wall and tightly packed vehicles. Wiping tears from her face, Mac stumbled, the emotional overload from the day swamping her.

"I need to stop, Jake. I can't keep going." She was

choking on sobs, and breathing behind the face mask was difficult.

Turning, he put both hands on her shoulders and stared down at her. She blinked wet eyes, focusing on the tawny hazel depths of his that were highlighted by the headlights stretching out behind them. They were pretty, if you could call a man's eyes pretty.

When did Jake become a man?

"Mac, focus." He gave her shoulders a gentle shake. "You're strong. Stronger than you think you are. And we need to keep moving."

"How much farther?" She whimpered. She was tired. So damn tired.

She just wanted this day to be over.

"The accident is just up ahead. It looks bad, so just concentrate on following me and try not to look, okay?"

Mac nodded mutely and they continued on, ignoring the coughing car occupants they were passing. She tried to overlook the occasional slumped passenger.

They were sleeping. Not dead. Definitely not dead.

Trudging onwards, her over-loaded mind wandered, attempting to forget the horrors the day had unfolded.

It was funny Jake had mentioned that time she'd sprained her ankle because it was the first, and only, time she'd noticed him as anything other than Chloe's little brother. She hadn't seen much of him that summer, which made his growth spurt even more obvious. Suddenly he was taller than her, his voice was lower, and although still gangly, the breadth of his shoulders hinted at the man he was about to become.

Yeah, she'd noticed him all right. And then Jason Aldrich had done a dive-bomb and reclaimed her attention and, two weeks later, they were going steady—all weird thoughts of Jake forgotten.

The urge to pee brought her back to the present. The closer she and Jake came to the accident, the less light there was because most vehicles had turned off their engines and headlights. Mac couldn't see beyond the wreckage of metal that was blocking the road. It looked like a semi-trailer truck had lost control, and several cars had become collateral.

"Do you think there's a rest stop ahead? I really need to use the bathroom."

Before he could answer, a gunshot rang out. Gasping, she ducked behind a minivan with Jake throwing an arm over her head, urging her lower to the ground.

"Jesus *Christ*," he mumbled as another shot rang out. "It's coming from behind us."

Blood was pounding so loudly in her ears that Mackenzie found it difficult to hear anything with the panic that was coursing through her. She wanted to crawl into the van, put her hands over her ears, and pretend this wasn't happening.

She started fumbling for the rear door handle of the vehicle, but she was shaking so badly she couldn't get a proper hold. Seeing what she was doing, Jake brushed her away and tried to open it, but found it locked.

"Come on." He grabbed her hand as they skirted the side of the van and approached the woman sitting in the driver's seat.

"Let us in!" Jake called, rapping softly on the window.

The woman shook her head, her eyes sad. A stream of blood was coming from her nose and it started gushing as coughing racked her body.

Mackenzie looked at Jake in despair. "She's infected, isn't she?"

He nodded grimly.

A pounding of feet on asphalt had them swinging around to face an oncoming tide of people, looking as though they were running for their lives.

"Fuck! Mac, come on!" Jake pushed her ahead of him. "Run!"

Adrenaline forced her bone-weary body into a sprint, Jake's hot breath inches behind. Screaming and more gunshots filled the air, competing with the relentless car horns. She slowed as they came abreast of the accident, but Jake shoved her roughly between the shoulder blades.

"Keep going. Run, Mac, run!"

She dodged an open door, and then suddenly the road was clear before them. The darkness ahead was complete, and Mackenzie's chest was heaving as she gulped for air.

Tiredness rushed back through her and she faltered, her chest tight. She tore at the inhaler in her backpack and sucked it with desperation.

Jake unslung the bag from his shoulder and pulled out the flashlight, switching it on and aiming it down the highway that stretched before them. Behind them, the wave of hysterical people also slowed as they hit the darkness beyond the wreckage of the accident.

"What were they running from?" She huffed, bending at the waist to ease a stitch in her side. She hadn't been kidding about being unfit.

"I don't know, but I think we need to get as far ahead of them as we can," Jake said grimly, walking forward.

Mackenzie was dizzy with dismay.

"Can't we rest?" she asked.

"The highway opens up ahead, we'll be able to get off and find refuge in a field." Jake stopped, waiting for Mackenzie to catch up.

"Want me to carry your backpack?" he asked, concern lacing his tone.

It was hard not to succumb to "damsel in distress" when every step rubbed her raw feet, her shoulders ached with the heavy pack, and she was tired. So tired.

And oh god, the pressure in her bladder was becoming unbearable.

"Maybe just for a bit." She shrugged her backpack off and passed it over, sighing in relief at the immediate lightness on her shoulders.

Reaching down, he grabbed a hold of her hand and wound their fingers together, like it was the most natural thing in the world. And they started off down the dark highway.

MACKENZIE all but ran for the line of trees bordering the field they'd just entered, the urgent need to relieve her bladder fierce. Ducking behind a bush, she gasped in relief, her lack of dignity the furthest thing from her mind.

"Don't wander too far," Jake called out.

Mackenzie smirked to herself. She was lucky to have gotten as far as she had. There'd been a very real chance she was going to wet herself. Thank god there were some random tissues tucked into the side pocket of her backpack.

"What time is it?" she asked Jake, emerging from behind the bush.

"You really should start wearing a watch," he said absently. "It's almost nine o'clock. Let's try to find somewhere to rest."

Mackenzie's legs wobbled, but she obediently followed Jake as he made for an outcropping of large rocks.

"This is a hell of an introduction to camping," she said

as they settled with their backs against a large, smooth rock, facing out over the moonlit field.

"You girls used to set up tents in our backyard all the time," countered Jake.

"Yeah. But we were never brave enough to actually sleep in them."

"You didn't happen to pack a sleeping bag in that backpack, did you?"

"Do I look like someone who owns a sleeping bag?"

His expression turned thoughtful. "You know, we passed a turnoff for a town, Essex, which should only be a couple of miles away. I'm pretty sure it's big enough that it would have a hiking store and it's our best bet to finding a car, too."

"We're not going to need hiking stuff after tonight, though. We're only a couple of hours from Sanford," she argued.

"We have old Mr. Murphey's hardware store, but nowhere in Sanford that sells a good range of gear. It can't hurt to be prepared."

"Prepared for what?"

"For anything."

Mac drew her knees up to her chest and rested her chin on them. "Like a bug-out bag? Because I hate to tell you, we're already bugging out."

The October days, although mild, still turned chilly when the sun set. Shivering, she rummaged through her backpack for a jacket.

"Any chance you have one in there that would fit me?" Jake asked.

"Peter wasn't the kind of boyfriend who left clothing at my place. Which is a good thing, because I don't need reminders of what a cheating jerk he is."

"He cheated on you?" Jake growled.

"Yeah. With his *wife*." Looking back, she had a track record of dirtbag boyfriends.

"You've always dated dirtbags," Jake casually told her.

Huh.

"Look, a soul mate would be great. But at this stage I'd be happy to settle for someone who doesn't lie about being married, you know?"

"Come here, Mac. Keep me warm and try to get some sleep," Jake said, pulling her back against his chest. She relaxed, bracketed by his legs, and closed gritty eyes.

"Are you cold?" she murmured.

"Not anymore."

———

JAKE JERKED out of his doze, tensing around the sleeping woman in his arms.

Mac. Jesus Christ, I'm holding Mac.

His ass and lower back were numb after hours of sitting on the cold, hard ground. But there wasn't a chance in hell he was moving. Not when the trusting, warm weight of Mackenzie reclined against his chest, and her silky hair—freed from its bun—cascaded over the arms he had wrapped tightly around her.

He welcomed—hell, he relished—the responsibility he felt for Mackenzie. Even when he dated other women, she was always somewhere in the back of his mind. Now, the instinct to care for her, to protect her, had strengthened to a tangible level. He could *feel* his dedication to her in the thrumming beat of his heart.

The sun wasn't yet visible, but the sky was lighter and birds were calling all around them. In the early morning calm, the events of yesterday had a hard edge of surrealness. But he'd watched enough end-of-the-world movies to know it was those who were prepared that survived.

And while this may not be the end of the world, he wanted to fully kit the both of them in Essex. He was happy enough to get laughed at when they arrived back in Sanford, when this all sorted itself out.

If it sorted itself out.

The woman in the minivan with blood pouring out her nose flashed through his mind.

Jake's stomach rumbled, reminding him of their meager food situation. It should be just over a mile to Essex, which he and Mackenzie could walk in half an hour.

"Wake up, sleeping beauty."

She stirred and then snuggled farther into him.

He fought the urge to dismiss reality, to stay sitting here as long as he could with Mackenzie in his arms. Because he knew that when they reached Sanford, he'd have to share her with Chloe, Kat, and Rachel. And those three were really shit at sharing.

Jake couldn't remember a time in his life when the four girls hadn't been attached at the hip. They had a bond that made them more sisters than friends, and they were fierce in their love for each other.

Absently, he lowered his head to sniff Mackenzie's hair for the hundredth time just as she sat up, her skull smacking into his face.

"Fuck!" he groaned, throwing his head back and pinching the bridge of his nose with his fingers, pain spearing through him.

"Oh god, I'm so sorry!" Mackenzie twisted in his lap to face him, her thighs straddling him.

He groaned again, nose forgotten.

42

He needed to get her off before she realized she was sitting on one hell of a boner.

Before he could displace her, a gush of blood had him yanking up his shirt and holding it against his face.

She moved closer, bringing her own hands to cover his.

"Are you okay?" she asked softly, eyes wide.

"Just a bloody nose. I'll be fine," he mumbled, excruciatingly aware of the juncture of her thighs nestled over his throbbing cock.

Jake knew the exact moment she comprehended his predicament. Those wide eyes blinked, and she audibly drew in a breath.

"Oh. Oh, okay." She stumbled to her feet and turned to face away from him, tugging the sleeves of her sweater down over her hands.

"Can you pass me the water that's in your backpack?" he asked, getting to his feet slowly. "This has already stopped bleeding."

She passed it to him without meeting his eyes.

"Don't get weird on me. It's just an erection. Happens most mornings." He grinned.

"No. Nope, not going there."

"It's a normal bodily function."

"Jake, stop! We are not talking about your dick."

"You just did."

She huffed and stalked toward the bushes she'd used last night. Laughing softly to himself, he rummaged through their food supplies and put together a passable breakfast of tomatoes, cheese and a bread roll he split into two.

Mackenzie came back, talking to herself.

"What's up?"

"Yesterday's eyeliner can be today's smoky eye if you

believe in yourself enough," she said. "And if there's no mirror around to contradict you."

He wasn't sure what to say to that.

"Don't say anything," she instructed.

"Babe, this conversation is above my friendship paygrade."

"And again with the *babe*."

"You don't like it?"

Instead of answering, she sat beside him and started eating.

He grinned again.

JAKE AND MACKENZIE had been walking for just over twenty minutes and, even with the Band-Aids she'd reapplied, Mackenzie was struggling.

"Want a piggyback?" he offered, only half joking. He'd carry this woman all the way to Sanford. Not that she'd take him up on his suggestion.

"I'm fine," she answered primly, attempting to cover her limping.

They reached a sign showing Essex was not far off, and a car passed them. Jake hitched out his thumb but was unsurprised when it didn't even slow down. The lack of people was unsettling. Had everyone locked themselves inside?

Or was everyone dead?

Jake shook his head resolutely. There's no way this thing had spread that quickly. And if this virus had wiped other countries out, they'd have heard on the news. Right?

Ahead, he could see the fields giving way to industrial-looking buildings.

"I think if we cut through this field and head north, we'll

end up near the center of town and bypass the outskirts," he said, shading his eyes.

"North, huh? Sometimes I wonder what happened to the people who asked me for directions."

"You what?"

"Talking about north, south, east and west is like a foreign language to me. I need you to say left and right, and then give me landmarks. Like, I'll tell someone they need to follow the street until they pass the bakery, and then turn left at the boutique that has the yellow dress in the window."

"The way your brain works never ceases to amaze me."

"Just me, being as indispensable as always." There was something about the lilt in Mackenzie's voice that made him pause.

"You're one of the smartest people I know, you know that, right?"

"Yeah, sure I am," she scoffed.

"It wasn't your dad paying your way through college, or some miraculous inheritance that covered your education. You got *two* scholarships, Mac. And now you're a kick-ass environmental lawyer."

She didn't respond, but from the tinge of pink to her high cheekbones, he knew she'd heard him.

They crossed the open expanse in easy silence and skirted a high school football field before cresting a small rise and seeing the sprawling grounds of the Essex Memorial Hospital spread before them.

"Oh, wow," Mackenzie said, stopping and leaning in against his side.

The grounds looked like an airport parking lot, with vehicles covering every spare inch. Stationary cars were clogging the road into the hospital and spilled back out onto the main road. People were abandoning their cars and heading on foot toward the ER, even though a white bedsheet hung across the entrance with the words "We Can't Help. Go Home!" spray painted on it.

There was a growing crowd in front of the closed doors, and it didn't appear they were letting anyone enter.

"Why aren't they helping?" Jake asked in frustration.

"Maybe they can't do anything. If there was a cure for this thing, then they'd be handing it out. And maybe the hospital staff is sick, too. If everyone in there is contagious, they're going to want to quarantine themselves."

"Everyone should quarantine, otherwise it's just going to keep spreading," he agreed.

"All these people..." Mackenzie squeezed her eyes shut. "I don't want to see them. I don't want them to be sick. I don't want to *get* sick."

"We are *not* getting sick, Mac. We're going to be fine. We just have to steer clear of contact with anyone and get back to Sanford."

Mackenzie seemed to have shrunk into herself, and she couldn't tear her eyes from the scene before them. He refused to let anything, even reality, stop them from getting home.

Holding her elbow, Jake marched them away and across to the main road, dodging a woman assisting an elderly man who was coughing blood into his hands.

He couldn't take much more of watching Mackenzie limp along. It was killing him to see her in pain. The road ahead was crammed with empty vehicles, and he made his decision. "We're going to take one of these cars."

"If this virus is airborne, then these vehicles have probably just had infected people in them. We can't risk it," Mackenzie said.

He spun her toward him, forcing her to stop. "Enough. I know you're trying to suck it up, but your feet are really hurting. I can't keep walking past vehicles, watching you suffer."

"Remember I told you about the West Northern case? They knew *nothing* about this virus, how it's carried, how long people are contagious for. We have to be careful."

Her eyes were wet with unshed tears.

Pulling her against his chest, Jake propped his chin on the top of her head, knowing he'd do anything for her. Anything except risk her life.

"You're right. That row of houses down the block have vehicles in their driveways. We'll take one of them. Someone carrying the virus could've been driving them, but at least they're not parked on their way to the hospital."

"We're just going to take someone's car?" She snuffled into the front of his shirt.

"It's a shitty thing to do, but yeah. Normal rules don't apply at the moment, and we need to do anything we can to get home safely."

Mac nodded and pulled back. "Okay, but maybe we should talk to some of these people to see what they know about the virus."

"All they know is that they *have* it. And I don't want us to be anywhere near them."

"But we could find out how long they've had it for, what their symptoms are. If they know anyone—" She paused. "Anyone who's died."

"I think we can assume that yesterday is when most symptoms became obvious, although who knows how long the virus was incubating. And the news reports I heard said they were flu-like symptoms, but that must've been before it progressed to the bleeding."

"I don't think they're sick for long before it kills them," Mackenzie said quietly, and he followed the direction of her eyes.

A young woman with a mop of curly auburn hair was sitting in a stationary car, her head tilted at an odd angle and the lower half of her face coated with blood. She wasn't moving.

In silent agreement, Jake and Mackenzie started moving again, crossing the road to avoid walking next to the line of parked vehicles.

Jake was conscious of a lack of sound—it seemed the entire town was muted. There was no noise of traffic, and even the mob of people at the front of the hospital were milling quietly or slumped listlessly against the walls.

A dog barked once, off in the distance, but there wasn't even a breeze to disturb the fall-colored trees around them. So they both startled badly when they stepped off the sidewalk onto a front lawn and a gravelly voice greeted them.

"You two looking for transport?" A grizzled man was sitting on his front porch, salt-and-pepper beard neatly trimmed and a shotgun resting on his lap.

Instinctively, Jake moved in front of Mackenzie. "We're not looking for any trouble. We just want to get home."

"You're not sick, are you?" It was more an observation than a question.

"No, sir."

"Well, you can't take my truck. But my neighbor fell over dead yesterday. He wasn't sick for more than half a day. So you can take his truck because he sure as shit won't be needing it." He spat on the ground at his feet. "By my reckoning, there's going to be a lot of shit no one's going to be needing," he said, tipping his chin in the hospital's direction.

"Has your neighbor been in his truck recently?" asked Mackenzie, stepping out from behind Jake. "Just in case, you know, his germs are in it?"

The old man chuckled. "Nah, he only left the house on a Sunday afternoon to visit the bar, and then again on Monday to get his groceries. He hasn't been in it for a couple of days."

"So you're okay if we just take it?" Jake flicked his eyes between the shotgun and the faded Ford F-Series in the next driveway over.

"Sure, son. Take it. The keys will be behind the visor." He nodded. "And you take care of that little missy of yours, you hear?"

"That's the plan, sir."

CHAPTER FOUR

Mackenzie collapsed into the passenger seat, staring out the window as Jake navigated his way into a deserted downtown Essex. She was exhausted. The last twenty-four hours had depleted her physically and emotionally. She couldn't handle much more and the idea of sitting still, doing nothing, in the safety of the vehicle was the closest thing to heaven she could think of.

She desperately wished she was home with Chloe, Rachel, and Kat; she didn't even have the energy to be disgusted with herself for acknowledging Sanford as home. She just wanted her three best friends.

Not that Jake wasn't a pretty good substitute. He'd literally been her knight in shining armor—it was his logical practicality that was keeping this shit show on the road. The shit show being her.

Unbidden, the memory of their conversation yesterday crept back into her consciousness, making her tummy do a funny tumble.

I know what I want, Mac. I want you.

She wanted to dismiss his declaration. Instead, she worried at it like a child with a loose tooth.

Jake was in love with her? It was just so unbelievable. Jake was Sanford's golden boy. He was quarterback the year Sanford High School had gone to state. Betty, at Trader Joe's, still slipped him candy at the checkout and he was twenty-three, not five.

God, he is twenty-freaking-three.

Mac could just imagine how Sanford would react—they'd want to burn her at the stake. Even *she* knew she wasn't good enough for Jake.

She'd literally grown up with Jake on the periphery; he was a constant, a touchstone of familiarity and the comfort of childhood. And while she was forging a new life for herself in Chicago, he'd grown into a man. A man with intriguing possibilities.

The pull of attraction was unsettling. Not only had she been in a relationship just yesterday, but this was *Chloe's little brother.*

She wondered where Peter was right now, if he'd made it to pick up his daughter. She was sad for him, but in a detached way. Like she'd known him years ago.

A small convoy of military vehicles rumbled up from behind and overtook them, not pausing as they continued on. Starting, Mackenzie blinked her eyes back into focus.

A man was crumpled on the sidewalk and a woman was sobbing, pulling futilely on his arm. She had twin rivulets of blood streaming unchecked from her nose.

"Jesus, people are literally dropping on the sidewalk!" Jake swore.

Mackenzie continued to watch the convoy as they drove slowly past.

A cavern of hopelessness bloomed in her chest.

Turning back to face the windshield, she closed her eyes. Was this life now? Watching people die and just driving past?

"That's the hiking store," said Jake, pointing at a bright blue building to their left.

"It doesn't look open."

Jake ignored her. "Are you ready to do some shopping?"

"I think it's called shoplifting, not shopping."

"Come on, Mac. Weren't you the one asking for a sleeping bag last night?"

"That was you."

"Okay, maybe it was," he conceded. "But if we're going to sleep outside again, wouldn't you prefer to do it in a sleeping bag?"

"I don't plan on sleeping outside again. Do we really need to do this? We're on our way home. We don't need camping supplies."

"We don't *need* camping supplies," he agreed. "But this is serious, Mac. Life isn't just going to go on like it did before."

Mackenzie shifted in her seat, finally taking the time to digest their new reality.

"You're right," she said slowly, thinking. "How long do you think the electricity is going to keep going? And even if some of the country's food producers survive the virus, what are the chances that the transport drivers will also survive? The distribution facilities? The warehouse and supermarket workers?"

He nodded, eyes somber. "This could all blow over tomorrow. Next week. And I'm happy to be called a fool for being a doomsday prepper. Because I'd much rather that than find out it's not going to blow over, and we don't have matches and flashlights and batteries for when the power goes out. When we don't have hunting knives and fishing rods to keep ourselves fed. Whatever happens, we're going to survive, Mac."

Jake had a determined tilt to his chin and Mackenzie felt a flutter of *something*, knowing he'd look out for her, care for her, no matter what. There was something primal—primitive—in his confidence, in his assurance of protection.

And hell, maybe she and the girls could finally sleep out in the backyard overnight.

"Okay." She nodded. "But we can't just smash the front window to get in, we don't want to draw attention to ourselves."

"Sit tight. I'll walk around to the back of the building and see if there's a window I can break into there."

She nodded again, locking the truck's doors as soon as he'd gotten out and watching as he walked with a long-legged stride around the corner.

Was it wrong to check out his ass? Definitely. *It's a really nice ass though.*

In less than five minutes, he was inside the store, unlocking the front door and gesturing for her.

"That was quick."

"The back door was wide open," he admitted. "No need for hero tactics. I don't think we're the first to have this idea."

Checking the empty sidewalk behind her, he pulled the doors closed and bolted them.

The store was enormous, with row after row of outdoor camping equipment; tents and canoes, hiking gear and para-phernalia she couldn't guess the use of.

Her eyes widened with overwhelm. "Where do we even start?"

"We'll kit ourselves first," Jake said. "Choose a backpack

that you can easily carry when it's full and then look for hiking boots. The women's hiking clothing is over there. Pick out two full outfits and a couple of extra pairs of socks. But do it quick, there'll be others who think of raiding this place."

The knowledge they could soon be joined by other survivors gave Mackenzie a jolt of trepidation. The fewer people they came across, the less the chance of the virus infecting them.

"Meet me at the front counter when you're done, and we'll get together some camping equipment. I'm hoping there might even be a small solar generator here."

Mackenzie hadn't even realized that solar generators were a thing. Shaking off that thought, she headed for the racks of women's clothing, a trickle of anticipation replacing the trepidation. Shopping, she could do.

Slipping behind a half-wall of shelves, she changed into a pair of black, fitted cargo pants and a gray waffle-knit Henley. The thick merino-wool socks were deliciously soft on her ravaged feet, and when she found a pair of hiking boots that had shearling inserts, she almost cried. It was like walking on clouds.

Coordinating a second outfit and some lightweight merino base layers, she then stuffed them all into a bright yellow backpack.

"Don't forget to grab a warm waterproof jacket," Jake shouted from across the store.

"I'm almost done," she called back. "Need me to find anything else?"

His head popped around the corner, grinning. "I think I have everything. I'm just going to look for a portable water purification system."

By the time Jake finally deemed them sufficiently

prepared, Mackenzie's backpack contained a flashlight, a first aid kit, a water bottle, sunscreen, matches, hand sanitizer, a survival knife, a compass—"Do you really think I'm qualified to use this?"—an LED headlamp, and a sleeping bag.

Jake had also put together a pack with tent and cooking equipment, along with the water purification system and solar generator he'd been looking for.

Mackenzie smirked at him. "You look like a packhorse."

"A *prepared* packhorse." He grinned back.

Jake was energized with purpose and Mackenzie took a moment to admire his assertiveness, the straightforward manner in which he'd taken control, allowing her a comforting warmth in his steadfast protection. Who knew making someone feel safe could be sexy?

His broad shoulders easily carried the weight, and her stomach fluttered at the man before her. He was gorgeous. And competent. Did she mention gorgeous? Her eyes roved greedily over the hard planes of his chest, down the thickly corded muscles of his forearms.

"Like what you see?" he drawled quietly, stepping so their torsos brushed ever so lightly.

Mackenzie's nipples hardened perceptibly beneath her top, and her breathing hitched. She couldn't tear her eyes away from the full bottom lip of his mouth. What would it feel like to kiss him? To kiss Jake?

The faint but distinct popping of gunshots in the distance had them jumping apart, breathing heavily. The hiking store had been a cocoon from reality, and Mackenzie had actually had fun playing at doomsday prepper. But it was time to get moving.

They exited the store, tossing all the equipment into the back of the truck.

They weren't *playing* at anything. As evidenced by the dead body of a man in the gutter across the road, who hadn't been there when they'd parked.

As she stood eyeing the corpse, a police siren split the still air, jolting her. Cowering instinctively against the side of the truck, she watched as a police car careened around the corner, its siren wailing. It was speeding far too fast for safety, and several youths were hanging out the windows, hollering with unrestrained joy.

"What the hell?" yelled Jake. "Mac, get in the truck!"

Scrambling to obey, she slammed and locked the door behind her, but the police car was already in the distance, the siren growing fainter. They sat silently, watching until the police vehicle rounded a far corner and disappeared.

"I can't wait to get home," Mackenzie surprised herself by saying.

Jake just nodded grimly and started driving.

THEY WERE CRUISING down the highway, Jake driving with a careless competence, when they came across the first deserted gas station with a handmade sign proclaiming No Gas.

Apart from two vehicles they'd passed going in the opposite direction, the highway had been just as deserted.

"Where do you think everyone is?" Jake asked, breaking off a piece of bread roll and chewing.

"They're probably either staying inside, or dead." Mackenzie wished he hadn't asked. *Everyone* couldn't be dead. Surely. "Do you think everyone is okay in Sanford?" she asked quietly.

Jake stared ahead, his jaw working. Finally, he

answered, "Yes." His eyes were trained on the empty highway before them. "They're going to be fine."

Mac couldn't bear to think of her best friends suffering.

With blood running down their faces.

She couldn't imagine a world without Kat, Chlo, and Rach. Her heart ached with a fierce need to be with them.

———

"ANY APPLES LEFT?" They weren't far from Sanford, and Jake's stomach was growling. He nudged at the bag sitting between them and then flicked his eyes to the fuel gage of the truck. "We're only just going to have enough gas to get us home."

Mackenzie hummed noncommittally and rummaged through the bag, finally pulling out a red apple, which she promptly licked.

The sight of her small pink tongue against the glossy skin of the apple almost had him veering off the road.

"What are you doing?" His voice was unnaturally hoarse.

"I licked it, so it's mine."

Jake emitted a low growl at the thought of licking the milky white column of her neck. Would that then make her his?

"If you think a bit of spit is going to stop me from eating that apple, you're sadly mistaken," he warned, reaching out a long arm and snatching the fruit from her.

"Hey!" she protested, swatting ineffectually at his shoulder.

He took a large bite and chewed loudly. "Tastes good."

"You're such a dick."

"I thought you didn't want to talk about my dick?"

The instant flush that warmed her face had his blood rushing south.

With her red cheeks facing the window, he adjusted himself discreetly. The constant proximity to her—without access to a cold shower—was like playing with fire. And damn if he didn't want to get burned.

Jake didn't want to push Mac, but he was desperate to know if she'd been thinking about yesterday's declaration. His adoration of her had been in a pressure cooker for years, and even when things seemed serious with that asshole Peter, he couldn't turn it off. There was *no* stopping the ground-shaking reverence of his feelings.

His heart was heavy with them.

The only reason Jake was on Instagram was so he could follow Mackenzie. The only reason he couldn't commit to a relationship was because no one else *was* her. Hell, he still had a T-shirt of hers she'd left behind in Chloe's room *six years* ago.

This wasn't a passing crush for him.

Casting her a quick side-eye, he sighed quietly.

Could she see past the fact he was Chloe's brother? Her *younger* brother?

"You've gone quiet," Mackenzie said, reaching over and grabbing the forgotten half-eaten apple from his fingers. He winced as the movement caused her top to pull tight against the swell of her breasts.

Fuuuuuuck.

"Just thinking," he said.

"About what?"

Wrapping your thighs around my hips and fucking the recollection of every previous man from your memory. "Probably best that you"—his voice cracked, and he cleared his throat—"don't know. Have you thought about where

58

you're going to stay? I'm assuming your dad isn't an option."

"You assume correctly. I wouldn't stay in his broke-down trailer if you paid me."

"You can crash with me."

It was her turn to give him a sideways look. "I'll stay with one of the girls. Chloe, if Ash isn't back yet. Or Rach, her long hours at the vet clinic make her a good roommate. Not sure if I can handle the hot mess that is Kat on a 24/7 basis, but I could manage for a couple of days."

"The offer's there." He shrugged.

They passed the Welcome to Sanford sign and fell silent, the steady whirring of tires on asphalt filling the truck.

Tightening his hands on the steering wheel, Jake swallowed. He hadn't allowed himself to think about what could've happened in the twenty-four hours he'd been gone. Dread settled low in his belly.

Coming around the last bend in the road before the bridge, Jake saw the local fire truck barricading it, planted sideways across the road and flanked on both sides by several vehicles. But it was the men standing on top of the fire truck with AK-47 assault riffle that had Jake's skin tightening, the hairs on his arms rising. He jerked the truck to the other side of the road, his foot easing from the accelerator.

"What are they *doing*?" Mackenzie breathed, transfixed. "Is that Buddy Robinson and Tom Brenner?"

"Looks like it." Jake pulled his truck to a stop fifty feet from the makeshift blockade.

He'd played football with Buddy, but Tom was a mean son of a bitch. Not knowing what to expect, Jake slowly swung his door open and made to step out.

"Hold it right there!" Tom yelled.

"Tom, it's me, Jake Brent. We just want—"

"I said, hold it right there!" Tom growled. "Quinn, check 'em out."

At the sight of Quinn—Jake's cousin—jogging out from behind the truck, his lungs expanded enough for a decent breath.

"Jesus, Jake. We were getting worried." Quinn puffed, coming to a halt at the open driver's door. "We expected you back last night."

"What the hell is going on?" Jake was unable to take his eyes from the Ak-47s pointed at them. "Can you tell them to put their fucking rifles down?"

Quinn waved his arm at Buddy and Tom. "It's all right, boys, it's just Jake and Mackenzie Lyons."

Tom grunted and climbed down from the truck, his weapon still at the ready. "It's not all right until they've been cleared."

"Cleared?" asked Jake.

Quinn's face clouded over, his brows drawing together. "It's been bad. Mayor Townsend is saying more than half the town is gone. He's set up a quarantine for everyone who comes down with symptoms, and so far no one's come out."

"Gone?" Mackenzie was leaning over Jake to hear Quinn better.

"Dead." He confirmed grimly.

Mackenzie choked on a sob.

"Chloe?" Jake asked roughly.

"Chloe, Kat and Rachel are all fine. At least, they were when I saw them an hour ago. Frantic over you two, though."

"Have you seen my dad?" Mackenzie said, surprising Jake. He didn't think she'd seen or spoken to her father in years, but he guessed the apocalypse overshadowed family estrangement.

"Get out of the truck," growled Tom, shoving in front of Quinn before he could answer, pulling a surgical mask over his mouth and nose. "No one's coming into Sanford unless they've been cleared."

Jake glanced at Mackenzie, concerned at how short of breath she appeared. "It's okay, let's just get this over with. Have you got your inhaler?"

She nodded, and he waited for her to use it, his heart rate mirroring her breathing as it calmed.

Tom and Quinn backed away so Mackenzie and Jake could come round to the front of the vehicle.

Jake took Mackenzie's trembling hand and squeezed. "We're almost home."

Her fear was palpable and Jake's throat ached with wanting to comfort her, with wanting to draw her into his arms and be far away from this fucking moment in time.

"And why the fuck aren't you wearing your mask?" Tom hissed at Quinn.

Quinn's features hardened. "Because it's *Jake*, and he wouldn't put the entire town at risk by coming in here if he was infected."

"Well, why the *fuck* does he have dried blood on his shirt?" Tom raised the rifle to his shoulder.

Jake's mouth went dry.

"I can explain." He stepped forward, raising his hands palm up.

"Don't come one foot closer." Tom slid the bolt of the rifle and loaded a cartridge into the chamber.

"Tell me that's not blood, man," Quinn entreated, his eyes flashing with panic.

"It's not! Well, it is—"

"Don't make this hard on us, boy. Just get back in the truck, turn around, and go," Tom ordered in a hard voice.

"It's not the virus. I'm not infected, I swear."

Sweat beaded on Jake's forehead, itchy and hot. The relief at having reached Sanford—at being so close to home —crashed swiftly, replaced by a desperation that tasted sour.

"It was me!" Mackenzie stepped forward, hands also raised in supplication. "I accidentally gave him a bloody nose."

"Back off, bitch," Tom threatened.

"Watch your mouth!" Jake exploded and turned to Quinn. "He's a fucking *electrician*. What makes him quali-fied to be doing this? Where's the police chief, or that new deputy, what's his name?"

"Deputy Davies. And they're both dead," Quinn said.

That silenced everyone. The sun overhead cast long shadows of their uneasy impasse.

"Do you have any symptoms? Fever? Headache? Aching joints?" Quinn asked finally, his voice threaded with a mix of angst and hope.

Jake shook his head, heart in throat. "I swear it, Quinn. Neither of us are sick."

"He's been bleeding from his nose. He ain't coming in," Tom growled.

"What if I vouch for him?" Quinn said.

"Your vouching means nothing if we're all dead."

"Okay, then we compromise. Let them over the bridge, but not into the Safe Zone. They can stay in one of the houses outside the boundary for forty-eight hours, and then we reassess." Quinn rolled his heavily muscled shoulders to release tension. "I'm not turning them away, Tom."

"Safe Zone?" said Jake.

"We can't defend the entire town, so Townsend has sectioned off a part as a safe area—the Safe Zone—and everyone is inside that boundary, except those who've been quarantined."

"Who are you defending the town from?" Mackenzie asked, shading her eyes from the glare of the sun and inching closer to Jake.

He pulled her against his side, his arm bracketing her shoulders.

"People like you," snarled Tom. "Infected people looking for safety and instead killing us all."

"We don't know they're infected," Quinn said firmly. "They aren't exhibiting any of the signs except the blood on the shirt, which they've explained."

"They can't prove it," said Tom.

"Neither can you. I'll escort them into the Evac Area and guarantee they'll stay there until we've cleared them."

"If they approach the main gate before I've personally cleared them, I'll shoot them on sight." Tom promised before swinging his large frame away and striding back to the fire truck, spitting on the ground as he went.

"Lovely welcoming committee you've got going," Mackenzie murmured. "Thank you for standing up for us."

"Not a problem," Quinn said. "But if it's all the same to you, I might hold off on the welcoming hug. Drive around to the left and I'll move the barricade, and then follow me. Jake, your home's inside the Safe Zone, but you can crash at my house. It's in the Evac Area."

Which meant Chloe was also in the Safe Zone. The tension in Jake's gut eased some. His parents were on vacation, and Chloe would be looking after their grandmother. Not for the first time, he wondered how his parents were faring.

Tom grudgingly waved them through the blockade, and they followed Quinn, riding a dirt bike across the bridge and into the outer suburbs of Sanford. The streets were disconcertingly vacant, save for a band of dogs that were nosing around a knocked-over trashcan.

Pulling up in front of Quinn's brick home, Jake pulled on the handbrake and turned to face Mackenzie. "We made it. Quinn'll let the girls know we're here, and we'll see them in forty-eight hours. We're safe."

Mackenzie wrapped her arms around her middle, and Jake noticed she was shaking. "It just doesn't feel real. It doesn't *feel* like home. And what if we are infected, and we're just not showing symptoms yet?" she whispered.

It'd been a niggling thought at the back of Jake's mind also, but he refused to give it credence.

"We're *not* sick, Mac. We're going to be fine." Leaning over, he cupped her face tenderly, stroking calloused thumbs over the smoothness of her cheek. "I'm not going to let anything happen to you."

CHAPTER FIVE

Mackenzie came awake in slow degrees, her body boneless and mind drifting. The keening woman on the highway, holding her dead child, jerked her into full consciousness.

Heart in throat, she squeezed her eyes together, wishing the oblivion of sleep would drag her back under. She wasn't prepared to face her life—the world—right now.

She'd tumbled into bed as soon as they'd arrived at Quinn's house and slept deeply. Dusk was now falling, so she assumed she'd only been asleep an hour or two. Just enough to take the edge off her exhaustion. Sighing, she relaxed back into the pillows and peered around Quinn's bedroom. It was beyond weird to be sleeping on sheets that he'd lain in not so long ago.

The fact they were in Sanford but still so far from Kat, Chloe, and Rach turned Mackenzie's yearning sharp, and she clenched her hands in the sheets. The need to be with them was a visceral tugging in her stomach.

Maybe if she just curled up under the covers for long enough, the world would right itself by the time she emerged. But when her stomach complained loudly, she knew she couldn't avoid reality any longer.

Swinging her legs over the side of the bed, she searched the room for her backpack. She'd been in such a daze when they'd arrived, she couldn't remember where she'd left it. Maybe the family room? She wondered where Jake was, if he were asleep somewhere in the house.

The need to see him hit her fiercely. She craved the sense of safety he instilled in her.

"Jake?" she called quietly, venturing downstairs to the open-plan living area.

He was asleep sitting up, muscle-corded arms spread along the back of the couch, legs thrown wide in an overtly masculine position and head tilted back, exposing a strong throat that had Mackenzie licking her lips.

Oh, my goodness. What am I thinking? What would Chloe *think?*

Clamping her lips firmly closed, Mac skirted his sleeping form, spying her backpack. She reached in and rummaged quietly for a clean tank top without waking Jake. Turning to face the wall, she whipped off her stale top and shrugged into the new one, turning as she did so.

Looking down, she gasped.

Jake was watching her intently, riveted to the exposed skin of her stomach before the material dropped into place. His throat swallowed before he raised his eyes to hers— there was pure, undiluted sex in his gaze and a liquid heat rushed straight to her core.

"Remember that yellow bikini you used to wear?" Jake asked huskily.

"Mm-hmm."

"I still think about that bikini." He finally released her from the intensity of his gaze as he sat up, stretching. The movement bared his own stomach, and Mackenzie flushed at his leanly defined muscles dusted with golden hair.

"Is there an air conditioner in here?" she asked abruptly.

"Just the fan." Jake pointed to the lazily revolving ceiling fan above them.

"Does Quinn live with anyone?"

"Nah, he's too hung up on—" He paused. "Never mind."

"Too hung up on who?" Mackenzie was intrigued.

Although Sanford was a small town and everyone knew everyone, Quinn was a few years older than Mac and she hadn't had a lot to do with the big, burly man, except to know he was a distant cousin of Chloe's and a part owner of Jake's mechanic shop.

And there was that one time Kat had been dancing on top of the bar at The Strumpet and, thanks to the copious volume of vodka she'd consumed, fallen. Hadn't it been Quinn who'd caught her?

Mackenzie's stomach rumbled again. Loudly.

"Hungry?" Jake grinned.

"Starving."

She walked into the kitchen, acutely aware of how closely Jake followed behind. Acutely aware of everything about the man. Having found a safe haven, there was now nothing to distract her from his declaration of love, and while she knew he was confusing love with lust, she couldn't deny her own attraction.

"Quinn has bacon, I can make us BLTs," she said, keeping her face stuck in the refrigerator to cool her suddenly warm cheeks.

They flared hotter when she felt him close in behind her, his chest pressed against her back.

"Sounds good." He plucked a beer from the shelf above her head and stepped back. "Want one?"

"Uh-huh."

Closing her eyes, she counted to ten. Mac was completely fine with being alone with Jake. *Completely fine.* They'd just spent the last twenty-four hours together. She could totally do this. Grabbing a beer for herself, she withdrew from the refrigerator and set about preparing their meal, resolutely ignoring the shiver of desire that sparked as their fingers brushed when he passed her the mayonnaise jar.

They'd discovered that Quinn wasn't much of a cook, and his almost-bare pantry reflected that fact. Even with the food they'd brought with them from the supermarket in Chicago, they'd have to venture into the neighbor's homes tomorrow to see what kind of food they could scavenge.

Mac shivered at the thought of heading back outside.

"Do you think Grams is okay?" she asked. She wondered about her father as well, but didn't voice it. He was a topic she avoided at all costs, whereas Jake and Chloe's grandmother had always been kind to her and she was genuinely concerned for the woman.

"She'll be with Chlo."

"Not your parents?"

"They're in Hawaii. I'm sure they'll be trying to get the next flight home, but with O'Hare out of action... I hope they wait until this is all under control."

His voice had an undercurrent of uncertainty that Mackenzie found hard to reconcile with the charmed, and charming, Jake.

"I'm sure they're fine," she reassured, although privately she wondered if *anyone* was fine anymore. "They're going to be thrilled to see me again."

"What do you mean?"

"I just said that out loud, didn't I?"

He quirked an eyebrow at her.

"Forget it."

"Forget what? You think my parents won't be happy to see you?"

"Not as happy as they were to get rid of me," she mumbled. When she turned to face him, the confusion on his features had her sighing. "Forget it, Jake. It's ancient history."

"Mom and Dad pretty much raised you, you were part of the family."

"Your parents are good people, and they took care of me when they could, which I'll always appreciate. But they did it because they felt obligated, not because they wanted to. Trust me when I tell you they didn't love the fact that Chloe chose me as a best friend."

Mackenzie wasn't sure she could articulate the many subtle ways his parents had made her feel she didn't belong. And to be honest, she didn't want to. She didn't want to relive those days of feeling like an outsider, and she didn't want Jake to think badly of his parents.

Because right now, as crazy as it seemed, she did feel like she belonged. Belonged with him.

The idea of being with Jake brought as much security as it did butterflies. She wished, for just a moment, she were any other girl. One who could fall into his arms with no reservations about her past or her history with this town. One who was worthy to bask in the glow of Sanford's golden boy.

Because she was tempted. Oh, she was tempted.

JAKE COULDN'T PULL his eyes away from Mackenzie, stacking the dishes from their meal in the sink. Her new tank was white and—*fuck me*—she wasn't wearing a bra. The curving outline of her generous breasts, the dusky shadows of her nipples, were enough to cause his head to spin. Every drop of blood in his body was now pulsing in his cock.

Registering the intensity of his stare, she blushed, a pretty pink spreading across her cheeks. Would she flush like that when her legs were locked tight around his hips?

"Jake?" She raised an eyebrow, and that slight smirk had him instantly imagining those lush lips wrapped around his—

"Earth to Jake." She rounded the kitchen counter to stand beside him, gently knocking her hip into the side of his thigh. "You need an early night, buddy."

She smelled warm and cinnamony—and god*damn*, his balls were aching.

"Here, I made you tea," he said.

"You know how I take my tea?"

"Two sugars, lots of creamer."

Those big green eyes of hers studied him over the rim of the mug. "Careful Jake, you're showing your hand."

"Babe, my hand is flat on the table, facing up."

Jake shifted, nudging her back against the counter and stepping closer, until he swore she could feel the beat of his heart in his chest. But he didn't touch her. Not yet.

"You know I'm in love with you, Mac. The question is, how do you feel about that?" he asked, low and husky.

Her grip was unsteady as she placed the mug behind her, but he saw the fluttering pulse in the hollow of her neck. He recognized the banked desire in her heavily lidded eyes.

He knew she was the other half of his soul, and because of this faith, it was inconceivable she wouldn't feel the connection between them. Circumstance, age, history... they'd all worked against him. But now, with life stripped back and nothing between them—no significant others, no distracting friends, how could she *not* feel it?

"Jake," she breathed, hands fluttering at her sides before coming to rest against his chest.

But she didn't exert any pressure signaling he should step back, and he reveled in the knowledge.

"This is all kind of... sudden," she hedged, biting on that plump lower lip, and *fuck* if he didn't want to suck it between his own lips. "Because of Chloe, because of Peter, I just haven't ever..."

"Haven't ever what?"

"I haven't ever thought of you that way before." Her eyes dipped to where her fingers were unconsciously kneading at his chest, kitten-like. She stilled.

"Don't stop," he urged gruffly.

Mac blinked inky lashes, and the moment spun out between them, consuming and full of possibility.

"I just—it feels wrong to be feeling like this. You're *you*. You're like my—"

"Don't say it. I'm *not* your little brother. Does anything about me feel little to you?"

The need to pull her closer was overwhelming, but until she gave her consent to explore their ratcheting attraction, he held firm. This had been one-sided for too many years.

"Jake? Can we talk about this in the morning? I'm exhausted and I can't think straight."

Hiding his disappointment, he moved back, catching her hands as they fell.

"Whatever you need. I'm not going anywhere." He

brought the backs of her hands to his mouth and softly kissed the almost translucent skin. "Get a good night's sleep. I'll just switch off the lights and then turn in too."

"Where are you sleeping?"

"Quinn has a spare bedroom. It's tiny as fuck, but the bed's comfortable enough."

"Do you think..." She paused. "You could sleep with me?"

She said it so quietly Jake almost thought he'd misheard.

Motionless, he stared at her.

"I'm not coming onto you!" Her eyes widened. "I just don't want to be alone tonight."

"Of course, babe."

MORNING LIGHT WAS SEEPING beneath the bedroom blinds as Jake groaned softly, drawing Mackenzie's slumbering body tighter. Burying his head in the crook of her neck, he acknowledged that a stiff prick had no conscience.

He'd promised himself she needed to make the next move—he was adamant he wouldn't push her. But *Jesus fucking Christ*. The soft, languid weight of her curled into him was more than any man could bear. Surely.

Another groan reverberated through him.

Jake needed to get out of bed before he did something he'd regret.

Disentangling their legs, he slid from beneath the covers, pulling them up so they covered the exposed curve of Mackenzie's shoulder.

Even her *shoulder* was sexy.

"Jake?" she mumbled sleepily. "What're you doin'?"

"Go back to sleep. I'm going to check out some of the neighboring houses and see if I can scavenge some food."

At that, she sat up abruptly, the covers pooling at her waist.

"You're leaving?"

"I won't be long. Quinn's always whining about a neighbor's rooster crowing at ungodly hours. Feel like eggs for breakfast?"

She visibly relaxed. "Just be careful, okay? And don't be too long."

"I'll be back before you know it," he promised, pulling on the jeans he'd discarded last night.

Jake didn't miss the way she watched the flexing of his thighs and hid a grin. Heading downstairs, he collected a shopping bag and tied a clean bandanna around his face. He knew the Evac Area was supposedly deserted, but it was better to be safe than sorry.

Outside there was a chill to the air, a deceptive stillness. Sanford was at once the town he'd grown up in and an unknown entity. Where forty-eight hours ago cars would be leaving driveways heading to work, school buses would be making their rounds, and joggers would be pounding the sidewalks—now, all was quiet.

Jake tried to remember which poet had coined the famous quote about the world ending not with a bang, but a whimper. English had never been his strength at school. Regardless, the undeniable truth of the poem was jarring.

Looking up and down the empty street, he turned to the right, deciding it would be best to check each house methodically. Quinn's neighbor had a neatly kept front yard with a rolled-up newspaper still sitting on the front porch. Picking it up, Jake noted it was from three days ago, the headline shouting about a celebrity who'd been sentenced

73

to fourteen days in prison because of some college admission scandal... nothing at all about the virus that was about to annihilate humanity.

It was incredible that the media outlets had been so willing to fall in line with the president's complete denial of Sy-V.

Raising his hand, he knocked at the front door and was immediately chagrined. There would be no one home. They were in the Safe Zone, or dead. Absently, he wondered how long it would take for old habits to be replaced by this new reality.

Sanford was a small town with little to no security concerns, and the doorknob turned, unlocked. Before he could set foot inside, a putrid stench of decomposition overcame him. Instantaneous retching had him gagging behind his bandanna as he fell backward, slamming the door closed.

Tears ran unchecked down his cheeks as he spat compulsively onto the ground, desperate to erase an odor so pervasive he could taste it. Stumbling to the street, he collapsed into the gutter, shaking legs unable to hold him standing as he gulped deeply of the clean air.

There was a huge distinction between knowing he could encounter dead bodies and *actually* encountering them. Surely that person—people?—had been dead longer than the two days they'd known of the virus? Or did the virus make them decompose quicker?

It was several long moments before Jake had the strength to stand and the will to continue on. Pausing at the front door to the next house, he steeled himself for what lay beyond before cautiously opening it, sniffing at the air with a curled top lip. The relief at not being hit in the face with a decomposing human body was palpable.

Shutting the door gently, he ventured down a hallway lined with photos, although he couldn't place the family. He wasn't sure if knowing or *not* knowing them would be easier as he walked through their home. Several pairs of shoes littered the floor and the kitchen still had dirty breakfast dishes in the sink.

Resolutely blocking out the personal details of the house, Jake went straight for the refrigerator and began loading his bag. The pantry had slim pickings, but there were canned vegetables and tuna.

It was the third house where he found the chicken coop out back, along with a verdant and well-ordered vegetable garden. Reaching under clucky hens, he collected several eggs, already debating whether he should poach or scramble them. Handily, an egg basket sat outside the coop so he could carry them back to Quinn's.

Feeling on a roll, he chanced one more house before heading back to Mackenzie. She had a sweet tooth, and he wasn't above using chocolate to fight his way into her affections.

He headed straight to the back door and was relieved to find it open. Although, learning how to pick locks was fast climbing to the top of his priority list. The kitchen cupboards were well stocked—but no chocolate—and Jake's bag was full before he'd even started on the second shelf.

He'd just clocked the stack of dog food cans when the clicking of nails on the hardwood floor preceded a warning growl that had his balls shriveling.

"Hey boy," he murmured in a low voice, slowly turning to face the dog.

A large German shepherd crouched in the doorway, hackles raised and teeth bared.

The growl escalated to a snarl and Jake continued

soothing platitudes at the canine while frantically evaluating escape options. He'd have to cross the dog's path to make it out the back, and it was blocking the doorway to the front.

There was only one other door, and Jake guessed—hoped—it led to the garage. "Easy boy, easy," he said, slowly backing toward it.

The German shepherd tracked his movements, and when it lunged forward on powerful hind legs, Jake flung himself through the door, slamming it just as the weight of the dog crashed into it.

Panting, Jake looked around the dim interior, confirming it was a garage. To the soundtrack of frantic barking, he located a light switch and found the space empty save a golf bag, a stepladder, and some gardening implements.

When the bare bulb illuminating the room flickered, and then went out, he swore. Blown bulb, or had the electricity gone out?

Striding to the automatic garage door, he ran his hand along the wall, searching for a button to open it. The dog was now ferociously scratching at the door and when Jake's hand finally ran across the button, he jabbed at it anxiously.

Nothing happened.

The electricity was out. But surely there was a way to manually open it? Frustration clawed at him. He should've gone back to Mackenzie after the third house. He'd already been gone longer than he'd planned.

Setting down his bag of food, Jake grabbed the step ladder and studied the door, finally seeing what looked to be an emergency cord hanging from the center rail of the garage door mechanism. Pulling it, he expected the cord to disconnect the door from the garage door opener, allowing him to lift it open.

Jumping from the stepladder, he pulled at the bottom of the door, to no avail.

"Fuck!"

He tried the cord again, and while it swung from the urgency of his action, the door stayed resolutely shut.

He slid to the ground, bowing his head between bent knees. He should've followed his gut and stayed in bed with Mackenzie. Screw the consequences.

Pun intended.

He sighed. Why was everything so damn *hard*? Nothing was easy anymore. He prided himself on being resilient and practical, but was it too much to ask for a simple home ransacking to go to plan?

Jake could wait for the electricity to come back on, assuming it would, or find a weapon of some description and brave the dog.

It was the thought of Mackenzie panicking at his longer than expected absence that had him getting to his feet and finding a garden shovel. The idea of maiming an animal made him grimace, but the option of being mauled to death wasn't especially appealing either.

Glancing back at the shopping bag, he decided he'd have a better chance of escaping unharmed without trying to carry it as well, as much as he hated the thought of returning empty-handed.

The door was shuddering as though the dog were throwing itself against it. Bracing himself, Jake raised the shovel and prepared to open it quickly. He hoped he'd startle the dog into charging into the garage while he was shielded behind the door, and he could slip past back into the house.

"Because everything else has gone so smoothly," he muttered wryly to himself.

Rolling his shoulders, Jake took a deep breath... and then hesitated.

Exactly how much would a dog bite hurt? He imagined its teeth were sharp enough to puncture cleanly through. It was the ripping and tearing of his flesh as the German shepherd pulled away that was concerning.

"Fuck it." Gripping the door handle, he pulled down... only to find it locked. It had locked automatically from the inside. "You have *got* to be fucking kidding me!" he roared.

Trapped, he turned in a slow circle around the garage, assessing his options. They were few. Resuming his sitting position—as far from the snarling beast as possible—he cursed not having the ability to search the internet on his phone.

Jake could understand telecommunication going down in an apocalypse, but surely it was just human decency to allow the internet to live on. How was anyone meant to know *anything* without it? He was pretty sure there weren't going to be books in Sanford Town Library telling him how to pick locks. Not that he could *get* to the library in his current predicament.

T.S. Eliot.

Remembering the name of the poet, he let out a whimper.

CHAPTER SIX

"Fuck. Fuck-fuck-fuckity-fuck."

Mackenzie resumed her pacing. Jake was taking *way* longer than she thought he would, and now the power had gone out. Not even yoga breathing was helping with the restless agitation consuming her.

It wasn't so much the lack of electricity that was terrifying—it was daylight, after all. It was the idea of what it represented. How did the world function without power? Did you even still have running water without electricity?

Spinning on her heel, she rushed to the kitchen, turning on the faucet and feeling light-headed with relief when water spilled out. Out of habit, she flicked on the teakettle and pulled a mug from the cupboard, only to realize the kettle wasn't boiling.

Of course.

Sighing, Mac slumped at the kitchen table. It was unnerving to be alone in the house, knowing only empty houses surrounded her. She was cut off from the rest of the town and the distance created an echo of unease.

When Jake had left this morning, she'd rolled into the

hollow of the mattress he'd vacated, breathing in the wholly masculine scent of him. It wasn't a cologne, which she'd always found overpowering with other men. No, it was just *Jake.* A smell that had something warm and unbidden unfurling inside her.

The idea of him, of *them,* was fluttery. Exciting. It had her chest tightening with a delicious sense of anticipation. For the first time, cocooned in the warmth he'd left behind, she'd allowed herself to imagine the possibility of them together.

And it felt right. *God,* it felt right.

He promised he wouldn't be long.

Resolutely, she stood and marched to the front door. Swinging it open, she hesitated on the threshold, hating the vulnerability that swamped her. Had it really come to this? She was a grown woman who was afraid to leave the house?

Mackenzie jumped as a sudden electrical whirring preceded the lights coming back on. Well, at least they had power again. Buoyed by this, she stepped onto the porch, letting the front door swing shut behind her. Outside was eerily quiet.

"Jake?" she called, walking down the steps and scouting up and down the street.

Nothing moved.

Turning left, she called out again, wondering if she was brave enough to enter any of the houses.

"Mac!"

Thudding feet on the sidewalk behind her had her spinning, arms instinctively raised in defense. She collapsed to her knees at the sight of Jake running toward her.

"Mac!" he yelled again.

"Where have you *been?*" she screamed, built-up tension exploding from her.

Panting, he dropped to his knees to embrace her, and she shoved him away, getting awkwardly to her feet.

"You left me! *Again!*" Her throat was tight as she struggled to rein in a torrent of tears.

"I'm sorry! I'm so sorry." His eyes were imploring and his fists clenched uselessly on his thighs. "I got trapped when the power went out. I couldn't get to you."

Gulping at air, she stared as he slowly got to his feet, reaching out until he gathered her trembling body into his.

"I would never leave you," he whispered into her hair with a tender fervency.

"I didn't know where you were."

"I know, I know," he soothed. "Come on, let's go inside. I promised you eggs for breakfast, didn't I?"

THEY ATE THE EGGS, each hyperaware of the other. Jake kept watching her as though he were worried she was about to have a breakdown, and she was jumpy if she couldn't see or hear him.

A fact she didn't think she was hiding very well.

Jesus. I need to get my shit together.

"So the poor dog is still in the house?" Mackenzie asked.

"I know you love dogs, and I feel like shit leaving it there, but it was vicious. I didn't really want my arm bitten off."

"It was probably just hungry. I think we should go back and feed it."

He looked at her dubiously.

"You know I have some sort of weird affinity with dogs. Remember that cranky old lapdog Grams used to have? That fluffball adored me."

"Mac, this was a guard dog, and it was good at its job."

"We can't leave it there," Mackenzie said stubbornly, crossing her arms for emphasis. She didn't miss the way his eyes lingered on her cleavage. "Bring one of Quinn's hunting rifles if you think we need the backup, but I bet the poor thing is just hungry. And I'm going, regardless."

"Why is your determination turning me on?" He groaned. "Fine. Let me find a weapon and we can assess the situation."

Mackenzie grinned.

She'd always wanted a dog, but her father could barely feed her most of the time, let alone an animal. And when she'd moved to Chicago, her apartment was too small and her hours at work too long.

She hadn't been exaggerating about her affinity with canines; it was almost uncanny. She attracted them and she'd never met one she didn't like. Or one that didn't like her.

Mackenzie had found some questionable lunch meat at Quinn's and was confident she could win the animal over. She had a bounce in her step as they walked to the neighbor's house, Jake grumbling by her side.

"You stand back here, and I'll open the front door, run back to you, and then we can call for it," he instructed.

"You're no use as backup if you're in front of me," she replied. "How about you wait back here, and I'll open the door? That way if the dog really is crazy, you can let off a shot to scare it away."

His jaw ticked, and Mackenzie knew he hated the sense she was making. She hid a smile.

"Fine." He huffed. "But be careful. Open the door and get the hell away as fast as you can."

Mackenzie had no intention of running away. She *knew*, with a bone-deep certainty, the dog wouldn't harm her. That said, she wasn't stupid. She wouldn't try to enter the house, and she'd back away if it barked.

Stepping up to the front door, she stilled and listened, but heard nothing. She knocked gently before swinging it open and taking a half step back, calling quietly for the dog.

"Mackenzie!" Jake hissed.

She ignored him, concentrating on the steady click of nails on the hardwood floor until the dog appeared at the end of the hallway.

"Well, aren't you handsome?" she murmured encouragingly. Coming toward her cautiously, the German shepherd stopped at her outstretched hand, sniffing. "Hey there. You hungry?"

The dog sat back on its haunches, cocking its head. Mackenzie dropped the sandwich meat at her feet and, although the dog eyed it hungrily, it waited.

"Eat," she commanded, and it wolfed down the meat in a single bite. "Oh yeah, you're hungry," she said, ruffling its fur and noting the tag on his collar read Dex.

Dex whined and nudged her hand with his nose before turning and heading back into the house. When she didn't immediately follow, he looked over his shoulder and yipped.

"Okay, okay. I'm coming."

Jake joined Mac as she entered the house, muttering about how the animal could still be dangerous while angling himself in front of her. They found Dex in the kitchen, sitting in front of a cupboard wagging his tail. Mackenzie opened it to reveal tins of dog food, laughing when Dex sat up on his back legs in a begging position.

"This sure is one ferocious animal," she said.

———

JAKE SIGHED. First the dog had tried to eat him, and now it was stealing Mackenzie's affection.

She'd insisted Dex come back to Quinn's with them and, while the animal studiously ignored him, it was quick to position itself between him and Mackenzie at every opportunity.

The afternoon had darkened with an incoming storm, and what could've been a cozy situation instead became Dex working his way between their bodies until his face—complete with lolling tongue—was on Mackenzie's lap, and his ass was pointed at Jake.

I'm being cockblocked by a damn dog.

After a late lunch, Mac had decided they'd earned a spot of day drinking, and when he'd seen Quinn's impressive whiskey collection, he'd been inclined to agree. Not knowing what was happening in the Safe Zone was bugging him more than he'd like to admit, and he was hoping the alcohol would take the edge off.

"What's up?" Mackenzie asked, rubbing Dex's ears. "You've gone quiet."

"Just thinking."

"About?"

"It's maddening that we're so close to home, but we're not there. It's like we're in a vacuum out here. We have no idea what's happening in Sanford, or out in the rest of the state. In the rest of the *country*." Jake took a long swallow of the whiskey.

It had shaken him more than he cared to admit when he'd learned the military had bombed O'Hare. How was it that, in the space of a day, the situation went from presidential assurances the virus wasn't a big deal to American citizens being killed by their own government?

And why had the roads been so empty? After the frenzy

to leave Chicago, Jake had assumed the deluge of people would be clogging every main road. But aside from the crowds they'd witnessed at Essex Memorial, people had been few and far between.

Were they quarantining themselves in their homes?

Or were they dead?

"It kind of feels like we're suspended in time here," Mackenzie said. "Everything happened so fast, and now we're just... sitting here."

"It's hard not knowing. And not doing anything."

"You don't like it when you're not in control," she observed.

"That's not it. I don't have to be in control all the time."

"I'm not saying it's a bad thing. It's just who you are. You're confident and you take charge. You make me feel safe." Mackenzie stared into her almost empty glass.

The rush of warmth Jake experienced had nothing to do with the whiskey and everything to do with her words. The fact she felt safe with him was *everything*. He wanted to beat on his chest in satisfaction.

"Don't go getting all cocky." She dislodged the dog, reached for the whiskey bottle, and refilled their glasses.

He knew he looked smug, and as her eyes narrowed on him, his shit-eating grin spread wider. "What else—"

"Shut it, Jake."

They continued putting a dent in Quinn's whiskey, reminiscing about their shared childhood and avoiding any more talk of the apparent apocalypse.

The dog, curled on the floor at Mackenzie's feet, opened one eye when Mac took two attempts to place her glass on the coffee table, and Jake was suddenly aware that she was more than a little tipsy. He stood, holding out a hand to her.

"You okay?" She tipped her face up to look at him, her nose crinkling adorably.

"I'm fine."

"Well, I'm glad you're fine, but I'm actually not. I'm not fine at all. Want to know why I'm not fine, Jake?"

Pulling her to her feet, he pushed a curl behind her ear. "Why are you not fine, babe?"

"Because *that*. That right there. You call me babe, and you *look* at me, and you make me *want* things."

The fact that Mackenzie had consumed her body weight in alcohol somewhat dampened the elation Jake had expected to sweep through him. When she stepped into him, pressing herself against his chest, he groaned.

"You are saying *all* the right things, baby girl, but you've also had way too much to drink."

"Don't drunks always tell the truth?" She smiled up at him, arching her back slightly and pushing her tits more firmly against him. Lust thumped low in his groin, warring with the indecision of how far he could let this go.

Taking matters into her own hands, she reached behind his neck and pulled his head down, the sweet scent of cinnamon clouding his already compromised judgment.

Common sense battled years, *years*, of wanting, but not having. Of denying how he truly felt. Of pretending the woman in front of him didn't light up his world, give life meaning.

Going on tiptoes, Mackenzie kissed him.

There was nothing tentative about her exploration as she sucked on his lower lip and then bit gently, demanding entry. He groaned, and her tongue slipped inside to stroke against his.

Jesus Christ, he was kissing Mackenzie.

Cupping her head, he tilted it, slanting his mouth more

firmly over hers and claimed her, his tongue thrusting as he took back control. Her soft mewl of pleasure—her unrestrained passion—had him desperate. He wanted more. He wanted *everything*. He deepened the kiss, recognizing that she tasted like his future.

They pulled apart, breathing heavily.

"My head is spinning," she whispered, and the slight slur to her words was a bucket of ice water.

Closing his eyes, he rested his forehead against hers, fighting for the strength to walk away. "You need to get some sleep." His voice was hoarse with a need he couldn't disguise.

"Nope. I need to kiss you again."

"Babe, you're drunk and not thinking straight."

"So? Take advantage of me."

Frustration rode him hard. "Not tonight, Mac," he said regretfully, palming her cheek and running a thumb over her lush bottom lip.

"But you love me."

Her petulance was adorable and fast weakening his resolve.

"Jake, will you love me when we run out of deodorant and I smell?"

"Yes, babe."

"Will you love me when we run out of toothpaste?"

"Yes, babe."

"Will you love me—"

"Mac, I will love you forever, no matter what. But right now, you need to get to bed, okay?"

"You're no fun sometimes, you know that?"

Smiling, he pushed her upstairs.

CHAPTER SEVEN

Why had she thought whiskey was a good idea? Mackenzie's eyes were gritty, and her head pounded. Groaning, she rolled over on the bed, thankful she was between the sheets alone. Had Jake slept with her last night?

The morning sun was entirely too bright, and she dragged a pillow over her head. Mac groaned again.

Hangovers sucked.

Mackenzie had a vague recollection of pushing herself against Jake's firm chest, of rubbing her achingly tight nipples shamelessly against him. And then—

"Oh, my god. I kissed him!" She bolted upright. "It was our first kiss, and I was *drunk.*" She moaned.

She'd kissed Jake.

And could barely remember a thing about it.

"Fuck. Fuck-fuck-fuckity-fuck."

SEVERAL GLASSES OF WATER, two Tylenol, and a shower later, Mackenzie felt somewhat more human.

Although sitting in Quinn's light-filled kitchen, she fought the urge to squint.

"Why is the sun so sunny this morning?" she grumbled to Dex, swallowing the last of her coffee. The dog, lounging at her feet, nosed her in commiseration.

Jake had emerged from Quinn's home gym twenty minutes earlier, all sweaty and tousled. He'd slugged a bottle of water and dropped a quick kiss on the top of her head before heading to the shower.

"Morning, babe," he drawled, coming back into the kitchen. "Feeling okay?"

She hid her face in her hands.

She'd basically mauled him last night, if she remembered correctly. There'd been such an intense need. Desire that made her dizzy. She'd wanted to be close to him, couldn't get close enough. Couldn't catch her breath, but *oh god* it'd been good. So good.

And now he stood there, fresh and *delicious,* and she felt like a used tea bag. And not even English Breakfast. Green tea or something equally hideous.

"I've been better," she admitted, peeking through her fingers at him.

Dex's sharp bark distracted them, followed by a soft rapping on the front door. She instantly tensed. "Isn't the Evac Area meant to be deserted?" she said, eyes wide.

Jake growled low as he stalked toward the front door, Dex on his heels.

"Jake? Mac? It's me, Chloe," came a muffled voice from the other side.

In two large steps, Jake flung open the door and enveloped the petite blond in a crushing bear hug, her relieved laughter stifled in his shirt front.

"Hi to you too, little bro." She grinned, disentangling herself and promptly launching herself at Mackenzie.

Tears, hot and salty, drenched Mackenzie's cheeks as Chloe, and then Rachel and Kat, engulfed her, arms banding them together as the sisters they were.

Yipping, Dex bounced around their heels until Jake relegated him to the laundry room.

"Shouldn't you be in the Safe Zone?" Mackenzie finally gasped around hiccupping sobs.

"As if that dickhead Mayor Townsend could keep us from seeing you," declared Kat.

A laugh exploded from Mackenzie. Kat may have the morals of a pirate, but she'd do anything for her friends. They hugged tighter.

Finally pulling apart and settling somewhat, the four collapsed onto the sofa together.

"I know it's only midmorning, but we brought wine. Jake, can you see if Quinn has wine glasses?" asked Chloe, reaching for the two bottles of pinot that Rachel had dumped onto the coffee table.

She twisted the cap of the bottle open as Jake returned from the kitchen with four glasses and another bottle of water for himself. "I don't love this pinot. But I also don't love being sober." Chloe poured generously.

"Here's to having the same taste in alcohol." Mackenzie said.

"And different taste in men!" Kat and Rachel chimed in.

The four women raised their glasses.

"So what's with the dog?" Kat asked. "I'm not surprised you've found yourself a mutt, but where did it come from?"

"It's a long story. But I think he's mine now," Mackenzie answered. "Are you allowed to be here?" She gulped at the light, dry wine in a bid to relieve her lingering hangover.

"Mayor Dickhead has us on lockdown, but we have contacts on the inside." Kat waggled her eyebrows.

"Quinn's on border patrol," Rachel clarified. "As long as we're back before his guard duty is over, no one will miss us."

"It took you long enough to get here," said Chloe. "I was worried out of my mind. Between you two and not hearing from Ash..." She looked down.

"It wasn't... straightforward," said Jake.

"We wondered if you'd have Peter with you?" Rachel ventured. "But Quinn said it was just the two of you."

With hindsight, Mackenzie wondered what her friends *actually* thought of her ex-boyfriend. Belatedly, she realized they'd never shown a huge amount of enthusiasm for her relationship.

"Turns out my *ex*-boyfriend has a wife," she stated calmly, surprised by how little the knowledge rankled.

The girls were aghast and suitably furious on her behalf.

"Look, I should've seen it coming. My dating profile said I liked champagne and men with beards. Which is basically a euphemism for 'I have good taste in alcohol and poor taste in men.'" Out of the corner of her eye, Mackenzie saw Jake run a self-conscious hand over the stubble gracing his face. "And the signs were all there. It was stupid of me not to realize."

"Don't be so hard on yourself," Kat consoled. "The mom in *ET* had an alien living in her house for days and didn't notice."

Rachel spluttered and Kat helpfully thumped her on the back.

"God, I missed you," said Mackenzie, tears threatening to spill again.

"Careful, babe, you're going to be calling Sanford 'home' soon," teased Jake.

Kat's eyebrows reached her hairline and Rachel mouthed *"babe"* at Mackenzie, who quickly averted her eyes.

I am going to strangle him. Slowly.

"Speaking of Sanford, seems like a lot has happened since I left," Jake continued, oblivious. "Townsend must've mobilized quickly to evacuate the entire town into a safe zone and enforce a quarantine."

"It's been a fucking debacle," Rachel said in her usual forthright manner. "Mom and all the other female councilors have been out of town on some kind of empowerment retreat, and the men on the council have become cavemen lunatics. With guns."

"The council called a town meeting not long after you left," Rachel continued. "They had a checkpoint at the entrance of the town hall and those with symptoms were diverted onto school buses and taken to Sanford Hospital. That's where they've set up quarantine. We were all given two hours to make sure we had everything we needed and be inside the Safe Zone."

"How are they enforcing the zones?" Jake questioned.

"They've armed pretty much all the men and have them walking border patrols."

"And they won't give any weapons to the women," Chloe said.

"Dickheads," spat Kat.

"Where are the boundaries?" Mackenzie was trying to get her head around the new makeup of her hometown.

"Main Street down to the river, town hall, the distillery

and the middle school, and a couple of residential blocks. They've made anyone who lives within the Safe Zone accommodate everyone who lives in the Evac Area. Except, of course, Townsend, who's living in his great big mansion all by himself."

"But the hospital isn't in the Safe Zone?" clarified Jake.

"Nope. Because who needs medical supplies in an emergency, right?" quipped Rachel sarcastically. As a vet nurse, she appeared to have taken personal affront to this decision. "They should've set up quarantine in the high school and maintained access to the hospital."

"And they've tasked all the women with setting up a community kitchen and a day care at the middle school. We're not even allowed to stock take the food and supplies in the supermarket and the hardware store. Apparently, that's 'man's work.'" Chloe frowned.

"So the council is running the show?" Jake asked. "Quinn mentioned the law enforcement was, uh—"

"Dead," completed Rachel. "The mortality rate of this virus is unprecedented. I can't remember a lot of the historical infectious diseases component of my degree, but this goes way beyond anything we've ever seen before."

"And there's no cure?" Mackenzie asked quietly.

"Who knows? The internet and all other communication lines have been out for over twenty-four hours, and except for you, no one has been in or out of the town."

"And all the dead?" Jake asked. "What are they doing with the bodies?"

It was a valid question, but Mackenzie still wished Jake hadn't asked. These weren't the nameless and unknown dead she'd already witnessed. These were the people of her community that she'd grown up with. Possibly even her father.

"No one has died since we've been in the Safe Zone," Rachel replied. "Anyone with symptoms was removed before they set the boundary up, and no one else has come down with it since. I'm guessing they're all at the hospital, or in their homes."

A shiver raced down Mackenzie's spine as she pictured the houses surrounding them. Full of bloody-faced corpses.

Glancing out the window, Chloe rose to her feet. "I hate to leave you, but we have to get back. If they know we've been here, they won't let us back in."

Jake stood too, throwing an arm over Chloe's shoulders. "What about Grams? How is she?"

"The council made everyone over the age of seventy-five move into the Willows Travel Lodge," said Rachel. "Because so many of us lived in the Evac Area and had to move in with people in the Safe Zone, the council did some consolidation. Something about it being easier to care for the elderly if they were all in the one place."

Mackenzie could imagine that in the shock and chaos, it'd been easy for the council to herd the townspeople wherever they wanted.

"Grams is hardly elderly." Chloe huffed. "I'm going to check on her as soon as we get back."

"Give her my love, okay?" Jake said. "We'll see you tomorrow."

As soon as they were alone again, Jake caught Mackenzie in his embrace, and he spun them around. Mackenzie's back met the closed door before she could think. She had time to gasp in surprise before his mouth descended on hers, urgent and so, so right. His lips, a contradiction of soft and firm, explored hers as though he were savoring her. Consuming her.

"Wow. Hi." Mackenzie pulled back and gasped in air. "Give a girl some warning next time."

"Consider that your warning," Jake growled, capturing her lips with his own again.

She gave in and opened to him on a sigh, his tongue plundering and possessing. Gripping her ass, he pulled her snugly against him, his straining erection tight against her belly as they kissed, wet and deep.

Jake was known to her, and not known. This wasn't the boy she'd grown up with. This was a man. One allowing his emotions to bleed through with his every touch, forging an intimacy that was so profound, she was questioning every-thing she knew.

Time spun out. She was lost to the rasp of his stubble, the rhythm of his lips, the firm claiming of his hands on her waist. Without his hold, her knees would've buckled; she was boneless. Lost to the hunger between them.

"I don't think I can stand." She panted.

"I got you, baby girl."

Reaching behind her thigh, Jake urged it up around his hip—notching them tight together. Mac moaned, grasping onto his shoulders to grind herself wantonly. Shamelessly. Anything to ease the aching throb between her legs.

More. She needed more.

Unhooking her leg, she reached between them, palming his erection through unrelenting jeans before tugging desperately at his belt buckle.

"Slow down, babe," he said into the crook of her neck, licking the sensitive skin.

"Slow down?"

"We're standing against a door," he said, his eyes hungry but resolve clear in his tightening jaw.

"This isn't going how I thought it would." She pouted.

"None of this is happening how I thought it would." He laughed, relieving the tension. "I told you I loved you when I thought you were with someone else. You don't remember our first kiss..."

"I didn't say I didn't remember!" she protested.

He smiled, his fingers gripping her chin gently and tipping her face up. "Babe, our first time together will not be against a damn door."

"Are you worried I'll think you don't respect me?" She looked up at him through lowered lashes. "Because I'm totally okay with you disrespecting me, Jake." His groan reverberated through her, making her nipples pebble tighter —begging for his touch. "And if you've waited for me as long as you say you have..."

"You have no *idea* how long I've waited for you," he ground out, grabbing her ass and turning her, guiding her palms above her head to rest flat against the door. "You still want this?" His whisper was hot in her ear, and he used his knee to nudge her legs into a wider stance. "Because I can give you slow and sweet in a bed."

"I want this," she managed, her heart too large for her chest. The hard length of his body crowded her, dominant and assertive.

She'd never wanted anything more in her life.

His hand wound through her loose curls, tugging her head back so she could meet his smoldering eyes. "Say it again."

She licked her lips, delighting in the way his pupils dilated farther. "I want this. I want you, Jake."

Between one breath and the next, he was biting her neck, pawing roughly at her breasts and pinching at her taut, aching nipples. She arched her back into his chest as his other hand delved low, pushing aside her top to expose her stomach and then gliding down. Down.

She hadn't realized he'd been holding back. She'd never have guessed behind his easy-going personality he harbored such dirty, beautiful desires.

Her pussy clenched in frustrated anticipation.

His palm was so large she had to spread her legs wider to accommodate him, allowing him access to her slippery heat. Growling, he tugged at her yoga tights, pushing them and her panties down as far as her position would allow.

"So. Fucking. Wet," he praised, when his finger finally dipped into her folds, causing her to shudder uncontrollably. "I need to taste how sweet you are."

Through hooded eyes she watched over her shoulder, fascinated, as he withdrew his hand and brought it to his mouth, sucking the finger inside.

It was the hottest thing she'd ever seen.

Locking their gaze, he dropped his hand to reclaim her, stroking assertively as his thumb circled her clit with agonizing gentleness.

Rocking into his palm, her eyes fluttered closed, only to have him still. Groaning, she shifted on her feet.

"Eyes on me, baby girl," he instructed.

"More." She panted. Pleaded.

"Of this?" he asked, thrusting one thick finger, and then two, deep inside her.

"Yes. Yes!"

The eye contact was just as effective as his talented fingers at opening her wide, exposing her vulnerabilities. He was in total control, watching as her orgasm gathered momentum and tightened, tantalizingly close.

"Jake!" she yelled as she teetered on the edge, desperate to fall.

Dex howled from the laundry room.

Shifting, Jake braced himself against the door, leaning on a forearm and allowing his weight to press her forward, engulfing her wholly.

"Shh, baby. Bite me."

Tensing at the pleasure-pain of imminent release, she bit down on the corded muscle, muffling her cries as he pumped his fingers sure and deep, quickening the pace until she didn't know if she could stand it any longer.

Just as she was sure she couldn't be strung any tighter, his fingers curled and stroked and the orgasm crested, before crashing violently through her. She shook, and when she opened her eyes, her vision was momentarily black. Turning, she sagged into Jake's arms, breathless and not entirely sure what the hell had just happened.

"You were worth the wait," he whispered into her hair.

———

GOD, this woman. She wrecked him.

Jake was finding it hard to concentrate on anything beyond balancing his primal craving with the need to hold his sated woman close.

Her breathy cries. The way her tight pussy had clenched around his fingers. The connection as he'd looked into the depths of her eyes.

And when she'd come, biting deep into his forearm, it was a wonder he hadn't exploded right along with her. As it was, his cock was painfully hard and his balls hung heavy and demanding.

Chest heaving, Jake held Mac close, trying to distract himself from the need running rampant through his veins.

He'd meant what he said—he fully intended their first time to be slow and sweet. In a bed.

He hadn't been able to restrain himself from kissing her and couldn't comprehend how it had escalated so quickly. But he really needed to slow things down. The last thing he wanted to do was scare her off.

To not have Mackenzie when she was unaware of his feelings had been unbearable. To not have her now—when he knew the intimate taste of her, when he knew the way she became lost to sensation—*that* was beyond unbearable. It was excruciating.

He didn't realize he'd groaned until she lifted her head, her small hand palming his cheek.

"Your turn?" she asked, reminding him of a satisfied kitten licking its lips and looking for more cream. Lifting the bottom of his shirt, she skated her hands over his abdomen and up, rubbing her thumbs over his nipples and making his own breathing catch.

"*Jesus.*" He closed his eyes and prayed for strength. "Let's make it to the bed this time."

Taking her hand, he led her to the bedroom, where he shrugged from his shirt, exposing his chest. Her eyes were fixed on the light sprinkling of hair that dipped into the waistband of his jeans, and she watched as he slowly unbuckled his belt. Popped the top button. Slid down the zipper.

"Like what you see?" He chuckled, but there was no mirth. No, it was dark and dripping with sexual intent, desire sitting low in his belly.

She didn't answer, enthralled at the sight of the jeans and boxers dropping down his thighs, pooling at his feet until he kicked them off to stand naked before her.

His cock, thick and proud, jutted against the defined

planes of his stomach and he swallowed, mouth dry, as he ran a hand casually up its length.

"Is that even going to fit?" she blurted, finally raising stunned eyes to his face.

"Yeah, baby girl, it'll fit," he promised. "Your turn. Lose the clothes so I can finally update my mental image of you wearing that yellow bikini."

"No pressure. I don't have the body of a teenager anymore."

"Thank fuck for that. Because back then I wouldn't have known what to do with all these gorgeous curves."

Under his blatant adoration, she shimmied out of her jeans and pulled off her T-shirt. His groan of appreciation, low and rough, filled the room.

"Strip, Mackenzie."

The coarse timbre of his order seemed to dissolve the last of her hesitancy. With fumbling fingers, she unclasped her bra, letting the straps slide down her arms and the cups fall away, revealing her full, high breasts and attention-seeking nipples.

His tongue flicked over his bottom lip, his gaze devouring every inch of her. He was so done with slow.

Shoving at the sides of her panties, Mac pushed them—letting them slip down her legs as she stepped forward to press against his front, tilting her head up to entice his head down. Obligingly, his lips captured hers briefly.

"Don't distract me," Jake said. "I need to see you."

"Well, I need to kiss you, and I'm not in the mood to compromise."

Grinning at her sass, he pulled her onto the bed with him.

His erection pressed hard against her belly, and he

wrapped his arms tight around Mac as he gave into her demand and kissed her senseless.

"I want to hold you tight and love you slow," he whispered with gravel in his voice.

Flattening her palms against his chest, she pushed away, sliding down his body until she was kneeling over him, eye level with his straining cock. Bottom lip caught between her teeth, she gazed up at him with a wordless promise.

His body corded with tension, the sound of raw need ripped from his throat as she descended, her mouth closing over his shaft and sucking deeply.

Jesus fucking Christ, he was going to blow his load right now. *Mackenzie Lyons* had her lips wrapped around his dick. Her head bobbed down and slick warmth encased him, a rhythmic sucking causing his vision to darken.

Tangling his hands in her curls, Jake tugged gently.

"Back up here, babe."

His engorged flesh popped from her mouth with a smacking sound, and he had to breathe through it. He *would not* come. This was his every fantasy come to life, and he was going to make it eclipse every clandestine late-night wank session he'd ever indulged in.

Pouting at his interruption, she crawled back up his body and nipped at his bottom lip. "You're no fun."

"Oh, babe. You have no *idea* how fun I can be." Jake rolled her onto her back and settled between the nirvana of her spread thighs. His skin was pulled taut with anticipation and he couldn't stop running his hands over every inch of her body he could reach. She was so smooth and soft and warm and *everything*.

She was *his* everything.

The realization this was actually happening halted his exploration.

"What's wrong?" she asked, blinking up at him.

"I love you."

"So you say." Mackenzie turned her head to break their eye contact.

Grabbing her chin, he repeated his statement. "I love you, Mackenzie Lyons."

"Can we get to the sex part yet?" She sighed.

"Fuck yes."

Dropping his lips to hers, he kissed her, tongues tangling as he reached between them to find the wetness between her thighs. His fingers delved into the slick folds and she arched beneath him, her moans breathy.

"Condom?" she asked.

Jake pulled away long enough to snag his jeans from the floor, grabbing a condom, and rolling it on in one smooth movement—the tremble in his hand exposing unacknowledged nerves. Mac didn't know it yet, but he was about to become the last person she ever slept with. And damn if he wasn't going to make it perfect for her.

Swallowing at a suddenly dry mouth, he reached for her, tugging her reclined form to the edge of the bed where her splayed legs bracketed him. Marveling at his rough hand traveling up the smooth whiteness of her inner thigh, he reveled in how plump and inviting her pussy was.

God*damn,* she was gorgeous. "Are you ready?"

"Are you seriously asking me that?"

"Mackenzie."

"*Jake.* Would you please just fuck me?"

Grinning, he fell onto the bed, one forearm holding him steady as he guided his cock into her tight, welcoming pussy. He threw his head back, groaning, as her inner muscles tightened and her legs wrapped around his hips.

Holding against the urge to thrust and claim, he rocked

his hips, entering gradually until he was fully seated within her, every synapse in his body threatening to burn out.

"Oh. My. God," she whispered, eyes wide.

He leaned forward to run his lips down the side of her neck, sucking at her sensitive pulse and inhaling her erotically spicy scent. When she bucked her hips, hands clutching his shoulders, he lost it.

Lost any semblance of control he'd been holding onto.

He drove into her, lost to the bite of her fingernails in his skin, the indents of her heels into the small of his back, the incredible tightness of her pussy. Guttural grunts tore from him, overlaid by her gasping pants.

"So good. So good," she chanted.

Both Jake's fists pressed into the mattress above her head, bloodless with strain, as he pounded his devotion into her. The pressure was building at the base of his spine, that intense tingle that had his balls drawing tight.

"Touch yourself. Rub your clit," he growled, dropping his head to the crook of her shoulder.

Mac shifted to accommodate his demand, throat elongating as she threw her head back into the pillow on a cry of pleasure. The powerful clasp of her pussy as she climaxed had his own release barreling upon him, his cock jerking in an almost painful orgasm, as his vision blackened and his heart skipped a beat.

When Jake slumped, spent, draped over her shuddering body, she was murmuring incomprehensibly and running her hands through his hair. A surge of contentment had him closing his eyes, wanting to stay in this moment—their sweaty skin pressed together, breathing uneven and legs entwined.

"You were worth the wait." She smirked.

CHAPTER EIGHT

They'd fallen asleep in a tangle of limbs and awoken in the late afternoon, warm and sated. Jake's hands roved over her every inch and his soft sucking kisses were drugging her. Tugging at her heart. Making her fall in love.

"Dex!" She jolted out of her stupor. "Is he still locked in the laundry room?"

"He has food and water." Jake said, nudging his erect cock into her hip.

She rolled away, giggling at his exaggerated groan.

"I'm getting cockblocked by that dog *again.*"

Tugging on Jake's abandoned shirt, Mac headed through the house to the dog, who was happily curled up on a haphazard pile of what looked like freshly laundered clothes, pulled from a nearby basket.

Sorry, Quinn.

"Come here, boy. Who's a good boy?" she crooned as he leaped to his feet, pushing his head against her palm. "Come on, let's go get Jake."

Dex padded behind her as she made her way back to

the bedroom, heading straight for a tidy pile of Quinn's clothes folded on a chair. Nosing them into a heap onto the carpet, he circled three times and settled down, his eyes already closing in contentment.

Jake was sitting on the edge of the bed clad only in his boxers, his feet planted wide on the floor. Shaking his head at the dog, he motioned Mac closer. "Come here, baby girl. I missed you."

"I was gone for two minutes," she said, but obligingly straddled him to snuggle into his lap, her arms wrapping around his shoulders and her lips finding his.

She could definitely give Dex a run for his money in the contentment stakes.

At that thought, she stiffened.

I'm fooling around—with my best friend's little brother —and the world is falling apart.

"Hey, where'd you go?" Jake murmured into her neck.

"This is... wrong... when everything..." She gestured to the window, at a loss for words. Succumbing to the desire between them had been successful at blocking out reality, but now?

Those with symptoms were diverted onto school buses and taken to the hospital, that's where they've set up quarantine. Rachel's words swamped like murky water. "I didn't ask if they'd seen my dad."

"They would've said if they knew anything."

"I don't even know why I care. It's not like I even speak to him anymore."

"When did you see him last?"

She shrugged, not meeting his eyes. "What do you think is going to happen?" she asked quietly.

His arms tightened around her waist. "We're going to

stay safe, and eventually, the virus will run its course. Or they'll come up with a vaccine."

"Why do you think we didn't get it? The virus? It was *everywhere*. I still can't believe how crazy it was out there."

Soft tears were tracking down her cheeks, and Jake pulled back to look directly at her when she sniffed.

"I guess we got lucky. Or we're immune. Who knows?" he answered. "You know what I do know? You need a hot shower."

Mackenzie sniffed again. "Is that your way of telling me I smell?"

"It's my way of looking after you. Come on, I'll get it started for you."

"You're not joining me?"

He got to his feet, hoisting her easily with his hands beneath her ass and her legs still wrapped around his waist.

"I'm pretty sure I could be persuaded." He grinned.

Closing her eyes under the cascade of water, Mac gave herself over to Jake, over to the idea of *them*. Her hands roamed his wet skin—tracing the veins in his biceps, the tight curve of his ass, the dip in his navel.

She wanted him. All of him. And she wanted to forget.

Dropping to her knees, she thrilled at his hands tangling desperately in her wet hair.

He was hot and salty, and Mackenzie worked her mouth over his hard length, stopping to swirl her tongue at his sensitive tip and lap at the pearling pre-cum before swallowing as deep as she could. Jake's hips bucked in response and she gagged, pulling back only to bob down again, sucking feverishly.

Pumping her fist in rhythm with her mouth, she set a punishing pace, unable to get enough of the absolute power she brandished—she might be the one on her knees, but the knowledge he was completely within her control was dizzying.

"Fuck, Mac. Babe. I'm going to..." His hands tugged in warning, but Mac grinned around her mouthful. This man was hers, and she wanted every part of him.

"MACKENZIE LYONS, get your ass back in here," Jake demanded gruffly, watching her through the doorway from a sprawled position on the bed.

"Patience is a virtue, you know," she said, drying her hair.

"A virtue I've used up. And Mac? Ditch the towel."

Mackenzie halted in the action of wrapping the towel around her body and smiled slowly. Shaking back her hair, she turned to hang it up, before letting it slip from her fingers and glancing over her shoulder to catch his eyes.

"Oops." Bending from the hips, she wiggled her butt as she picked up the towel, smirking at the strangled groan coming from the bedroom.

"I swear to god, Mackenzie!"

The need saturating Jake's voice was a magnet, drawing her to him. Mac didn't stop moving when she got to the bed, climbing on and laughing at the way his eyes latched on her bouncing breasts.

His big hands cupped her as his thumbs caressed across her nipples, causing her to gasp.

His hands were large, square and capable—working hands that had slightly rough abrasions on the pads of his fingers, causing a delicious friction that had her grinding down on his already thickening cock.

"Jake, I need you. *Now*." Mackenzie said.

"What was that you were saying about patience?" He

ducked his head to capture a nipple in his mouth and sucked deep. She bucked, her core slippery with the need to have him inside her.

She appreciated that Jake wasted no time in sheathing his cock, and then she was sinking onto his lap, hovering millimeters from satisfaction.

Dex growled, and Mackenzie saw he'd raised his head. She paused.

"*Now* you're slowing down?" he asked.

"Did you hear that?" She cocked her head to the side. "Did we lock the front door?"

"Townsend himself could be on the doorstep. I don't give a fuck. I need inside you, baby girl."

"No, seriously—"

The dog shot to his feet, barking as he raced from the room.

"Fuck! That's Quinn." Jake groaned, clenching his hands in frustration on her hips. "Hurry, he'll use his key if we don't answer."

Mackenzie and Jake arrived at the front door, breathless and rumpled, opening it to find Quinn patting down his pockets, no doubt looking for his keys.

"There's a dog in my house?" Quinn asked, looking pointedly at the now quietened Dex.

"Took you long enough," said Tom Brenner, stepping forward with his AK-47 held purposefully, adding extra menace to a man who already exuded plenty.

"Jesus, Tom. Put the rifle down," said Quinn. "They're not sick, see?" He gestured.

"Come with us." Tom grunted.

"Sure, once you put your weapon away," Jake said with a deceptive calm. The rigidity of his stance didn't lessen until Tom reluctantly lowered the rifle. "It hasn't been forty-eight hours. What changed your mind?"

There was a blunt edge to Jake's question, and Mackenzie placed a warning hand onto his arm. It probably wasn't the wisest idea to piss off an armed man.

"Council has called a town meeting. Mandatory attendance," explained Quinn. "And it's been twenty-four hours. If you're not sick now, chances are you're not going to be."

"Okay," Mackenzie stepped from behind Jake. "But I'm bringing my dog."

Quinn raised his eyebrows.

"Your neighbor's dog," she amended, reaching down to pet Dex, who was leaning against her leg after having been reassured they weren't under attack.

"He's Stacy's. *Was* Stacy's." Quinn grimaced. "I saw her getting on the bus to the hospital."

"I don't give a damn about the mutt," Tom snapped. "You've got five minutes to grab your stuff, and then we're leaving." He stalked back to the SUV.

Quinn's eyes caught and held Jake's, a silent communication going on between them.

Mackenzie watched Jake's shoulders finally loosen, before he turned to her. "Let's get our things."

It was a short and silent trip as they followed Tom and Quinn into the Safe Zone, passing empty streets and a burned out church. Their vehicles were waved through a checkpoint of sorts before parking outside the town hall, where small groups of people were making their way into the meeting. Suddenly Mackenzie's nerves had nothing to do with the crisis, and everything to do with this town and her history with it.

Bitterness had a taste, and she swallowed convulsively.

Sanford was a small town with a long memory, and most of the population had no problem transferring her father's sins onto her shoulders. It didn't matter that she'd never passed out drunk in public, borrowed money with no intention of repaying, or whored around breaking up marriages. It didn't even matter that she had the endorsement of the town's golden girl, Chloe. Although, to be fair, Kat's antics probably negated any favorable feelings that association with Chloe provided.

No, Mackenzie herself didn't matter in the slightest. All the townspeople saw was the daughter of Carl Lyons —the high school football star turned alcoholic, who'd slept with more women, married and otherwise, than anyone was comfortable discussing. Who was she kidding? They *loved* talking about how much better they were than him.

Snide comments, obvious snubs, hurtful jokes—she'd endured them all.

There was a reason she didn't come home often.

Wondering if she'd see her father inside town hall, she decided she didn't care either way. They hadn't seen each other in years. From the time she'd turned twelve, she'd spent more nights on the rollaway bed in Chloe's room than in her own house.

"You good?" Jake asked, tucking her against his side as they walked through the imposing double doors, Dex tight on their heels.

"Just, this town." Mac sighed.

Jake squeezed her in response, apparently well aware of her feelings. It was flustering, the way he *knew* her. As though he didn't so much know her past as he knew her *memories*.

She had a sudden thought that the reality of her couldn't live up to the depth of his love. Because she had no doubt, he *thought* it was love. And she knew she couldn't possibly inspire such devotion.

They walked past a small group of middle-aged women in a row of seats, one of whom was her father's neighbor, who promptly turned her back.

"Ignore her," Jake murmured, leading her onward.

"I hope these people go to church because I don't want them in hell with me."

His laughter was a rich, low baritone that did funny things to her stomach.

"Jake! Mackenzie! Over here," called Chloe, waving at them from where she was already sitting with Rachel and Kat.

An immediate flash of guilt stung Mackenzie at the sight of her best friend, knowing what had transpired between her and Jake. How on earth was she going to have *that* conversation with Chloe?

They barely had time for quick hugs before Mayor Townsend, an imposing man with a chiseled jaw and barrel chest, called the meeting to order.

"It's a sad day to be standing before you," he said, "as your leader and defender, and see our population so decimated. Make no mistake, these are grave times and it's going to take strength and drastic measures to see us through."

"Jesus. Has he always been so self-important?" Mackenzie whispered to Kat, whose snort of amusement earned them glares from the row in front.

"The council and I are meeting tomorrow to draw up new laws, which will be implemented accordingly," Townsend continued. "In the meantime, I need several men to volunteer to go on a raid tomorrow to get supplies for the town."

A raid? Mackenzie's forehead creased.

Rachel had the same reaction, and she wasn't afraid to put it into words. Her hand shot into the air. "I understand we need to get supplies, but do we really need to call it a raid? That sounds overly aggressive."

"You're a woman, and I wouldn't expect you to understand. But aggression is the way of the world now, missy," Townsend stated, his voice dripping in condescension.

Rachel leaped to her feet. "Don't call me *missy*. And—"

"This town is going to operate on order," Townsend spoke over her, aided by the microphone. "And anyone who interrupts will be removed."

"This is a *meeting*, not an assembly for a dictator!" Rachel yelled back.

"Charles, remove her." Townsend waved an unconcerned hand in Rachel's direction and continued to strategize a raid on their nearest neighboring town.

Mackenzie hid a grin as Rachel raised an imperious eyebrow at the man who came to escort her out. "Seriously, Charlie? You've been my mother's assistant for almost a decade and now you're his lackey?"

"Don't make this harder than it has to be," Charles Nixen said, glancing back toward Townsend.

"Oh, don't worry, we'll *gladly* leave this shit show." Kat pulled Mackenzie and Chloe to their feet. "For anyone who wants to join us later, we'll be at The Strumpet!" She winked at the gaping mouths surrounding them.

———

JAKE FOLLOWED THE WOMEN OUT, stopping briefly to pull Quinn aside.

"Do me a favor? Find out who's going on this raid

tomorrow and ask them to look for asthma inhalers at the drugstore."

"Mackenzie?"

"Yeah, she has backups, but—"

"I'll make it happen," Quinn said in a low voice.

When Jake emerged onto the sidewalk, the four friends had linked arms and were marching up the middle of Main Street, heading for the bar attached to the whiskey distillery.

God, they'd always been a force to be reckoned with when they were all together. Jake grinned wryly to himself. He'd spent his whole life on the outside, looking in at the fierce bond they shared.

Mackenzie glanced back over her shoulder, looking for him, and he quickened his step.

Inside The Strumpet, Maggie, the platinum blond who'd managed the bar for the last decade, was wiping down the counter.

"Not at the town meeting, Mags?" Jake asked, sliding onto a bar stool as the girls headed for the bathroom, and Dex came to sit at his feet.

"Townsend can kiss my ass," Maggie said.

"Good to know that the world can go to hell, but you'll still be behind the bar."

"Where else would I be? I live up top. Donny's out back cleaning glasses." She motioned to her nineteen-year-old son. "Rather be here than put to work out there, running Townsend's little empire. Now, what can I get you?"

"Whiskey, straight up."

"No can do. A rep from the distillery has requisitioned all the whiskey, thinks we'll need it to trade with."

"A rep? I thought old man Harvey was in charge of the distillery?"

"He's just the manager. Remember James O'Connor? I think he was a couple of years above you at school. He works for the corporation who owns the distillery and was doing a site inspection when this all went down." Maggie poured him a beer. "He's not a bad kid, and to be honest, he's probably got the right idea, but half the locals want his head on a stick. This town survives on whiskey, and folks are mighty pissed they can't get it."

Out of habit, Jake reached for his wallet and pulled out some bills, pausing as Maggie raised her eyebrows.

"Pretty sure that's just useless paper now." Maggie laughed. "It's on the house. It's all on the house until we run dry, or Townsend takes it over. Put away your money, it's no good here."

"Darling Maggie, did I just hear you say everything's on the house?" cried Kat, strutting behind the bar and flinging her arms around Maggie.

"Get on with you, girl." She laughed, slapping a dish-cloth against Kat's ass as Kat bent over in front of the wine fridge and pulled out two bottles of white wine.

"Ladies, are we good with white?"

"Better grab a red too," called Chloe, settling at a high-top table.

Grabbing his beer, Jake joined his sister and pulled out a stool for Mackenzie. He caught the look Chloe flashed between them and didn't give a damn, instead pulling Mackenzie's stool closer to his own.

Chloe's reaction was forgotten when Mackenzie looked up at him from beneath her thick lashes, a secret smile dancing on those tempting lips of hers.

It was killing him not to claim her, not to tell the whole damn world they were together. That she was his. But she'd made him promise they'd keep it between themselves.

He'd agreed, for now. He understood her recalcitrance wasn't just in telling Chloe, but the fact she didn't trust in what was between them. That it was real.

But she would.

"ISN'T it funny how eight glasses of water in a day seems impossible, but I can do eight glasses of wine over a bowl of stale peanuts?" Kat dumped glasses and wine bottles on the table, upsetting said bowl of nuts.

"Are we going to talk about what just happened at the meeting?" Rachel asked.

"Nope. We're getting drunk." Kat opened a bottle and poured generously.

"It sucks, and we will talk about it," Chloe said, putting her hand on Rachel's arm. "But not right now. It's been forever since we were all here together, and I just want to forget everything. Forget that my jerk of a husband didn't come home when I asked and pretend the world hasn't fallen to shit and he's on his way back now."

"Sounds good to me. My mom is also on her way back from that retreat, and is healthy, and ready to take Townsend down a peg or three." Rachel's voice was only slightly wobbly.

They clinked glasses as townspeople began filtering into the bar, the meeting obviously over.

"Rachel Davenport, you're a bitch just like your mother," sneered a voice from behind them.

Rachel spun around and Jake got to his feet, deliberately placing his beer on the table before turning.

"Vivienne Oxley," he drawled. "I don't remember inviting you to join us."

"I wouldn't join you if you *paid* me!" she spat. "I just

115

wanted to let Rachel know that she's not so high and mighty now that her mother's not here, and she better learn her place."

"Learn my place?" Rachel laughed, high and brittle. "Vivienne, you're Townsend's *secretary*. Where exactly do you think that places you?"

"On the side of power, that's where."

"Just fuck off, Viv. You still haven't gotten over the fact that Rach beat you out for a spot on the marching band in high school, which is kind of sad." Mackenzie gave a small shrug of her shoulders and took another sip of wine.

"What exactly made you think you'd be welcome back in Sanford, Mackenzie Lyons? Your father's a deadbeat piece of trash and you're no better," Vivienne scorned.

Mackenzie's knuckles went white holding her wineglass and Jake's blood pressure spiked. He'd never in his life been tempted to harm a woman, but this small-town bitch was pushing his limits.

Mackenzie pushed herself away from the table and stood before Vivienne, head held high. "Vivienne, you are a disappointment to the sisterhood."

"Oh, that's right, you four are some kind of girl squad."

"You know what? We are. And to be a part of our girl gang, you need to be fluent in smart-ass, sarcasm, and adult language. In addition, questionable morals and nudity may be required. All of which I don't think you're capable of. So, I'll say it again, fuck off."

Jesus, and now he had a hard on. Jake surreptitiously adjusted himself as Vivienne flounced away. Sassy Mackenzie was a major turn on.

The color was high on her cheeks, and her chest heaved. Was he imagining he could see the outline of her nipples?

He took a long swallow of his drink, attempting to get himself under control.

"Oh, Mac, it's so good to have you back." Chloe sighed, slinging her arm over Mackenzie's shoulder.

"Look, I'm a nice girl. So if I'm a bitch to you, you need to ask yourself why," Mackenzie said.

Jake grinned and settled in for the evening.

MAGGIE WAS CALLING LAST DRINKS, and Jake was relieved. The girls had gone through several bottles of wine before starting on shots of peach schnapps, and it was only going downhill from there.

"Can you *believe* James had the nerve to come back to town and take away all our whiskey?" Rachel slurred.

"Screw the whiskey. I can't believe he's back. Have you seen him yet?" Mackenzie asked. "Because when *I* see him, I'm totally slapping that pretty face of his."

"You're not slapping anyone." Jake chuckled, removing the empty shot glass from her lax fingers. "So this James O'Connor from the distillery is the same James who—?"

"*Don't* say it." Mackenzie placed a finger over his lips. "You'll just hurt Rachel's feelings if you mention how he stomped all over her heart."

"Gee, thanks, Mac," Rachel said dryly.

But Jake had lost all interest in the conversation. Mackenzie's finger stayed pressed against his lips, and god himself couldn't have stopped him from opening his mouth and sucking it inside.

Wide-eyed, Mackenzie almost slipped from her stool, popping her finger free in order to rebalance herself. When her gaze flashed back to his, he licked his lips.

"Come on, ladies, time for bed," sang Chloe. "Let's have a sleepover at my house!"

"I'm assuming I'm not invited to this slumber party?" Jake said.

"Absolutely no little brothers allowed." Kat skipped toward the exit. "Good night, darling Maggie!"

The little brother comment was irritating, but Mackenzie appeared not to have registered it. She was still fixated on his lips, shaking herself when they twitched in amusement.

Reaching for her backpack, she stumbled and swore.

"I forgot what a dirty mouth you have on you," he murmured against her ear before picking up both his own backpack and hers.

"You don't know the half of it, Jake Brent," she purred, wiggling her eyebrows up and down mischievously.

"Come on then, I'll walk you all home." He sighed with feigned annoyance.

Chloe's house wasn't a long walk, but Jake had a new appreciation for mothers with toddlers as he shepherded them home.

"Kat! *What* are you doing?" He huffed as she scampered into someone's front garden.

"Maureen Park is a judgmental old bag, and she doesn't deserve to have this adorable gnome in her garden. He wants to come home with me."

"Put the gnome back, Kat."

"No."

"Kat."

"No!" And she ran off down the sidewalk, gnome in one hand and high heels dangling from their straps in the other.

Rachel and Chloe took off after her, disappearing through Chloe's front door half a block down.

Mackenzie sidled under his arm as they kept walking, Jake purposefully shortening his strides to match hers. He didn't love the idea of leaving Mackenzie at Chloe's and going back to his own house alone, but he also didn't want to fight those three banshees for custody of her.

He sighed. Sharing the love of his life with the rest of the world sucked balls.

CHAPTER NINE

───────────

"Why do I have an ugly-ass gnome in bed with me?"

"Kat, go back to sleep," Mackenzie mumbled, pulling a pillow over her head.

"You don't understand, we have a *gnome* in bed with us."

With an energy Mackenzie couldn't fathom, Kat sat up in the double bed they were sharing and waved the offending object in the air. Her movement jostled the mattress and instant nausea had Mackenzie moaning.

"What?" Kat pulled the pillow away from Mackenzie, exposing her to the morning light. "I can't hear you when you're under that thing."

"I said go. Back. To. Sleep."

"But I'm awake."

"Make yourself unawake."

Mackenzie knew she was fighting a losing battle. One of Kat's less loveable quirks was that no matter how debaucherously she'd behaved the previous evening, she awoke ridiculously chirpy.

"I'm never drinking again," Mac vowed, dragging

herself into a sitting position and leaning against the headboard.

"Are you going to be sick?" Kat asked brightly.

Mackenzie answered with a murderous expression.

"I tell you what, you tell me what's going on between you and Jake, and I'll get some water and Tylenol." Kat wiggled her eyebrows mischievously.

"What?"

"Don't play coy with me, Mackenzie Lyons. I saw the finger sucking that went on last night."

"The *what*?" But hazy images were assaulting her memory, and she half considered making a run for the bathroom. "Maybe I *am* going to be sick."

"Sit still and spill your guts, and then I'll get you water and drugs," Kat singsonged.

"You're evil."

"And you're keeping secrets. Spill."

"We... we've been intimate," Mac confessed in a rush, throwing hands over her heated face and peeping at Kat through her fingers.

"Been *intimate*? What are you, some eighteenth-century damsel?" Kat was choking with laughter. "I think what you meant to say was that you were fucking."

"It was *really good* fucking."

"Does Chloe know you have the hots for her little brother?"

"It's not like that! And can you not refer to him as a 'little brother?'"

"It helps that he towers over all of us and is built like a beautiful Greek god," Kat mused.

"Kat! Stop. Do you think Chloe saw?"

"Sometimes the hardest thing to see is what's right in front of you."

"Stop pretending you're wise," Mackenzie grumbled, "and go get me water."

As Kat bounced out of the room, Mackenzie gingerly lay back down, hoping slow movements would ease the roiling in her stomach.

The guilt of keeping this from her best friend wasn't helping matters.

"Fuck-fuck-fuckity-fuck."

HAVING SOAKED herself into sobriety in the shower, Mackenzie decided she was capable of starting the day. Entering the kitchen, she did a double take at Kat.

"Wait, what? Are you cutting that coffee with whiskey?" She watched as Kat poured a generous amount of alcohol into her caffeine. "Not that I'm judging. But if that's the new normal, I'm in."

"Jesus, Kat. Seriously?" asked Rachel, refilling the percolator with water. "Even the smell of that whiskey makes me want to barf."

"I'm on cafeteria duty this morning. I need it," Kat insisted, recapping the whiskey bottle and stirring her mug. "I don't cook. I hate cooking. And now Mayor Dickhead has me cooking for the whole freakin' town."

"So, we're not having breakfast here?" Mackenzie asked, looking at Chloe for clarification.

"People are pretty much eating in their homes until they run out of food, and then having meals at the middle school cafeteria. And because the council has taken control of all the businesses on Main Street, we have to rely on rations they dole out," she explained.

"But this has only been going on a few days. Surely

most people haven't run out of food in their own homes yet?" Mackenzie said.

"We had a thirty-hour blackout the day before yesterday, which spoiled pretty much everything in fridges and freezers." Kat took a sip of her coffee. "The supermarket has a backup generator, so everything there was fine, but here? We're living on cereal with no milk, pasta and a couple of random cans of food."

"I wouldn't be surprised if Townsend orchestrated the electrical failure, so we'd have to rely on him more," Chloe added dolefully.

"So how do we get rations?" Mackenzie grabbed a mug for herself.

"The council puts up a chore list and you have to report to some kind of duty, which is monitored by a councilman. At the end of the duty, they give you a tag, which you redeem for rations," Chloe answered.

"A tag?"

"Get this, it's a cattle tag. Like, one of those things they put in a cow's ear to identify it," said Rachel sardonically. "Todd Berryman is a councilor, and he's got a cattle stud, so I'm assuming that's where they got them from."

Mackenzie was digesting this information when Jake and Dex appeared at the glass door leading from the kitchen onto Chloe and Ashton's outdoor deck.

"Hi, ladies," he announced as he opened the door and they entered. "How are we feeling this morning?"

Mackenzie's persistent weight of guilt multiplied—she hadn't even noticed Dex wasn't with her, let alone wondered where he might be. Now she wasn't just keeping secrets from her best friend, she was neglecting her dog, too.

"Stop being so sober and non-hungover," Chloe

demanded. "And you could knock before you enter, you know."

"It's a glass door, Chlo. You saw me there. And, by the way, it wasn't locked. Tell me you locked up last night?"

A sheepish expression was her only answer.

Mackenzie bent to smother Dex's head in kisses, wishing she was alone with Jake and could smother *him* in kisses.

"Can you pour me a coffee, Rach?" Jake pulled out a chair at the table and sat down next to Mackenzie. "Morning gorgeous," he whispered, his warm breath making her catch her own.

Mackenzie narrowed her eyes at the dramatic waggling of Kat's eyebrows and concentrated on breathing evenly, ignoring Jake.

So much for him playing it cool in front of Chloe.

She was lusting over her best friend's little brother. What was *wrong* with her?

She jumped guiltily when Chloe accidentally dropped a mug, bursting into tears.

"Chlo! What's wrong?"

"I feel like shit. And I can't find my favorite mug. And it's killing me that I don't know where Ash is." Chloe snuffled.

"Wherever Ash is, he's trying to get home to you," Jake reassured.

"He's right," Rachel interjected. "That man is mad over you."

Chloe didn't wipe the tears that were sliding down her cheeks, and Mackenzie jumped up to hug her. "He'll get back to you, Chlo."

"Okay, enough of that. We need to get going." Chloe sniffed, pushing Mackenzie gently away. "You all need to report to your duties so you can get rations to share with me, because I'm not doing mine today."

"Got something better to do?" asked Jake.

"Anything would be better than crèche duty with Vivienne. But yes, I do. I want to check in on Grams. And remember that community garden she helps take care of? I think it's just inside the Safe Zone, and I'm hoping no one else has thought to check out the vegetables."

"Oh, you know what? It would also be good to see if there are any seeds there. We should probably try to plant some vegetables ourselves," said Mackenzie. That sounded like an apocalypse-survivalist thing to do. "How is Grams?" She suddenly realized she hadn't seen Jake and Chloe's grandmother at the town meeting. "She wasn't there last night, was she?"

"Not that I saw," he agreed. "But maybe with everything that's going on, they just forgot to let the residents at the lodge know about the meeting."

"It doesn't seem like Townsend has forgotten much at all," said Mackenzie. "Doesn't all this seem just a little too *organized*? How has the council implemented all these changes in such a short amount of time?"

It was a rhetorical question, but Kat bounced in her seat. "Oh, I know! Maggie was telling me last night. Apparently, there's a group of men on the council who used to meet at The Strumpet, and instead of playing fantasy football, they had this weird version of 'How I Would Run the World.' Like, they'd come up with strategies of how they'd run the town in the case of an apocalypse. Kind of like, now..."

"That's.... psychopathic, right? Who plays fantasy apocalypse?" Mackenzie's question was met with silence, which was eventually broken by Chloe.

"You guys better leave now. No cars, remember?"

"We're walking?" The pounding in Mackenzie's head intensified.

"Yep, Townsend has put a ban on using gas, and he has crews going from home to home, siphoning everything they can get," Chloe said.

Jake stood in alarm, his chair crashing to the floor behind him. "Have you drained your car and hidden the gas?"

"Calm down, Jakey. Quinn sorted it for us yesterday. We've got four jerricans hidden." Kat grinned.

"Meet at the school later?" Chloe asked as they traipsed outside.

"Yep. And as a lunch lady, you don't need a tag to get fed!" Kat laughed, walking ahead with Rachel.

Jake fell into step beside her, and Mackenzie watched as Chloe turned and walked in the opposite direction, stalling until Chloe rounded a corner.

"I should warn you now, I'm not good at keeping secrets," Jake said, bending his head forward to catch her eye. He ran a thumb over her bottom lip and a corresponding warmth flashed straight between her legs.

The husky depth of his voice had her wanting to turn around and head straight back to bed. With him. She was light-headed with lust and excitement and, maybe, a little too much caffeine.

"Hurry up, you two!" Kat called from ahead, jolting Mackenzie from her daze.

With a grin, Jake linked his fingers through hers and tugged her forward. His palm was broad and calloused, and her hand felt tiny within his. He was strong and confident, and she was almost sad she hadn't noticed him growing into this man. She'd been present, but still missed the transition.

How was it that, mere days ago, he'd been an unremarkable part of her life, and now... now.

Now, she was a mess of confusion.

Mac thought she'd been in love with Peter. But it'd never taken her breath away to think of him. Made her heart stutter to be near him. And it was almost alarming to think of how easily he'd slipped from her life.

Whatever this feeling was for Jake, it was equal parts excitement and bone-deep contentment. It felt right.

Her steps faltered. It *did* feel right. So, was it really so wrong? Maybe they could give whatever this was a chance.

Noticing him watching her, she blushed.

"Sleepover at yours tonight?" she asked, unexpectedly coy.

"If I can wait that long." He smirked.

———

JAKE LOOKED up from the census form he was being made to fill in, struggling to concentrate. He'd never been great at this kind of shit at school and now, with Mackenzie sitting at the next table over, there wasn't a chance in hell he could focus.

Not when her soft curls were falling over her shoulder, and her brow was furrowing in an adorably cute way as she chewed on the end of the pen she was holding.

Jesus. Get your shit together, man.

She wanted to spend the night with him, but as they'd approached town hall, she'd also reminded him about keeping their relationship a secret. Which was making him crazy because he wanted to shout from the rooftop that Mackenzie Lyons was giving him a chance.

Shaking his head, he returned his attention to the document in front of him. Why the hell they had to fill out a census was beyond him. Sanford was like any other small town. Everyone knew everyone else—it wasn't like anyone was going to gain new information from him ticking a box about his age and occupation.

Who thought of getting residents to fill out this kind of data when the world was falling apart? How had the council evacuated half the town, established an armed perimeter and put together job lists for the survivors in just a couple of days?

Playing fantasy apocalypse over a couple of beers couldn't have equipped the council to pull this off, surely.

He glanced over at John Jefferies. Jefferies was the owner of the local car dealership and a longtime town councilor. Now, he was standing at the door to the room they'd been ushered into, looking for all the world like a guard. Complete with an AR-15 self-loading rifle slung over his shoulder.

"Hey! Jefferies," Jake called, leaning back nonchalantly in his chair. "What's with the gun?"

"What's it to you, kid?"

"Just seems strange, that's all. We're supposedly in a safe zone, so why do you need to be armed?"

"None of your fucking business."

There was open belligerence in Jefferies' response, and a flash of warning prickled down Jake's spine. Eyes sharpening, he straightened. Since when did one of the most upstanding members of the town act like an asshole?

"You asked me if I was carrying when I came in. If I had been, would that have been a problem?" Jake asked in a deceptively mild voice.

It didn't deceive Mackenzie, who'd raised her head and was watching their interaction with concern. Catching his eye, she raised her eyebrows, silently asking what the hell he was doing.

What the fuck *was* he doing? He'd never been one to question authority. He'd never had reason. But right now? He found it concerning as hell that the town council was militarizing itself.

"All residents have been ordered to hand in weapons, so yeah, it would've been a problem," Jefferies said, walking over and planting his feet, stance wide, in front of Jake.

Jake resisted the urge to rise to his own feet. "But it's okay for the guy who owns the used car lot to carry?"

"Careful, son. Now's not the time to piss me off. Finish the census and get to whatever job you've been assigned for the day."

Jake contemplated his response. Did he push this further or wait and watch? Before he could decide, Jefferies was called away, closing the door with a click behind him.

"What was that about?" Mackenzie said. "I don't think antagonizing the man with the gun is a smart option."

"I have faith in Townsend's contingency plan. Hell, I voted for the man. But Jefferies' attitude is something else altogether."

"You voted for Townsend over Rachel's mom?"

Maree Davenport, Rachel's mother, had been a prominent councilwoman for many years, and her discontent with Mayor Townsend was legendary, their tussles focusing on Maree's progressive attitude and Townsend's stubborn desire to remain in the last century.

"I'm not against Maree's ideas. I just think Townsend is a better leader. He gets things done," Jake said. "We had no warning this virus was even in the country, and then within a day, all hell broke loose. We saw how crazy things are out there. But here in Sanford? Townsend has things locked down tight."

"That's putting it mildly. He's acting like a dictator."

"Maybe. But he's keeping us safe."

Mackenzie went back to chewing on the end of her pen.

"You two finished?" asked Jefferies, stalking back into the room. "Because you've got guard duty, and I need to show you the route before the current shift ends."

"Um, I haven't ever held a gun before," Mackenzie ventured, surprised she was being given the option of guard duty, but not unhappy about it.

"Not you. You report to the kitchen."

Mackenzie raised an eyebrow. "I didn't say I didn't *want* guard duty. Just that I'd need to be taught how to handle—"

"Men do guard duty. Get going to the kitchen before I reassign you to the laundry."

"What? So the women are being pushed into the domestic roles, without taking into consideration what other skills they may have?" she questioned hotly.

Eyes narrowing, Jefferies swiped up Mackenzie's census form. "And what skills are you suggesting"—he glanced down at the paper—"an environmental lawyer has to offer us right now?"

"Skills can be taught," she responded evenly. "And my background gives me an insight into how a pandemic will affect the environment. Affect our community."

"I don't need a degree to tell you the effect is a shitload of dead people." Jefferies sneered.

Jake's stomach clenched at the thought of Mackenzie carrying a rifle and patrolling their town. No way in hell did he want her in that kind of danger. However, as much as he believed Townsend was doing the right thing in protecting their community, he wasn't going to stand for someone speaking to Mackenzie that way.

That said, the firearm Jefferies carried had Jake at a distinct disadvantage and, for the first time, he understood the need other men felt to carry. A weapon gave power.

"It's fine, Jake, I'll go to the kitchen," Mackenzie murmured, and he realized that while he'd been silently fuming, she'd stood up and walked to his side. "We need information about how all this is working," she added for his ears only.

"Good girl," Jefferies said. "And you, son, come with me."

"Do I get an AR-15?"

"When your shift starts."

Slipping from the room, Mackenzie seemed to take all the available oxygen with her. With a tight chest, Jake wondered why, in a "safe" town, he was decidedly uneasy about her safety.

"THIS STREET MARKS the northern perimeter of your watch." Jefferies jerked his chin. "Radio in when you get to this point, and then head back. Your rations get docked if you're caught standing still. We need our guards on the move at all times."

Jake nodded. He absolutely agreed with the importance of keeping the infection out of the town, however uneasy he may feel about implementing some of their policies. But turning people away who needed help didn't sit right. Jefferies had been adamant there was no possibility of quarantining strangers looking for sanctuary.

They were under orders to turn away anyone and everyone, and shoot if they didn't take no for an answer.

"Seriously? You're condoning shooting innocent people looking for help?" Jake said.

"We're looking at the big picture, son. And your orders are to fire on anyone who doesn't comply with our rules."

Jake knew he'd be hard-pressed to turn away another human in need, let alone raise a weapon to one. He resolved to speak to Townsend about it.

"What about Willows Travel Lodge? It's just around that corner," he said.

"What about it?" Jefferies snapped, an odd look flashing across his fleshy features. "It's not part of your watch."

"I heard some of the older residents are being housed there. I wouldn't mind checking in with my grandmother."

"Not your concern. When you're on guard duty, you're focused on the safety of this town. Is that understood?"

Jake nodded, knowing he'd check in on Grams, regardless.

"Not good enough, son. You'll respond with a 'yes, sir.'"

Who the fuck did this power-hungry prick think he was?

Jefferies grinned at the swift and obvious rise of Jake's anger. "Son, we don't give out chances. And only men we trust are allowed to guard this town. So are you going to 'yes sir' me, or are you going to walk your ass to the laundry?"

Grinding his teeth, Jake forced out a strangled "yes, sir," hating the triumph it elicited from Jefferies as he sauntered away.

"Make sure you check in over the radio with every circuit," Jefferies threw back.

Shouldering his borrowed rifle, Jake glanced once again toward the travel lodge before turning to retrace his perimeter.

He completed several loops of his circuit, keeping track

of each new voice who responded to his radio communication. He knew all the men, and the knowledge relaxed him. Jefferies might be a massive dick, but the town was in safe hands.

"Jake Brent, it's good to see you, son." Townsend strode over to meet him.

Jake took a moment to register the difference between Townsend calling him son, and the way Jefferies had used the term.

"Mr. Mayor." He adjusted the hold on his rifle and wondered why Townsend was here. "What can I help you with?"

"Walk with me a bit. It surprised me to hear you'd left town, especially to bring that Lyons girl back."

Back straightening, Jake gritted his teeth. "Why would that be surprising? *Mackenzie*"—he emphasized her name—"is a family friend."

"Of course," Townsend placated, slapping him lightly on the shoulder. "It just wasn't a smart move to have left when you did."

Jake said nothing, and they continued walking.

"I'm glad you made it back. You're an asset to this town, Jake. I need men like you to help me keep Sanford going. I was hoping you could tell me about what you saw out there. Did you see any kind of government authority?"

Jake recounted his trip to Chicago and back, unsure which details Townsend would think important. He was more interested in asking some of his own questions.

"What's happening with the quarantine at the hospital?" Jake asked.

Townsend halted, and Jake stopped and faced him.

"Come on, Jake. You just told me about the hospital at Essex. Everyone sent to the hospital was already dead, they just didn't know it yet." The mayor's tone was slightly chiding, as though Jake should've figured that out already.

"Why haven't you told the rest of the community? They need to know what happened."

"Not yet. That would just create more unrest and chaos. We need to maintain order."

Townsend resumed walking and Jake fell in at his side. It surprised him to find he wasn't shocked at the knowledge; unconsciously, he'd guessed at the fate of those who'd been "quarantined."

"What about outsiders who come to Sanford for help? Why are we turning them away without offering to quarantine them?"

"You just said it yourself, son. Outsiders. This is a new world, and we can't trust anyone. Until Sanford is fully established and running smoothly, we're committed to being insular. No one in, and no one out."

When he asked what "fully established" meant, Townsend stonewalled him.

"I meant what I said, Jake. We're reshaping the world as we know it, and Sanford needs men like you. I'm holding a meeting with select individuals in the next couple of days, and I'd like you there."

Taking Jake's acquiescence for granted, Townsend once again slapped him on the shoulder before striding off back to Main Street.

Jake watched him go, a mixture of pride and loyalty stirring in his gut. He'd step up and help with guiding his hometown through their new reality.

"Jake! Wait up," called Quinn, jogging over as he rounded the corner onto Grove Street.

"Can't stop, man. If I don't walk, I don't eat," he joked. "Do they really dock your rations if you stand still?"

"Fucking pricks," Quinn muttered, panting.

"Since when are you out of shape?"

Jake took in the sweat-stained front of Quinn's t-shirt. Quinn was a big man, easily over six feet, but he was heavy with muscle and took his fitness seriously.

"Fuck off. I've been working out. Thinking of seeing if anyone else wanted to start some workout sessions." Quinn rubbed his bearded jaw and sighed. "Seems to me we could be facing a survival-of-the-fittest-type scenario. And some of these townsfolk—Jesus, they couldn't run to the bakery for a pie sale without having a heart attack."

"You're right. If it's fight or flight, I don't reckon many will stay to fight," Jake said.

"Kat's going to tear me a new one when I tell her to do a push-up," Quinn mumbled to himself, a rare smile lightening his features.

"You ever going to tell that girl how you feel?"

Quinn shot him a dark look. "Just because you finally made a move on Mac doesn't make you an expert on feelings."

Jake chuckled, readjusting his rifle. "That's not public knowledge, okay? She doesn't want everyone knowing."

Quinn gave him an inscrutable look. "Okay."

"Hey, did you find out what's happening with this raid to Dutton?"

"That's why I came to find you. Malcom Preston pulled out and they're a man short. I recommended you. They're leaving at sundown, thought it would be better to travel at night. Far as I know, their priority is to secure one of the fuel tankers from the Western Star depot. But once they have that, they're happy enough to detour to a drugstore. Makes sense to stock up on all kinds of medication."

Jake kicked at a stone in his path, watching it bounce off

an overflowing trash can on the sidewalk. Apparently, the council could organize a raid, but not trash collection.

"I'm in. Do we even know what's happening in Dutton? Maybe they've got a group of survivors who won't be happy about sharing their supplies."

"I don't think other communities are as organized as we are, which is why the raid is happening so quickly. Townsend wants to get in before they get their shit together."

Jake wanted to feel bad about taking supplies from another community, but he thought Townsend had the right idea. Until military or government help arrived, they needed to focus on the survival of Sanford.

"I keep expecting tanks or helicopters to arrive any minute, but until then, I guess it's up to us. Anyway, the group is meeting outside the school at one o'clock to finalize plans for the raid. Jim Boston is the one running the show, I'll let him know you're good to go."

"Thanks, bro."

"Later."

Jake continued his perimeter walk, noting the bite to the fall wind that sent leaves and several plastic bags swirling across the road in front of him. With no street sweepers in operation, the roads were already looking derelict. If this was just a few days of neglect, what would it look like in a few weeks?

Pulling his jacket tighter he walked on, counting down the minutes until he saw Mackenzie again.

CHAPTER TEN

Mackenzie hadn't been back to the middle school since, well, since middle school. Not that she minded being back now. There was a comfort to walking the halls of her childhood.

Those years were some of her happiest—her father got his shit together for a while, meaning she had clean clothes and a full belly. She'd had her three best friends, and enjoyed learning, reveling in the warm feeling of approval from her teachers.

And really, if you had to hangout somewhere during an apocalypse, then a school with bright paintwork and motivational posters wasn't a terrible choice.

The cafeteria hadn't changed at all. It had a nostalgic scent—not altogether pleasant—but reassuring all the same. Now that she was on the other side of the lunch counter, Mackenzie was gaining an appreciation for where the smell originated.

"Here I was thinking that eggs came from chickens and were cracked out of shells," Mackenzie said to Rachel. "Who knew they were actually powder in a box?"

"It's ridiculous how many foods have been dehydrated and reduced to powder," agreed Rachel. "It's not like kids need to eat real food, right?"

Not that they were begrudging the huge stockpile of food. Thank the lord for well-organized lunch ladies.

When Mackenzie had arrived an hour ago, a team of women were clearing and washing breakfast dishes, and another several were debating what they were going to produce for lunch. For over three hundred people.

Rachel had thrown up her hands and stomped away. "I'm a vet, not a goddamn cook. I say the men find their own fucking food."

For the first time since this began, Mackenzie's spine straightened with a sense of purpose. Sanford might not need an environmental lawyer, but food? She knew food.

She'd spent a childhood getting inventive with sparse ingredients, making it stretch as far as it could. As an adult, she'd taken pleasure in knowing her bank account could support a full grocery cart and indulged in cooking elaborate gourmet meals.

She'd decided on frittatas for lunch—it was easy enough to make in large quantities and would help what fresh food they had stretch farther. The other women were mostly grateful to have someone directing them, although a few gave her distasteful looks and she didn't miss the hissed *trailer trash* that was lobbed her way.

"Is cilantro too much to ask for?" Mac muttered, running a finger along the food shelves as she walked up and back.

"The only spice that school cafeterias have is 'bland.' You're wasting your time," said Rachel, who'd relented and was energetically slashing at sweet potatoes.

"What are you two nattering for? Lunch needs to be

ready to be served in forty-five minutes." Mrs. White tsked, a sixty-something widow who'd presided over the Sanford Women's Club for the last decade and, having arrived several minutes ago, was intent on presiding over the cafeteria kitchen, too.

She turned to the industrial sink, where women were rinsing the breakfast dishes and stacking the dishwasher, hindered somewhat by Jean Fiskette, who was washing tomatoes. "My dear, now is not the time to be washing fruit for the frittata," she scolded, picking up a stray dish towel and swishing it in Jean's direction. "It needs to be chopped, and pronto."

Jean's face fell, tears falling unchecked.

"Oh dear. No need for tears," Mrs. White soothed, her kindness marred by an underlying briskness. "I know these are trying times, but we need to get on with our jobs."

"My Bill, he's in quarantine, and no one will tell me how he is," Jean whispered, wringing her wet hands.

Cocking her head, Mackenzie stilled in her perusal of the shelves, listening. The quarantine issue had been playing on her mind all morning. She didn't necessarily want to see her father, but she'd like to know where he was. Having not seen him at either the town meeting or the bar last night, she suspected he'd been taken to the hospital.

"Why has no one gone to check on the hospital?" she asked.

The other women ignored her.

"She has a point," Rachel interjected. "We're all wondering what's happening, and Townsend tells us they have it under control. But why hasn't anyone gone to check?"

Mrs. White gave them a side look and tutted at them to keep her voice down.

"Because," Jean whispered, "the last people who announced they were going to check didn't come back. And Townsend has instructed that anyone who leaves the Safe Zone isn't allowed back in."

"I'm sure we'll hear news when there is some," Mrs. White said.

"I heard the bus drivers who took them away didn't come back either," one of the women at the sink said.

"Enough chitchat, ladies. We have work to do. Back to it," Mrs. White scolded.

"What do you think is happening at the hospital?" Mackenzie murmured, sidling up to Rachel. "Three-quarters of the town are up there. They wouldn't even all fit inside. How do we not know what's happening?"

"I heard they were using the undercover parking lot, which would make sense. But I honestly don't think..." She paused.

"Don't think what?"

"Mac, you've seen how fast this virus progresses once symptoms present. I just don't... I don't think there are going to be any survivors. It's been four days. I doubt anyone at the hospital is still alive," she finished somberly.

Looking at the quietly sobbing Jean, Mackenzie swallowed, intensely grateful the people she cared about most in this world weren't at the hospital.

Which was instantly followed by a slug of shame. Did she really not care that her father might be dead? They hadn't had a relationship in years, and she harbored a deep resentment for the shitty parenting he'd afforded her. But it was disconcerting to feel so little about his welfare. What did that say about *her*?

What would Jake think of her being so callous?

Jake.

Warmth infused her chest. She totally had the hots for her best friend's little brother. How had this happened? Closing her eyes, she ran a finger over her lips, a fierce longing almost making her tremble, even as the weight of their new world pressed down.

Even if she was starting something with him—and, to be fair, their recent between-the-sheets (and against-the-door) antics indicated that convincingly—she still wasn't prepared for the whole of Sanford to weigh in.

She'd had enough of the town's judgment to last a lifetime.

Her stomach gave a little flip, remembering the way he'd sucked her finger last night.

Just as quickly, a prickle of guilt washed over her. People were dead. Dying. And she was behaving like a lovesick teenager. Not to mention deceiving her best friend.

"I know things are fucked up at the moment, but I am *seriously* disturbed that Vivienne Oxley is the one who's in charge of looking after the kids in the crèche," Kat announced, wandering back into the kitchen. She'd played hooky not long after Mackenzie had arrived. "She doesn't have a maternal bone in her body. She's like one of those insects that eats its mate once they've had sex." Kat jumped up to sit on the counter.

"Hygiene, Kat," Rachel reprimanded. "Get off the food prep worktop."

"You know what I overheard?" Kat continued blithely. "Jim Boston's got some biohazard suits. Fuck knows where he got them from, for the raid they're going on tonight."

"Stop calling it a raid," griped Rachel. "And get off the counter. Make yourself useful and go check that batch of frittatas in the oven."

Kat ignored her.

"You know what *else* I heard?" Kat's voice lowered and took on a gravity that had both Mackenzie and Rachel pausing. "Old Mrs. Murray was beaten when they found out she'd hidden gas."

"What?" Mackenzie gasped, frittatas forgotten. "Is she okay?"

"Some bruising on her face, and maybe a broken wrist," Kat said somberly.

"Are the whole of the council on drugs?" Rachel exploded. "My mother would *never* have allowed this shit to happen."

"Hopefully she'll be back soon and can reason with them," Mackenzie said.

"They're beyond reasoning with. They're power-hungry chauvinistic assholes," Rachel spat, swiping her eyes to hide brimming tears.

"Why isn't help coming?" Kat questioned. "Mac, you said you saw the military in Chicago, didn't you? And a convoy in Essex? Surely, we'll get some kind of information soon. A vaccine. *Something*."

They quietened as Mrs. White passed by, and Mackenzie's gaze swung intuitively to the kitchen's back door just as Jake walked through. His eyes scanned the room until he found her, a dimple popping in his cheek with that cocky grin. Tipping his head, he gestured for her to follow before backing away.

Glancing around furtively, Mackenzie responded on light feet, slipping around boxed supplies and disappearing from the room unseen.

Jake was pulling her to him before the door had even snicked closed and, although she wanted nothing more than to bury her head against his chest, her thoughts were so far from romantic it wasn't funny.

"What is it?" he asked, his finger lifting her chin so his concerned gaze could capture hers. "Not wanting to get frisky in the dirty alley behind the cafeteria?"

"I'm scared," was all she could muster. Mac didn't know how to put into words the overload of emotion and information.

Jake responded by tugging her closer, wrapping strong arms around her as he settled his chin on top of her head. "The virus isn't going to breach Sanford."

"It's not the virus that has me most worried," she admitted. "I mean, it *is*. But it's the effect it's had on everything. We have no idea what's happening, and the council is acting crazy."

"What do you mean, crazy?" He pulled back, his brow furrowed. "The council is keeping us safe. They've got a plan to get us through this."

Mackenzie weighed her response. It unnerved her that Jake wasn't seeing where she was coming from. "Who is going to keep us safe from the council?"

Jake cocked his head. Sitting heavily on a stack of overturned milk crates, he patted another for Mackenzie to join him. "Why would we need to be kept safe from the council?"

Unable to sit still, she paced before him. "Don't you find the level of control they're exerting disturbing?"

Surely, he could acknowledge that. Nothing about this new world was normal, but having a gun-toting, self-promoted militia "protecting" them *wasn't* normal.

"I know that no one has breached the blockades set up along the roads leading into Sanford," Jake said, "and men are risking their lives in patrols to ensure our safety."

"Exactly. *Men*. What's with all the patriarchal bullshit about keeping women in the kitchen? And don't you wonder if the patrols are more about keeping *us in*, rather than others out?"

"We're not prisoners, Mac." Jake's voice had hardened, and he was looking at her like he didn't know her. "Where's this coming from?"

"Kat just heard that Mrs. Murray was assaulted because she didn't hand over all her gas."

"I'll admit someone got carried away, but the council were requisitioning gas for a reason. Everything is unprecedented at the moment," he defended.

Mackenzie breathed out in frustration, coming to a stop in front of him. "She was *beaten up* for hiding gas!"

They stared wordlessly at each other, knees touching, but a world of difference between them.

"I don't like the council taking everything," she said finally, watching her boot make patterns in the loose gravel. "If we can gather supplies of our own, we won't have to rely on the council."

"Absolutely not."

Her head snapped up. "*Excuse me?*"

Since when did Jake have the right to speak to her like that? To dictate her actions?

"Absolutely not," he repeated.

"Just because we're, whatever we are,"—she waved an emphatic hand between them—"doesn't mean you can tell me what I can and can't do."

"You go outside the Safe Zone, and you could be shot trying to reenter."

She gaped at him.

"There's a reason for everything Townsend is doing, Mac."

Her head was spinning, and she slumped down onto the crate. She didn't care about the reasons. She cared that men in their town thought they could punish with impunity. She cared that Jake *agreed with them*.

"So get that idea out of your head, Mac. I forbid you from leaving the safety of the Safe Zone."

"I beg your pardon?" Mackenzie snapped. "You *forbid* me?"

An imminent headache began knocking with persistence.

"I don't want to fight with you," he said, grasping at her suddenly chilled hands. "You know I just want to keep you safe. I couldn't bear it if anything happened to you."

The word *forbid* was echoing between them, and she couldn't force her hands to grip his in return.

He carried on, oblivious. "I came to let you know I'm going to go on the raid to Dutton. We leave late this afternoon."

Pulling her hands away, she pressed her back against the wall to create some distance between them.

Distance that physically pained her even as her insides were flayed with each word he spoke.

"It's not a raid," he amended. "It's just a scavenging trip to get a fuel tanker."

Disbelief made her rigid. "I can't go out there, but you can? What if you get infected?"

Regardless of her anger at his pigheaded and misdirected intentions, Mac was petrified for his safety. Petrified that he was leaving her. She stood on unsteady legs, and he followed suit.

"I won't. We're taking precautions, and we'll make sure not to get too close to anyone. The fuel depot is on the edge of town. I'll be back before you know it," he promised.

But she was not to be deterred.

"So Townsend's now a general and you're his little soldier, going out on commando missions?"

"It's a quick trip to do a little recon and grab some gas. I promise it's not a big deal."

"Not a big deal?" she cried, pushing her hands against his chest to make him back away. "The world is dying out there. It's chaos. And you *know* it's not safe."

"Mac! Are you out here?" came Kat's voice.

They both started, turning toward the back cafeteria door.

Kat's head popped around, scowling when she saw them. "Seriously? We're trying to feed a shit ton of people right now and you're having a deep and meaningful conversation?"

"I'm coming," Mackenzie mumbled, trying to push past him.

"Hey. Hey! Babe, you're not leaving like this."

"You're right, I'm not leaving you, *you* are," she retorted, sidestepping him. "See you when you get back." She tossed over her shoulder as she went inside.

———

JAKE WATCHED HER GO, reeling at how fast his dreams had crashed at his feet. How many nights had he lain awake over the years thinking of Mackenzie? Dreaming of kissing her, touching her. None of those fantasies had come even close to the real thing.

She was beyond his wildest imaginings.

And now she was so pissed at him she hadn't even met his eyes when she'd said goodbye.

"Fuck!"

Checking his watch, he groaned inwardly, before spinning on his heel and heading around the front of the school to meet with Jim Boston.

The next few hours with Jim and the other six men reassured Jake of his decision. Jim had a family to come home to, so he wouldn't be taking any unnecessary risks.

When the meeting finally broke up, he had half an hour before they were to head out, and Jake was hoping he'd catch Mackenzie in the cafeteria before the dinner rush started.

Walking into the familiar room, he had the instinctive urge to check for incoming spit balls. God, they'd been unruly kids.

Smiling, he glanced around and waved when he caught sight of Chloe attempting to wrangle several small children.

"This is much harder than it looks." She huffed, putting her hands on her hips and surveying the damage they'd caused with cups of red Jell-O.

"I'm not saying it looks easy, but, sis, you're a teacher. Shouldn't you be all over this?"

"I'm a high school English teacher. These terrors are five and under, way outside my experience. Give me hormonal teenagers any day."

"So who has the teenagers?"

Come to think of it, he hadn't seen many kids around at all.

"I've seen a few groups roaming around but, to be honest, I'm not sure how many are left," she admitted.

"And their parents?" He waved at the children.

"Dead."

"Did you get to the community garden?" Jake asked, changing the subject.

Chloe's face brightened. "It was a goldmine. I've got a

wheelbarrow of vegetable seedlings that the kids and I are going to plant tomorrow."

"And Grams? I didn't get a chance to stop in and see her."

"The doors were locked, and no one answered my knocking. I went straight to town hall, and Jefferies tried to tell me they were probably *napping*," she said doubtfully. "I'm going back after dinner. Want to come with?"

"Can't. I'm heading out with the group going to Dutton." Jake waited for Chloe's reaction. His big sister wasn't known for holding back her opinions and, like Mackenzie, he knew she'd be worried about his safety.

"Okay, just be smart," she surprised him by saying. "And if you get the chance to talk to anyone, can you ask about Ash? If he was making his way home, he'd have to come through Dutton."

"Of course." He pulled her into a hug. "I'll be back later tonight."

He found Mackenzie alone in the kitchen, stirring an enormous pot of meat and vegetable stew that, despite its appearance, smelled delicious.

Coming up behind her, he slid his arms around her waist, dipping his head to kiss the back of her neck. She stiffened, but then relaxed back into him. He smiled against her skin.

"I'm still mad at you," she said, continuing to stir.

"I know, babe."

"And when you get back, we're going to have a serious discussion about your attitude. We're a team. You can't go around telling me what to do."

"We are way more than a team, baby girl," he murmured into the sweetness of her neck. "But you're right." He turned her to face him. "I should've talked to you about it. I know it's a shit show out there, but I'm going to be careful."

"I know *you'll* be careful, but what about everyone else? You're going on a stealing mission for the stupid council. Don't we have gas in our own depot?"

"It was due to be refueled when this all happened, and we think the tankers were held up at Dutton."

He realized Mackenzie was no longer relaxing into his embrace. She was definitely still pissed.

"It doesn't mean you have to go," she said.

"You know I'd do anything for you, but..."

"Anything?" She raised an eyebrow.

"Babe, please don't ask me not to go. I've committed to the team, and I can't back out now. I promise we are taking every precaution and you'll wake up tomorrow morning with me in your bed."

He could see the indecision warring on her face, his insides warming because he knew her anger was born from fear. Fear for him.

The girl didn't know it yet, but she was totally falling for him.

"You do what you have to do, Jake." She turned her back to him, resolutely stirring the stew.

He hated he was upsetting her. But he *had* to be proactive about their situation.

"I'll see you in a couple of hours." Moving to her side, he reached out to grasp her chin, tilting it so he could kiss her lips.

She twisted her head, and he grazed her cheek instead. Steeling himself, he stepped back, hoping she'd at least look at him before he left.

Her eyes stayed downcast as he walked away.

CHAPTER ELEVEN

Mackenzie was in a daze walking home from the cafeteria. Night had fallen while she'd been inside planning for tomorrow with Mrs. White, and she was wrecked. Her legs were leaden, and it was as though the air had a density that made it impossible to move at any pace.

Not that she was in a hurry.

She couldn't *believe* Jake's recent attitude and that he'd left on that stupid raid. He was taking unnecessary risks. And he was leaving her. Which, she had to admit, was a small part of why she was so mad. Okay, maybe not so small.

Ever since she'd returned to her apartment to find him waiting for her, Jake had become her rock. *He* was safety for her.

Was it only a few days ago? It felt like a lifetime.

A lifetime in which she'd aged immeasurably. Her body was struggling with the physical demands she'd placed on it —first walking back to Lincoln Park and then fleeing the city. Even the walk from Chloe's house to downtown Sanford was more exercise than she was used to. Having always maintained the same curvy build no matter how much pizza she did, or didn't, consume, she'd seen no reason to cut into her Netflix time by exercising.

Which meant, in addition to a bone-deep weariness, her muscles were aching with fatigue. Putting one foot in front of the other was becoming an effort. She seriously needed to reconsider her attitude about getting fit.

The overhead streetlight flickered, and instinct made Mackenzie pick up the pace. The last place she wanted to be right now was alone in a darkened street.

She had no idea where the closest power plant was, and how much manpower it relied on. If there was no one to manage it, how long would it continue to supply electricity?

The workings of the world were not something that Mackenzie had ever bothered herself with. Regardless of how neglectful her father was, she'd grown up taking for granted that water would come out of a faucet when turned on, and electricity would light a room when she flicked a switch. She'd never stopped to consider the *how* of these functions.

Sure, she knew where the town's water treatment plant was because it was right beside a park she used to frequent in her early teens. But how did the water get there? How did it get distributed through the town?

The lack of knowledge tightened her chest with help-lessness.

Tears threatened, but she swallowed them back. She shouldn't have let Jake leave the way he had—she didn't even say goodbye.

She was just so *tired*. She couldn't even attempt rational thinking in this state. Thankfully, the lights of Chloe's front porch beckoned, and she mustered the energy to jog—albeit slowly—up the driveway, greeted by an overenthusiastic Dex.

"I WOULDN'T HAVE THOUGHT to put an apple into this, but it's good," Rachel commented, crunching her way through a salad Mackenzie had prepared using produce Chloe had scavenged from the community garden.

They had decided that for as long as they had supplies, they would eat together at home.

"I have a feeling our food choices are going to get a lot more creative going forward," Mackenzie answered. "The cafeteria is pretty well stocked, but putting together three meals a day for three hundred people is going to put a major dent in those pretty quickly. Townsend should get everyone to dig up their front gardens and plant vegetables, instead of putting together raiding parties."

"Do you think we need to be thinking so long-term?" Chloe asked. "I mean, not everyone died, right? We're still alive. So it stands to reason there are still scientists and government people out there, working on a cure and getting civilization functioning again."

Rachel narrowed her eyes with skepticism.

Looking between the two of them, Mackenzie felt the tug of that rising tide of helplessness again and sought comfort by petting the ever-present Dex, whose tongue lolled in appreciation.

"Things will go back to normal eventually," Chloe insisted. "They have to."

Mackenzie uttered a noncommittal murmur and Rachel shoved a forkful of spinach leaves into her mouth, chewing with unnecessary vigor.

"Thanks for making dinner Mac, but I'm going to go to

bed," Chloe said, pushing her half-eaten plate away. "I've got a headache."

"And you're worried about Ash," Mackenzie said. "You're going to cry in the dark, aren't you? Want me to come curl up with you?"

"Love you, but no. I just need to be alone."

Mackenzie and Rachel watched with concern as Chloe left, shoulders slumped. There was no way she could add to Chloe's emotional burden right now, even if the secret of Jake was a burning itch.

"I just got busted sneaking food to Maggie at The Strumpet by that asshat Charlie Nixen." Kat said, bursting through the front door and flinging her shoes off as she entered the kitchen. "He's such a do-gooding weasel. And honestly, did he really think he was going to tell me what to do? He can't even tell himself what to do. I'm pretty sure he still lives with his mother. Jesus. He's lucky that Quinn was there and saved his skinny ass." Dropping into the seat beside Mackenzie, Kat started picking tomatoes from her plate.

"Saved him from what?" Rachel asked.

"Me. I had him backed up against the jukebox. Honestly, if you're going to get all righteous about rules, you better have the balls to follow through."

Rachel snorted. "You probably scared him half to death."

"Back up a bit," Mackenzie requested. "Why were you sneaking food to Maggie?"

"Townsend wouldn't give her rations today because she didn't go to the town meeting last night," Kat answered through a mouthful. "Apparently he thinks it's 1939 and we're living in Soviet Russia."

"Are you kidding? He can't deny people food!" Rachel

was outraged.

"He thinks he can," Kat said. "Maggie is putting together a group of people who also think this is bullshit, and we're going to meet soon to figure out a way to handle the assholes."

"The sooner the better," Mackenzie said. "When? Where?"

"I know we don't speak of James O'Connor, but he's offered the distillery as a safe place for us to meet without being found out," Kat replied.

Rachel stared at Kat, brows lowered.

"I know, I know. He's a jerk, that's old news. You know what *isn't* old news?" She sang, "That Mac has a *boyfriend*."

"Kat!" Mackenzie huffed, tugging her plate away. "Can you keep it down? Chloe's just in her bedroom."

"You two better not have discussed the juicy details before I got here." Kat snatched another apple slice from Mackenzie's plate.

"Hang on," Rachel interrupted. "What do you mean, *boyfriend*?"

Mackenzie shrank back in the seat as she became the sole focus of Kat's formidable energy.

"Come on, little hussy. Tell us everything," Kat demanded, leaning into Mackenzie's personal space until their noses touched.

Kat sat back expectantly and Mackenzie despaired at the telltale flush she knew would be staining her face.

Pressing the backs of her hands to her burning cheeks, Mac took a deep breath. "Okay. But this is going to require wine. Lots of wine."

Grinning, Kat bound up to rummage through the fridge, loudly denigrating Chloe's choice of Sauvignon. "I'll drink it if I have to, but tomorrow, we'll get Maggie to stock us up on the good stuff."

When their glasses were full, Kat gave Mackenzie an exaggerated well-go-on-then widening of her eyes, but it was Rachel who jumped in.

"Can one of you please tell me what the hell is going on? As far as I knew, the only boyfriend is the douche back in the city."

"That *ex*-boyfriend is yesterday's news. Today's news headline is all about Jake Brent," Kat declared.

Rachel's head tipped, obviously thinking, before she took a swallow of her wine. "Makes sense. That boy has been in love with you forever."

"Can we agree to refrain from calling him a boy?" Mackenzie begged. "He is *not* a boy. And what do you mean, he's been in love with me forever?"

"I thought everyone knew he had a crush on you, and we'd just decided not to talk about it," said Rachel.

"Does Chloe know?" Mackenzie cried, eyes wide.

"Not sure," Rachel mused. "Does she know now?"

"No! No one knows."

"Ooh, so it *is* a secret. I love me a good secret," said Kat.

Dropping her head on to her folded arms on the table, Mackenzie groaned. "I can't talk about this if you're not going to take it seriously. This isn't just a random hook up."

"I didn't say it was random!" Rachel protested.

"I know. I know I'm being sensitive about it." Mackenzie sighed. "This feels different from anything else I've had before. I just really need to know you're not going to make a joke out of it."

"Darling girl,"—Kat flung her arms around Mackenzie's slouched shoulders—"you can't honestly think we'd ever make fun of something that's important to you. We love you. We adore Jake. We are one hundred percent behind you two getting married and making babies and living happily ever after."

"I'm totally down with a niece or two," Rachel agreed.

"So, let's discuss the sex!" piped up Kat.

"This is going to make me regret being celibate for the last twelve months, isn't it?" Rachel despaired, taking a large swallow of wine.

MACKENZIE AWOKE the next morning disoriented, somehow expecting to be waking next to Jake. Instead, she was being spooned by Kat.

By unspoken agreement, the four friends had again spent the night at Chloe's, instead of heading to their own homes.

Careful not to disturb Kat, she slipped out of her loose embrace and headed to the bathroom, almost running into a rumple-haired Chloe.

"Morning," Chloe mumbled.

"Have you seen Jake?"

Chloe shook her head.

"I thought he might've called in when he got back, to let us know everything was okay."

"I haven't seen him," Chloe said.

An insidious dread unfurled in Mackenzie's chest, pushing aside any residual sleepiness and making her throat tighten.

Why didn't he come and see her when he got back?

"Maybe it was really late, and he didn't want to wake us," Chloe said.

Nodding mutely, Mackenzie closed the bathroom door with a shaking hand. She fought to hold back the fear, but it bloomed, suffocating and consuming, as she slid down the door and folded onto the tiled floor.

She couldn't explain it, but she *knew* something wasn't right. Wrapping her arms around her middle, she attempted to hold in the knowledge. If she didn't admit it, if she didn't let it out, Jake would be okay.

———

PRESSING his hand against his side to stop the slow flow of blood, Jake gritted his teeth against swearing out loud. Any noise he made could betray their position. Closing his eyes against a wave of dizziness, he attempted to even his breathing.

Night was finally breaking into a gray dawn, weak splinters of sunlight made its way through the dust motes to light the barn they were hiding in.

In the farmhouse beside them, the motorcycle gang of marauders who'd chased them from downtown Dutton were drunkenly smashing and pillaging, unaware their quarry was within such close proximity.

Over the course of the long night, they'd thrown anything flammable onto the front lawn and created a roaring bonfire, which was only now burning itself out. The thick smoke that had billowed into the sky was finally dissipating and the revelers that had crowded it were mostly passed out or asleep.

The three gang members posted as sentry had Jake biting back his pain. Those three weren't drunk, weren't loud, and weren't forgetting their mission. Already one of them had called out, asking when they were going to be moving on.

"That drugstore is ours. This whole town is ours. And

those fuckers stole from us!" He flicked a cigarette butt in impatience. "We should be hunting them."

"We still got whiskey here, settle down," was yelled from inside.

"Fuck, I wish they'd move on," whispered Jesse, squatting beside Jake to check the crude dressing he'd applied to the gunshot wound on Jake's side.

He was lucky the bullet had only passed through soft tissue. Now that the bleeding was pretty much under control, the only concern was infection. And the pain. It hurt like a bitch.

"We need to get you some proper medical attention," said Jesse.

"Pharmacist, doctor. Same-same." Jake grinned and then winced as Jesse inadvertently jostled him.

When Jim had suggested the team split, with one taking the fuel tanker and the other heading farther into town for recon, it was a solid idea. They didn't need eight men to jack a truck, and it was well into the evening; night had fallen, and all had appeared quiet.

Even with everything that had happened, Jake couldn't regret his decision to go to the drugstore. Not when it meant he'd not only secured more medication for Mackenzie, but they'd met Jesse. The pharmacist had been holed up in the store since this began, surviving on bottled water and candy.

Jesse had said it was only a matter of time before someone found the tools to break down the safety barrier to the dispensary, and so, when Jake, Rob and Lee had turned up, he'd agreed to help stock them in exchange for going with them.

Dutton was a town in flames. Most survivors had already fled, leaving behind bodies and a motorcycle gang that had ridden into town and liked what they'd found. Lawless chaos had them thriving with a reckless abandon.

What society had once stifled and judged, now the virus had set free. The gang roamed like modern-day Vikings, raping and pillaging—reinforcing Jake's protective instincts toward Mackenzie tenfold.

"How's Lee looking?" Jake asked, glancing over into the shadows where the man was slumped.

"Not good." Jess sighed. "The wound is messy, and I don't know which internal organs have been affected. We're going to have to make a move sooner rather than later."

They'd had this conversation several times over the course of the night. When they'd ducked into the barn ahead of the motorcycle pack, they were only looking to hide out until the gang had passed them by. They couldn't have known their pursuers would also stop. And stay.

In waiting for the gang to move on before they made their own move, they'd lost the advantage of darkness. But with Lee seriously injured, they couldn't go any farther without some form of transport, and there was no way of starting a vehicle without alerting the gang to their whereabouts.

"We can't risk being followed back to Sanford. And we don't have a hope of outrunning them, even if Lee and I weren't in this condition," replied Jake.

He thought briefly of Rob, who'd been shot in the leg in their escape and then run down by the motorcycles—the ringing shot of a bullet confirming his fate—before forcing his mind to Mackenzie. Thinking of her was the only thing that had gotten him through the night. The way her skin flushed a pretty pink, the pout of her ravished lips, the way she tasted. God, her *taste*.

He groaned, remembering.

"Hang in there," Jesse instructed, misunderstanding.

"Tell me again what your college roommate told you," Jake said, needing to take his mind off a worrying Mackenzie and a possibly dying Lee. Plus, this was the other reason he was so glad to have found Jesse —information.

"Jono. He's still living in Chicago and works as a rep for Pharmotech. He's dating this girl who's a scientist with the company, and he called me the day before everything went to shit saying something big was about to go down, but there would be a percentage of the population who were immune.

"His girlfriend believed that if you didn't get sick in the first day or two after this happened, then you weren't going to. The virus had been incubating for weeks; there might be some communities that haven't been affected, but they'll be rare cases in remote parts of the world.

"So the whole of Earth's population has been incubating the virus for weeks or, with anyone still alive, being a carrier for it."

"So we're immune?"

"She seemed to think so. And it's a theory that holds if you take me as an example. I was in contact with people showing symptoms for two days before I closed the drugstore. I even dragged a sick man out of the store and into his car."

"And you're fine."

"Well, fine if you don't consider I'm being hunted by a gang of psychopaths."

They lapsed into a silence that was broken by the muscular roar of approaching motorcycles.

"Fuck. There are more?"

"It's only another two," confirmed Jesse, peering

through the slats of the barn. "But one of them has a second rider."

His sharp intake of breath had Jake shuffling awkwardly across the ground to join him. "Is that—?"

"A captive? Looks like it."

"Do you know her?"

"No, but I've only been in town for six months."

They watched as the rider dragged the woman off the bike, her hair wild and eyes frantic. She was a brunette, little more than a teenager, wearing an oversize sweater and sporting a vicious black eye. Whatever had happened prior to her arriving here, it was clear it had knocked any fight out of her. She was shaking with obvious fear, but didn't struggle.

The man holding her had greasy hair and a greasy smile, with the kind of meth-lab cunning that would see him thrive in this new world order.

"Got ourselves a fresh one!" he crowed, presenting her like a trophy.

"Jesus fuck," Jesse breathed.

"We have to help her."

"*How?* There are a dozen of them. Fourteen now."

"I don't know, but we have to do *something*," Jake insisted, watching as the men circled the woman like the prey she was.

His mouth was cottony, his throat parched. It was hard to think past the pain.

His eyes followed Jesse, who moved to crouch over Lee's prone form before looking back at Jake with a grim expression. "He's gone."

"God*damn.*"

The woman's scream split the air, causing the hairs on

Jake's arms to stand on end. Spurred into action, he surveyed the interior of the barn.

"There. That ride-on mower. Push it out the side door and get it about a hundred yards away. The side of the barn'll shield you from their view. There's a gasoline can next to it. Use this rag as a fuse, and then run like hell to that stand of trees back there. When it goes off, I'll run out and grab her and meet you at the trees."

"You're kidding, right?"

"You got a better plan?"

"Jake, you've got a gunshot wound. You can barely walk, let alone run."

"That's why you're the one pushing the mower, and I get the easy job of rescuing the girl."

There was silence for one beat. Two.

"Okay."

"Okay," Jake confirmed with a grim smile. "I've still got a full chamber in my rifle. You take it and I'll take Lee's Glock. We'll head into that heavy forest where they won't be able to follow on their bikes, and then double back to get to that neighboring farmhouse we saw. Hopefully, there'll be a vehicle there."

"We can't just take this one?" Jesse gestured to the beat-up pickup parked in the barn with them.

"There won't be time to open the barn doors to get it out. We're going to have to do this part on foot."

"You're sure you can do this? We can take five and think of an alternative." The woman screamed again, and Jesse winced. "You're right. Let's do this."

Striding to the workbench, Jesse rummaged until he found a lighter, turning to wave it at Jake before inching open the side door. It swung silently, revealing a crisp, clear morning.

Jake picked up Lee's pistol, covering the man's face with his jacket as he did so and vowing he'd return to bury him. As Jesse heaved the mower through the door, Jake stepped outside and crept up the side of the barn so he could peer around the corner.

Someone had added fuel to the fire, and it was again roaring, the heat buffeting against Jake's face. The woman's arrival had caused those in the house to come out so that all fourteen of the men had her encircled.

They cheered as the one who'd brought her pushed her to her knees, holding her immobile with a harsh grip on her hair. Another stood before her, unbuckling his belt.

"Go. Go!" Jake whisper-shouted at Jesse.

It was a long three minutes before Jesse glanced back, raising his thumb. He crouched to light the rag and then took off at a dead run.

Even though he was expecting the explosion, the blast still rocked Jake, and he lost precious moments. Darting forward, one hand holding his injured side and the other the Glock, he headed straight for the circle of men who'd scattered in shock. Several headed for their motorcycles while others ran toward the explosion, firing their weapons ahead of them.

Amid the shouts and choking smoke, Jake spied the woman, kicked to the ground by her captor while her would-be rapist stood by, perplexed, his dick hanging limp.

Jake reacted without processing his actions, cocking pistol and firing it close range into the back of the man's head. His eyes caught and held on those of the captor, who stared back with crazy intent.

"If I don't get her, neither do you," the man snarled, spittle landing on her forehead.

Time slowed, the thumping of blood in his ears the only sound Jake heard.

"*Please,*" the woman mouthed, her eyes a desperate entreaty as the captor's gun barrel jammed against her skull. And fired.

"No!" A flash of bile threatened and Jake swallowed it, jerking back from the red pulpy mess before him.

The man straightened and pointed the gun at Jake. Jake raised his own weapon—hand steady—and the two stared, unblinking, at each other.

"Looks like we got ourselves a good ole fashioned Mexican standoff." The man grinned, revealing tobacco-stained teeth. "Go on, then, git." He waved his weapon. "I'll come across you again, boy, don't you worry."

Walking backward, his weapon trained unwaveringly, Jake made his way to the trees where Jesse waited.

CHAPTER TWELVE

"I've been making a list," Rachel said, head bent over the notebook she was writing in at the kitchen counter. "I think you were right when you mentioned heading into the Evac Area for supplies."

Stirring creamer into her coffee, Mackenzie hummed absently. She'd used her asthma inhaler in the bathroom, and even now her heart was racing. The gathering fear was a black storm, eclipsing all else.

Even Dex couldn't distract her.

"I'm thinking tampons. Toilet paper." Rachel looked up pointedly. "Condoms." When Mackenzie didn't respond, Rachel closed her notebook and sat back. "What's up?"

Chloe entered the kitchen, tying her hair in a messy topknot and glancing between the two. "Something wrong?"

"It's Jake," Mackenzie blurted. "He didn't come home last night."

"How do you know? Have you been over to his house?" Chloe asked.

"No." Mackenzie stalled. "It's just... I'm worried."

"What aren't you telling me?" Chloe's eyes flicked over her suspiciously.

Hot guilt crept up Mackenzie's throat, and she suddenly wished she'd told Chloe about her relationship with Jake as soon as it had become a possibility. Since when did she keep secrets from her best friend?

Since the secret involved her little brother.

Mackenzie's chest tightened, and she felt for the inhaler in her pocket.

The thrumming tension she endured every time she thought about Chloe knowing snapped. No matter the consequence, she couldn't carry the guilt besides the worry.

"Mac? What are you not telling me?" Chloe said.

Dex stood beside Mackenzie, leaning against her leg and nudging his nose into her lap. "Chlo, I should've said something earlier. I'm so sorry..."

"Sorry about what?" She took a step toward Mackenzie, clearly agitated. "Do you know something about Ash?"

"It's not Ash, it's Jake."

"What about Jake?"

The confusion on her face was wrenching for Mackenzie. She'd betrayed her best friend's trust. Why? Why couldn't she have just told Chloe what was happening? Why had she assumed Chloe wouldn't approve?

"We're together. Seeing each other." Mackenzie clarified when Chloe's confusion deepened.

"You're what?"

Mackenzie took a breath of her inhaler, unable to meet Chloe's eyes. "I'm sorry we didn't say anything sooner..."

"We? You and my brother are a *we*?" Chloe stumbled back, her eyes bouncing between Mackenzie and Rachel.

"Did you know about this?" She demanded of Rachel.

"You hadn't suspected?" Rachel asked carefully.

"No, I hadn't suspected! She's my best friend, and he's my little brother. The world is fucking falling apart. When the fuck did they have time to become a *we*? This is ridiculous!"

Mackenzie's cheeks burned in shame and her heart hurt. Chloe's complete lack of acceptance—her anger—was agonizing.

"Chlo..." she begged.

"I don't... no. No. I'm not having this conversation now. I'm going to see Grams." Chloe practically ran from the kitchen.

Mackenzie turned helplessly to Rachel, who said, "It's okay, I'll go with her. She'll come around."

Rachel gave Mackenzie a quick hug before following Chloe out of the house.

NO ONE from the recon team had returned.

After confirming that Jake wasn't at his own home, Mackenzie had gone straight to Jim Boston's house where she'd found his wife, Caroline.

"He should've been home hours ago," Caroline worried, wiping down the kitchen counter while simultaneously feeding a toddler. "Tabitha has already been here. Rob didn't come home either. As far as we know, none of them have come back yet."

"So no one's heard anything?" Mackenzie asked.

"Not that I know of. I was just about to head to town hall to see if there's been any radio contact." Caroline wiped down her son's face and lifted him from the high chair, setting him lightly on the floor. "I just need to get the kids sorted."

After instructing her reluctant teenage daughter on her

babysitting duties, Caroline set off on foot with Mackenzie toward town hall.

"We need to find some bicycles," Mackenzie said, stretching out stiff legs. Her muscles were still protesting the unaccustomed exercise and, although healing, the blisters on her feet were sore. "All this walking isn't good for my health."

"The sports store isn't in the Safe Zone, but we could ask Townsend if he'd send a truck out and bring some bicycles back in," agreed Caroline. "Jim was talking about organizing some groups to head into the Evac Area to get supplies. And just to check things out. We'll need to clean out fridges and round up pets. And there'll probably be bodies that have to be removed and buried."

Mackenzie shuddered. As essential as it was to gather supplies, Jake had told her about the stench from the dead body in Quinn's neighbor's house. It was awful to think about how many houses hid similar gruesome discoveries.

Lapsing into silence, they walked on, dodging overflowing residential rubbish bins littering the curb sides. Mackenzie wrinkled her nose. The fetid scent of decay was cloying and her stomach lurched, reminding her she hadn't eaten breakfast. Her stomach heavy with dread, she hadn't been able to face the thought of food.

Anxiously, Mac tapped her fingers against her thighs as she walked. *Please let him be okay. Please let him be okay.*

They were within sight of town hall when they saw an SUV speed up from the opposite direction. The vehicle came to a stop and several men jumped out, striding into the building.

"That's the recon team!" Caroline exclaimed, breaking into a run.

Forgetting her aching limbs, Mackenzie raced after her.

Please let it be him. Please let it be him.

Her chanting thoughts accompanied the thud of her feet as she ran through the wide doors of the town hall, out of breath. Caroline was already throwing herself at Jim and Mackenzie searched desperately for Jake. Thinking she may have run straight past him she swung in a frantic circle, once. Twice.

He wasn't there.

"Where is he?" she gasped.

Townsend emerged from a corridor followed by several councilors, heading straight to the returned men.

"What happened to regular radio communication?" he barked. "Did you get the tanker?"

"Gavin's taken it around to the back enclosure," Jim answered, rubbing at weary eyes. "Our radio got dropped and won't work, and when the group split they took the other one. Have you heard from them?"

"We haven't heard from anyone!" Townsend was getting red in the face. "Who gave you permission to split the group?"

"You don't dictate our every decision," Jim growled, standing toe to toe with Townsend. "This was my mission, and I made the call. I don't give a damn if you have a problem with that. Medication is going to become a priority, so they went to see what they could get from the drugstore."

"And now we've lost three capable men, an SUV, and the weapons they had on them!" Townsend fumed, refusing to back down. "I'm the mayor, and I call the shots."

"This is a democracy, damn it!" yelled Jim, his hands balling into fists. "We didn't just risk our lives for you, we did it for this community."

Townsend took a deliberate step back, a cold smile flashing across his features. "You don't seem to have noticed, but this community stopped being a democracy days ago. We're in a state of emergency and you better believe I hold the power."

Expecting Jim's reaction, Jefferies and another two councilors moved forward with their guns raised. "How about you rethink that attitude of yours and hand over your weapons?" Jefferies suggested, waving his rifle at the four returned men. "We don't want to have to make an example of you."

"Make an example of what?" cried Caroline, stepping closer to Jim. When he tried to block her in an attempt at protection, she pushed his arm aside. "Of townspeople having an opinion? For having the courage to brave what's happening out there to bring us back supplies?"

She was met with silence.

"Oh, for god's sake, this is ridiculous!" Caroline focused on Jefferies. "Last month you were friendly as could be selling us a car, and now you're pointing a gun at me?"

"Get that AR-15 out of my wife's face," Jim growled.

"This all goes away if you hand over your weapons," Townsend said.

"And if we don't?"

"Then we take them forcibly and you'll be removed from the town."

Gavin had entered from the rear of the building in time to overhear Townsend's threat and moved forward with his weapon held out in surrender.

"I don't know what's going on here, but I don't have a problem," he called. He laid his gun on the floor and backed away, eyes darting between Jim and Townsend. "Come on, man, what are you doing? Whatever it is, it's not worth being thrown out over."

Heart racing, Mackenzie held her breath as Caroline

laid a hand on her husband's arm. The couple exchanged a look before Jim nodded his head once, unshouldering his rifle and placing it on the floor. The other men from the raid followed suit.

"That was the right decision, son." Townsend watched smugly as the councilors removed the weapons.

"Fuck you," Jim snarled, spinning on his heel to leave.

"Hold up. We still need to debrief," commanded Townsend.

Jim didn't acknowledge him, continuing his retreat.

"Jim! What happened?" Mackenzie called.

He halted at the door to the town hall and turned, seeing her for the first time. "That asshole needs taking down a peg or two." He seethed. "How dare he threaten to throw me out of my own town?"

Although visibly shaken, Caroline tried to calm him, leading them all to a table with bench seats beneath an enormous sycamore tree.

The other men from the raid—Henry and Trent— joined them.

"Can you believe they de-armed us?" Henry spat. "We need to call a town meeting and vote in a new leader. Either that, or shoot the bastard."

Mackenzie flinched at the unbridled fury. She understood what had just happened was hugely significant to the future of their community. But right now, all she wanted was news about Jake.

As the men continued to spill their anger, she waited for a break so she could ask her questions. When none came, she knew she'd have to make herself heard.

But could she? This town held no respect for her father and had never cared either way for his daughter. Added to that, she hadn't lived here in years. Did she have the strength to speak up enough to be listened to?

Heart thumping, she realized she did. If she'd learned anything since this began, it was that she had an inner strength. And if anything was going to make her realize it, it was her feelings for Jake.

"Hold up a minute!" she said, attempting to get their attention.

Trent threw a glance in her direction before continuing in his tirade.

The sense of smallness, of hopelessness, threatened to swamp her.

"Stop!" She pushed in front of Trent and jabbed a finger at Henry's chest. "Quit your bitching and *think*. Where's Gavin? Someone needs to move that fuel tanker. It's not Townsend's, and we can use it as leverage.

"And before you call a town meeting, you need to pull together a core group of people you trust and put together a strategy. A plan. You have to offer the community an alternative. But before that,"—she paused and took in a deep breath through her nose—"you need to tell me what the hell happened to the rest of the recon group."

Conscious of the sudden attention, Mackenzie wrapped her arms around her middle to hide the shaking of her hands. She was a little stunned at the force and confidence of her outburst.

"Fuck. Yeah, I forgot about that for a moment." Henry sighed and sat heavily on the bench seat.

"Trent, find where Gavin left the keys and move that tanker. Take it to the lane behind my house until we think of a better spot," Jim instructed.

"I'm not following orders from a chick," Trent

answered, eyebrows pulled down sullenly. "I say we go back in there and throw Townsend out."

Before Jim could retort, Caroline all but pounced on Trent. "She's not *some chick*, Trent Wilson. You've known her all your life. And I'm telling you right now, you go blustering in there without a plan, you'll end up shot.

"Townsend was right in saying he has all the power, because he does. He's armed, and he has control of our supplies and resources." Caroline's eyes flashed when Trent went to interrupt. "Shut the hell up and listen."

"What do you know about any of this? You're a fucking stay-at-home mother." Trent sneered. "I'm not listening to you."

"You'll listen to me," Jim growled. "Find the keys and move the tanker. They're right, and if you lost some of that arrogance, you'd see it."

Mackenzie saw the defiance burning in Trent, even as he nodded curtly and strode away. She didn't miss the venomous look he shot her, either.

"Sit down and I'll fill you in," Jim said, pulling Caroline against his side. "Jake, Rob, and Lee split from us when we got to the fuel depot. We could still see their taillights when fucking Gavin dropped the radio and broke it. They were heading into town to check out the drugstore—Jake was set on finding asthma inhalers, and we decided it was a smart move to stock up on other medicines."

"Jake, what?" Mackenzie's strangled voice was low, and a cold sweat broke out across her brow.

Jake went to get asthma medication. For her.

She hadn't realized she was wheezing until Caroline wrapped an arm around her.

"There's no need to get worried just yet. We don't know what's held them up," Henry offered.

It was a hollow consolation. Everyone knew that *something* had to have happened, otherwise they'd have made it back to Sanford.

"We'd planned to meet up in an hour, but they never showed," continued Jim. "We waited until dawn and couldn't agree whether we should look for them or get the hell home. In the end, we came back and tried the radio from here. We stopped at the checkpoint on the way into town to make contact, but got nothing."

"We need to try again," Mackenzie cried.

"We will. But we tried for an hour with no response. By then, we were tired and hungry, and headed straight here."

"Right then, back home for food and rest," Caroline said, taking charge. "You too, Henry. Mackenzie, pull together anyone you trust, and we'll meet at the distillery at one. I've been talking with Maggie, and it's long overdue we started some form of resistance."

Lumbering to his feet, Jim pulled Caroline against his chest. "I love you, woman, you know that?"

Mackenzie's heart squeezed uncomfortably, their show of affection leaving her bereft. She was brittle with worry and guilt, that insidious dread weighing her down.

And now she needed to face Chloe.

THEIR MAD DASH through the forest had Jake's wound gushing with blood again. With Jesse's help, he concentrated on putting one foot in front of the other. Don't think about killing a man. Don't think about the pain. Definitely don't think about the girl.

Jesus fuck don't think about the girl.

Having closed his eyes tightly in a moment of anguish,

he stumbled over a fallen branch, and it was only that his arm was slung over Jesse's shoulder that he didn't sprawl into the leaf litter on the ground.

"Come on, we're almost there," Jesse encouraged, huffing with exertion.

There was no sign they were being chased. Not that it slowed their escape.

Jake could've wept when the red-roofed house came into view. His lungs were burning and the pain in his side was beyond anything he could imagine.

Abandoning caution as they approached, Jesse called out a hopeful greeting that was met with silence. There wasn't so much as a twitch of the curtain in the kitchen window.

"Think anyone's home?" Jesse asked.

"Maybe, maybe not," Jake answered. "Probably smart to hide from two strange men."

"Wonder if they'll appear when we start their pickup?"

"I think we should knock. Seems the polite thing to do. And I'd kill for some water."

Standing at the back door, Jesse knocked, and they waited, straining to hear anything from within. Jake swiped at drops of his blood from the sidewalk with his boot. After a minute of silence, Jake tried the doorknob. Locked.

"It's not worth breaking in just for a glass of water. I can use that garden hose, and then let's get the fuck out of here," he muttered, already making his way over.

They drank greedily, water running down their chins.

"Want to clean up some?" Jesse asked, eyeing Jake's blood-caked clothing.

"Nah, I don't want a wet shirt. It's damn cold enough as it is."

As if to emphasize his point, a bitter gust of wind swirled orange leaves around their legs.

"So if there's no key, you can hot-wire the pickup, right?"

"Learned how in the first week of my apprenticeship," Jake confirmed.

"Handy skill."

"Handy enough," Jake said, swinging open the door to the vehicle and smiling when he saw the key chain dangling from the ignition. "Speaking of handy skills, you don't know how to pick a lock by any chance, do you?"

Jesse looked at him in confusion.

"Never mind. You okay to drive?"

Loathe to admit to the woozy swimming of his head, Jake made his way to the passenger door, absently noting the trail of blood his supporting hand was leaving on the side of the truck. Hauling himself inside, he closed the door and collapsed back into the seat. "You can follow the road signs to Sanford, right?"

"Sure. You okay?"

Concern was evident in Jesse's voice, but Jake had closed his eyes. Adrenaline was leaching from his ravaged body, and he didn't have the strength to keep them open.

He felt the truck rumble to life, and then—nothing.

JESSE'S HAND shaking Jake's shoulder had him jerking back to consciousness, a burst of anxiety spiking his blood. The image of the girl, her eyes pleading, flashed in his mind.

"They don't look friendly," Jesse said, and slowed as they approached the blockade to Sanford, cautiously eyeing the armed men guarding it. "Sure they won't shoot first and ask questions later?"

"Just pull up here and let them come to us," Jake said. "This isn't the truck I left in, so they won't know who it is. We'll be fine once they realize."

I hope like hell they won't shoot first and ask questions later.

"Jake!" called Buddy, coming around to the passenger window and looking in with concern. "We've been trying to get you on the radio for hours. Where are Rob and Lee?" He gestured at Jesse with his rifle. "And who's this?"

"He's a friend, and he's safe. Let us through."

"He has to quarantine..." Buddy wasn't convincing in his role of authority.

"Fuck off, Buddy. He's safe, and I need medical help."

"You been shot?" Buddy asked.

"It's not bad. Let us through," he repeated.

"Rob and Lee?"

"Dead."

Jake held the other man's stare until he backed away, waving at the men at the blockade to allow them passage.

"I'll let Mayor Townsend know you're back," Buddy called out.

Jake ignored him.

"Where to?" Jesse asked.

"My sister's place."

"Those men at the checkpoint are radioing ahead. Don't they expect you to report in?"

"I need to get stitched up. And report to my girl."

Jesse didn't hide his smirk. "Sure thing, boss. Point the way."

An involuntary jumpiness had Jake's foot bouncing, a fierce need to see Mackenzie coursing through him. Now that they were so close, he couldn't contain his eagerness.

The rumble of the truck was loud in the suburban street

as they coasted to a stop in front of Chloe's driveway. Before Jesse had turned off the ignition, the front door to the house was flung open, Chloe and Mackenzie spilling out.

Fumbling with the door handle, Jake tried to jump out to greet them, but staggered.

"Jake! What happened?" Chloe cried, reaching him first and taking in the carnage of his clothing, her expression horrified. "Rach, where's Rachel? We need her!"

Without sparing his sister more than a cursory glance, his gaze landed on Mackenzie, who'd slowed her sprint toward him and was now standing back, eyes wide and unblinking. He could see the fear and uncertainty all over her face, and it killed him.

"I'm okay," he said, walking toward her with his hand outstretched as though she were a wild fawn that could startle and flee.

"God, Jake..." Her trembling palm covered her mouth, and she took a faltering step backward.

Noticing the dried blood on his outstretched hand, he looked down at himself, conceding he should've taken Jesse up on his suggestion to get clean before they got in the truck. He looked worse than he felt, which was saying something because he felt like shit.

Chloe pushed between them, stopping him from hauling Mackenzie into his arms.

"You're not okay. You've got blood all over you!" Chloe shrieked, frantically patting him down to find the source of his injury.

Catching Mackenzie's gaze over Chloe's shoulder, he willed her to come forward and claim him. Now, more than ever before, he didn't want to play the charade of friends. He wanted her enfolded in his embrace. He wanted to soothe the wild look from her eyes and kiss all the concern from her furrowed brow.

Most of all, he needed her to acknowledge the intense desperation they felt toward each other. To prove it was real. *They* were real.

Instead, Mac stood mute, hugging her torso, gnawing on her bottom lip.

"Let me look at you," demanded Rachel, pulling Chloe away and running practiced eyes over him. "What happened?"

"I got shot. It went through my side," he said, pulling his shirt up to expose the makeshift bandages covering the wound.

No one else noticed that Mackenzie choked on a sob. But for him, everything else was background noise. Every sense he possessed strained toward her.

"No way, Romeo," Rachel hissed at him beneath her breath. "I need you inside so I can look at this." She glanced at Chloe. "Get your first aid kit for me. And please tell me it contains Dermabond, because he's not going to like me stitching this up."

Behind Chloe's retreating form, Jake captured Mackenzie's hand, pulling her against him as they moved into the house, forgetting entirely about his traveling companion.

"Um, hi?" Jesse had exited the vehicle and was standing awkwardly on the curb.

"Who the hell is that?" Chloe asked, stopping in her tracks and looking over her shoulder.

"Shit, sorry. This is Jesse," said Jake, turning back around to wave his new friend forward, acutely aware that Mackenzie had again put distance between them. "Jesse, this is my sister, Chloe."

"Well, come on, don't just stand there," she chided him. "Are you hurt too?"

"No, ma'am,"

"Don't ma'am me." She huffed, waiting for him to reach her side before marching him after the others into the house.

In the kitchen, Rachel instructed Jake to lie down on the counter so she could inspect the wound, muttering to herself as she ran hot water and Chloe returned with the first aid kit.

"What can I do?" Mackenzie asked.

"Cross your fingers that this kit has skin glue," Rachel said, rummaging through the medical box. "Otherwise, this is going to hurt like a bitch."

"So reassuring," he quipped dryly.

"You're the one stupid enough to get shot."

"Not the only stupid thing you've been doing lately," Chloe muttered, glancing darkly between him and Mackenzie.

Mackenzie visibly tensed. So, Chloe knew about them and, apparently, wasn't happy about it.

"Not the time or the place, sis," he said.

"Who shot you?" Mackenzie asked, her lashes heavy with unshed tears.

Jake grimaced as Rachel began cleaning his wound, so Jesse answered for him, explaining about the motorcycle gang and how Rob and Lee were dead.

Mackenzie and Rachel traded shocked glances.

"I've never heard of an MC in Dutton," Chloe commented, finally looking away from Jake's hand clasping Mackenzie's.

"They're not locals," Jesse said. "They arrived about a

week ago and have taken over the town. It's bad. They've killed most of the surviving locals and have ransacked everything." Jesse accepted a glass of water from Chloe and continued.

"We found a barn to hide out in, but with both Jake and Lee shot, we didn't have a hope of outrunning them." Jesse nodded toward Jake's wound. "I bandaged them both up as best I could, but we lost Lee." He paused. "And then one of the gang members brought in a girl, and we couldn't just do nothing."

"What do you mean, brought in a girl?" Mackenzie asked, her eyes flicking between Jake and Jesse anxiously.

"A captive," Jake confirmed, concentrating on holding still as Rachel pulled the skin around his wound together and applied the skin glue. "Jesus, Rach, this hurts more than it does in the movies. Aren't you meant to be plying me with alcohol to numb the pain?"

"Suck it up," she retorted. "So you saved this chick?"

Jake closed his eyes, so he didn't have to see Mackenzie's face when he shook his head.

"We created a diversion and tried to rescue her, but these guys—" Jesse drew in a pained breath. "They're psychopaths. They, uh, shot her before we could get her away."

"Have you been to town hall?" Mackenzie asked, wincing on Jake's behalf as Rachel poured antiseptic over her handiwork and then turned him on his side to attend to the exit wound.

"Came straight here," Jake said. "Jim and the others got back okay?"

"Yes, but Townsend threatened to throw Jim and his family out of the town if he didn't fall into line."

"Fall into line?" Jake lifted his head from his bent

elbow, ignoring the agonizing throb in his side. "That sounds extreme. Are you sure you didn't misunderstand?"

"It wasn't a misunderstanding," Mackenzie said firmly, pulling away from him. "He literally said he'd throw them out of town if they didn't follow the rules."

"I know the rules might seem severe, but they're for our protection," he insisted.

"He's turned Sanford into a dictatorship!" Mackenzie exclaimed.

"And he isn't going to give up his power willingly," Chloe muttered. "We've got a meeting planned at the distillery in a couple of hours to work out how we're going to handle it."

"Not quite the safe haven I promised you, huh?" Jake addressed Jesse.

"Better than Dutton."

"Jake, do those motorcycle guys know about Sanford? Know where you're from?" Mackenzie asked. The worry etched on her features caused his stomach to clench.

The front door slammed and Jake jerked, causing Rachel to curse.

"Who is it?" Chloe called.

"Who do you think?" asked Kat, coming into the kitchen with her nose crinkled in confusion. "Whoa! What the hell's going on in here?"

Her eyes bounced from one to the other, stopping on Jake's prone form. "Jakey! When did you get back? What's happened?"

"Long story." He grunted. "You about finished, Rach?"

"Not my best, but not bad, considering what I had to work with," she responded, standing back. "And you'll live. I hope you brought back some antibiotics from the drugstore."

"Where've you been, Kat?" Mackenzie stood firm as Kat tried to push her away from Jake's side to better see.

Jake sat up with a groan and, ignoring Chloe, pulled Mackenzie to stand with her back between his knees. He was beyond relieved to feel her body relax into his as he wrapped his arms around her, resting his chin on her shoulder.

"I've just come from Main Street. Townsend has lost his shit. Hey, who are you?" She jabbed a finger in Jesse's direction. "I leave for a couple of hours and we adopt a stray? Lucky you're cute."

Jake chuckled as Jesse noticeably reddened, shifting from foot to foot.

"I'm Jesse."

"Kat," she responded, losing interest quickly. "So anyway, they caught a couple of teenagers scavenging toilet paper from the Evac Zone and then selling it. Stupid kids got caught because they tried to sell some to Jefferies." She shrugged, rolling her eyes. "And Townsend has accused them of looting and, get this, *tied them to stakes as punishment*."

Mackenzie cocked her head. "Are you being dramatic, or did that really happen?"

"Swear to god. It's Lucas Hernández and that other kid who works at the Dairy Queen, Jimmy Fowler. Townsend said they'd serve as a lesson to the town, and he's leaving them there for twenty-four hours."

"He can't do that," Rachel blazed.

Kat raised her eyebrows. "He can if he's got men standing guard with guns."

Mackenzie was vibrating in his arms, and Jake immediately assumed it was with terror. He tugged her tighter against him.

"We need guns," Mackenzie stated, pulling away from him so she could turn and look at everyone.

Not terrified. Furious.

"Now who's being extreme?" he asked. "Since when do you want to carry?"

"Since Grams disappeared," Mackenzie replied, tipping her chin at Chloe.

"What happened to Grams?" he growled, facing his sister.

"That's just it, we don't know," Chloe snapped, and then softened when she registered his anguish.

Why hadn't he checked in with Grams before he'd left on the raid? "What *do* you know?"

"Rach and I went back, but just like before, it was locked up and no one answered our knocking. So we found a side door unlocked and got in... but no one was there. It was empty."

"And then Tom Brenner caught us coming out and said we were trespassing, and if we didn't shut up about the old people, we'd wish we had," added Rachel.

"What the fuck?" he breathed out.

"And *that's* why I want a gun," Mackenzie said. "We need to make a list of everyone we think would have firearms, and whether they're here in town with us. If they're not, we need to know where they live."

"Lived," Rachel corrected quietly. "But everyone already handed in their weapons when this first happened."

"Get real, Rach. This is the United States. The only people who handed in weapons are the ones who already have a second or third one tucked away," Mackenzie countered. "We meet with Jim in two hours. By the end of today, we should all be armed."

CHAPTER THIRTEEN

Tension strummed tight within Mackenzie as she glanced around the lunchroom of the distillery at those assembled. Maggie and her son, Donny. Jim and Caroline. Jesse, Henry, Buddy and Quinn. Gavin and Trent. And James.

God, no wonder Rachel was still heartbroken over the man. He really was gorgeous.

She reached under the table to grasp her friend's hand and squeezed in silent support. She was pretty sure this was the first time Rachel had laid eyes on her high school boyfriend since he'd left town without saying goodbye, the night before their senior graduation.

Jake stood behind her, his injury making it uncomfortable for him to sit. The weight of his hand on her shoulder was reassuring for her, but antagonistic to his sister. Chloe sat at the other end of the table, resolutely ignoring them. The pain of her disapproval was a sharp cut into Mackenzie's already hurting heart. What if Jake hadn't come back? What the hell was happening with their town?

The virus. The motorcycle gang. The council. Threats pressed in on all sides and anxiety expanded in her chest, making it difficult to breathe and causing her to reach for her inhaler.

"Are all the doors locked?" Maggie asked James, rising from her seat to stand before the group.

"We're secure," he confirmed.

"Right. Well, let's get down to business. It's fair to say things have escalated quickly with the council, and if we don't stop it, we could be in some serious trouble," Maggie said. "I've mentioned to some of you that key members of the council used to indulge in fantasy world-building, kind of like playing fantasy football.

"Before anyone even knew this virus was a possibility, they'd already spent hours upon hours imagining how they'd structure their own post-apocalyptic world. The parts I overheard in The Strumpet were the essence of toxic masculinity. And our current situation has them with all the power; they control the food, and they've got all the weapons."

"Not all the weapons," Rachel cut in. "We rounded up two rifles and a handgun."

"And there'll be more," Mackenzie spoke up. "We just didn't have the time to search farther."

"I've got a hunting rifle I didn't turn in," Jim admitted, and Henry also raised his hand.

"Good," Maggie said. "Our biggest problem is that the council is already an established authority, and in times of turmoil people want to follow the familiar."

"Hang on," Jake interrupted. "Are you suggesting we overthrow the council?"

"I'm suggesting we give the town another option," Maggie countered calmly.

Jake crossed his arms. "Don't you think we should sit

down and have a conversation with Townsend before we stage a coup?"

"Our place in this town is a given, not a negotiation," growled Jim.

Mackenzie shifted in her seat, apprehensive of Jake's dissent.

"I'm not arguing with that, Jim. What I'm saying is that outside of Sanford, there's a virus that's killed a huge percentage of the population, as well as a lawless and dangerous motorcycle gang. I think our best bet is to bunker down, stick together as a town, and stay safe."

"That's just the problem, though. We're not safe with Townsend," Mackenzie said quietly, glad she didn't have to look at Jake as she opposed him. "They're tying kids to stakes."

Jake's hand flexed on her shoulder.

"They tied them up because they're kids. If they were adults, they would've shot them," interjected Gavin.

Mackenzie noticed with increasing unease that Jake didn't disagree with Gavin.

"And what have they done with the people in the travel lodge?" asked Chloe. "Where's Grams?"

"They're threatening to throw us out of town," Caroline chimed in.

"They're being unnecessarily heavy-handed," Jake agreed. "And we need answers to a lot of things. But I don't think overthrowing the council is the right move."

"Let's start with something smaller," Maggie placated when the nervous energy of the room escalated. "James, why don't you run us through some of your suggestions?"

Rachel stiffened beside Mackenzie as James's large form straightened from where he'd been leaning against a wall.

"I don't think we need to go in guns blazing," he addressed Jake, before sweeping his eyes over those assembled. "I just think we need to be prepared. We need to decrease our reliance on the council, and have plans in place in case we need them."

James was steady and reassuring, and Mackenzie took her first deep breath in what felt like forever. This was what she needed. To make plans and gain back a semblance of control.

Her breathing faltered when Jake's hand left her shoulder, the absence of connection robbing her of oxygen.

"I agree that making plans is a smart move, but I'm beat. I'm going to head home and get some rest," Jake said, his voice strained with an undercurrent of pain. "You coming, Mac?"

Her heart throbbed with indecision. She ached to be with Jake, to be held in his embrace and block out the rest of the world. But the rest of the world didn't give a damn about what she wanted. She could *want* to be with Jake, but she *needed* to take control of her life—to wake up and smell the coffee.

Damn it, *why* had she skipped her non-fat latte with caramel drizzle on that last morning in Chicago? Who knew when, if ever, she'd have Starbucks again?

"Mac?"

Mentally shaking herself, she swallowed before turning in her chair to face him. "I'm going to stay, just for a bit. I want to help..."

He raised an eyebrow, indicating he could also use her help.

Between him and Chloe, she was going to drown in guilt. Dex whined at her feet, sensing her distress.

"I got you, Jakey." Kat bound out of her seat and slung an arm around his waist. "I want to sneak some food to those kids who are tied up. You can help distract the guards."

Jake's eyes held Mackenzie's. A plea? A challenge? And she was the one to drop her gaze. She turned slowly back as he and Kat left, battling the desire to run after him.

"You okay?" Rachel murmured.

She nodded, avoiding looking at her friend in case the tears that threatened spilled over.

For the next hour, they discussed strategies, including stockpiling their own supplies and organizing a roster to sneak into the Evac Area when Quinn, Buddy or Henry were on guard duty to scavenge and note what was out there. Their primary task was subtly canvasing the town's residents to find out who was on board with the council and who they could recruit to their cause.

"We need to be smart about this," Maggie said. "We can't stage a rebellion without offering an alternative to the town. Let's organize another meeting in the next few days, and in the meantime, think about how you'd like to see the community run. We need as many ideas as possible."

"And it goes without saying, keep this meeting to yourself," Jim instructed. "The last thing we need is Townsend getting wind of any opposition."

"You don't think your little confrontation with him today alerted him to the fact there's opposition?" Henry asked. "He's going to be watching you like a hawk. You need to lie low and steer clear of the rest of us."

"Yeah, okay," Jim grumbled. "I'll play submissive. But we need more information. The council confiscated the ham radio that Roland Oxley had, and we need to know what they're hearing on it. Do you think Jake can find out?"

He looked between Chloe and Mackenzie, neither of whom looked at the other.

189

"You're right about needing information," Rachel intervened. "Because Townsend's fascist system of oppression pales compared to knowing what's happening with the virus."

"Okay, well, if that's it," Caroline said, standing, "I'm going to check in on Tabitha. She's a mess after learning about Rob."

Everyone dispersed, until it was just James left with Mackenzie, Rachel, and Chloe.

"Oh, hell no," Rachel muttered, her chair legs squeaking as she pushed back abruptly. "I'm out of here."

"Ladies, nice to see you." James doffed an imaginary hat and followed Rachel.

"Think he knows he's about to get slapped?" Mackenzie said, and then flashed her eyes to Chloe. It was *killing* her that her best friend was upset with her. "Chlo, can we talk about this?"

"Now you want to talk? Well, that's a nice change," Chloe snapped, before softening marginally. "Since when do we keep secrets from each other?"

Hot guilt prickled over Mackenzie. "I know. I'm sorry."

"You're my best friend, Mac. We share everything."

"It just kind of... happened. On our way back to Sanford."

"My parents took you in. Jake was like a brother to you. After everything Mom and Dad did for you, how do you think they'd feel?"

That was a punch to the gut. Chloe's parents *had* taken Mackenzie in, but it wasn't done for her. They did it to control their own reputation. They were the good Christian family who took in a stray, but their generosity had been a contract with hidden terms of compliance.

And falling in love with their son was definitely a breach of contract.

"Mom and Dad think of you as a daughter, Mac."

"Oh, come on, Chlo. You don't really believe that, do you?"

"What?" Chloe's face was the picture of puzzled hurt. "You practically lived with us. Mom put so many hours into helping you apply for your college scholarship..."

Mackenzie sighed. She was so *tired*. "Your mom and dad are good people, and were always kind to me. But they don't love me, Chlo.

"They took me in so that you wouldn't be best friends with a street kid. They helped me with my scholarship to get me out of Sanford. Not for me, for *them*. I'm sure they didn't mean to make me feel like an afterthought, but that was what I was."

"Mac!" Chloe was stricken. "I didn't know you felt like that."

"It's fine. Honestly, it is. I'm grateful for everything they've done. But trust me when I say they don't think of me as a daughter."

"Maybe not, but I think of you as a sister," Chloe whispered. "I'm so sorry I've been a jerk about this."

In seconds, they were out of their seats, a tangled mess of arms and tears and apologies.

"If it comes to choosing between Jake and you, I'll choose you."

Chloe had been the one constant in Mackenzie's life. She'd shown Mackenzie what love and kindness and empathy were.

"Don't be dramatic," Chloe sniffed. "Although you have no idea how weird it is to think about you being with my little brother. That's going to take some getting used to. To be honest, it was more about not wanting to lose you to him, and also..."

"Missing Ash?"

"I feel hollow," she admitted. "Just... empty. I don't know where he is. *How* he is. I'm just empty and aching, and I don't know how to get through this without him."

Mackenzie tightened her arms around her best friend. "I can't imagine how you're feeling, but I know you're not alone in this."

"I have one condition."

"No talking about sex?"

"No talking about sex."

———

JAKE SHIVERED IN THE DARKNESS, lengthening his strides as he made his way toward town hall. Winter was coming. And he damn well hoped Townsend had a plan to ensure they had the power to stay warm over the bitterly cold months.

Just another thing to add to the list he wanted to discuss with the mayor.

After Chloe had revealed yesterday that Grams was missing, it was only Rachel knocking him out on some heavy-duty pain relief that had stopped him from going to Townsend before now.

He waved at Buddy on guard duty as he rounded the corner and thought again of Mackenzie and Chloe's crazy talk of sneaking out to see what was happening with the townspeople quarantined at the hospital. He was relieved Chloe had come around to the idea of him and Mackenzie being together, but the two of them conspiring was never a good thing.

He and Mackenzie had fought, again, when he'd told them not to be stupid. And that was without him voicing his ambivalence about spying on the council. He agreed they needed to know what communication was coming across the ham radio—but he didn't want to be sneaky about it.

What he had with Mackenzie had seemed rock solid, and now it was literally crumbling apart in front of him. The powerlessness that coursed through him sparked an undeniable anger. He loved seeing how confident Mac was becoming in herself, but it also drove him crazy. How could she not see that all he wanted was to keep her safe?

As though conjured by his thoughts, he saw two figures dash into a lane just ahead. Even in the light of the street-lamps and without the shadow of Dex trailing them, he'd know Mackenzie and Chloe anywhere.

What the hell were they up to?

He broke into a run, but halted three strides in with a groan.

Christ, his wound hurt like a bitch.

Holding his side, Jake awkwardly jogged in the direction they'd taken and, two streets of labored jogging later, he was greeted with a soft bark from Dex trotting out from behind a dumpster.

"Bad dog!" Mackenzie scolded, appearing from the shadows of the bin. "You're terrible at hide-and-seek."

"Hide-and-seek?" Jake raised a skeptical eyebrow as Chloe also emerged. "What the hell are you two up to?"

"Don't be mad," Mackenzie said, approaching him with her hands out.

His eyes flashed to the guilty look on his sister's face, and he clenched his fists in frustration. "Tell me you're not trying to sneak out."

"Not trying, little brother. We did. And snuck back in,"

Chloe said, her chin tilted in defiance. "We had to see what was happening at the hospital, and if you stopped pretending to be Dad for just a second, you'd realize—"

"You what?" Jake's blood pressure rocketed.

Not only had they risked themselves by going into a quarantined area, they'd risked getting shot at by guards. And they'd lied to him.

Because they sure as hell weren't helping Kat pack up her things so she could move into Chloe's like they'd told him they were doing.

"What about the words 'shoot on sight' do you not understand?" he hissed between his teeth, forcing himself to take a step backward before he grabbed Mackenzie and shook her.

"Buddy was on guard duty. He wouldn't have shot us," said Mackenzie.

"You were putting your lives into the hands of Buddy?" he asked incredulously. "I cannot *believe* how stupid you two have been."

"Don't you *dare* call us stupid," Mackenzie bit out. "Stupid is blindly following along with Townsend and his cronies."

They stared at each other in silence, and the sinking in his gut told him she wasn't backing down from this. She honestly thought she was in the right.

"Fucking hell!" He swiped a hand across his face.

"There's no one alive there, Jake," Chloe whispered, coming to stand at his side. "It was just, piles of the dead. We couldn't get too close because the smell..."

He did not want to imagine the stench of rotting corpses. He didn't want to even know about them. He already had the face of the girl they'd been unable to save permanently etched into his memory. "Stop," he said.

"And we heard motorcycles in the distance," Chloe continued.

"Stop!" he shouted.

Both women took a step back, Mackenzie placing a hand on Dex's head when he whined.

"You don't even realize how reckless you're being," he said. "I can't protect you when you lie to me and put yourself in danger."

Both his hands were in his hair, fisting at it in torment.

Everything was unraveling. And he didn't know how to stop it.

Chloe said, "You can't tell me—"

"Not now, Chloe. This is between Mac and I."

"There isn't going to be a you and I, if you keep acting like this," Mackenzie stated, her voice surprisingly firm considering the hectic color that had bloomed on her cheeks. "I'm well aware I'm not as capable or competent as I need to be for this new world, but you're not even letting me try to change. You want to wrap me in cotton wool and hide me away."

"I want to *protect* you. Don't make me out to be the bad guy in this!" he exploded.

"I don't need your protection!"

"Well, what do you need, Mac?"

"Nothing. I don't need anything from you."

JAKE TURNED his back and left, leaving Mackenzie and Chloe in the dark alley as he stormed toward town hall. Swallowing against the tightness in his throat, he used anger to mask the breaking of his heart.

Nothing. I don't need anything from you.

He wasn't stupid; he knew he had a tendency to want to fix

things. But that was a good thing, right? He wanted to help people. Mackenzie didn't get it. She didn't understand he wanted to carry the burden for her. He loved her, for fuck's sake.

"What's got your panties in a twist?" Gavin called out as Jake stalked into the foyer of town hall.

The council had turned it into a base for their operations, and it was where most of the men spent their time, although Jake was surprised to see Gavin hanging out. From his presence at the clandestine meeting at the distillery, Jake had assumed Gavin's agenda was aligned differently.

When Gavin joined Trent and a couple of other guys hassling Vivienne Oxley about serving them beer, Jake frowned. Were the two men assimilating in order to gain information, or had Maggie been wrong to speak so candidly in front of them?

With every female member of the town's council out of town when Sy-V hit, town hall had literally become a boys' club; they'd assembled tables, chairs and sofas, and were clearly not hindered by the rationing the rest of the town was on with food and alcohol.

"Vivienne, time for you to leave," demanded Tom Brenner.

"Who's going to monitor the ham radio?" Vivienne demanded.

"Jennings has it figured out."

"Jennings knows shit. It's my brother's radio, and I know what I'm doing."

"Shut it, woman! It's not your place to be telling us what to do," growled Tom.

"Don't speak to me like that!"

"Bitch!"

Tom raised a hand to strike her, and Jake waited for one

of the nearby men to intervene. The sharp crack as Tom's open palm met Vivienne's cheek was definitive in the sudden quiet.

Vivienne gasped, hands flying to cover her reddened face before she spun and raced from the room. Shocked, Jake didn't know whether he should follow to check she was okay, or stay to confront Tom. The fact the other men were complicit in their silence made his skin crawl.

Before he could act, Townsend emerged from his office. "Jake! Good, you're here."

Jake followed the mayor into his office and remained standing, even after Townsend gestured for him to sit.

"You're not going to let him get away with that, are you?" Jake said.

"Son, we have bigger concerns than Tom Brenner." The older man looked worn, his usually ruddy complexion gray. He poured two tumblers of whiskey and passed one to Jake. "There's a lot at stake, and I need men like you I can count on. I can count on you, Jake, can't I?"

"Of course."

"I knew I could. Just like I know I'd be able to count on your father if he were here. Now, we need to have a discussion about that missing tanker of fuel, and Jim Boston. Is he going to be a problem for us?"

Unease caused Jake to pause. "I don't know anything about the tanker, but I know Jim isn't happy. I can handle him. He won't be a problem. I have to tell you, though, I'm not comfortable with everything that's been happening. Where are the kids who were tied up out the front?"

"We let them go yesterday. You didn't really think we'd leave them there overnight, did you?"

Some of the tightness in Jake's chest eased.

"And what about the old folk who were at the travel lodge? Where are they?"

"That's—" Townsend was cut short by Gavin, knocking on the door and entering without an invitation.

"The door was closed for a reason!" Townsend thundered. "Get the fuck out."

"Sorry, sir. Sorry. Brenner wanted me to let you know he made contact again with the survivors in New York."

"Why didn't you say so?" Townsend shot to his feet.

"Reception was patchy, and they're gone now, sir. But they repeated they'd spoken with someone from the CDC and confirmed the immunity theory."

Gavin was sliding back out when Townsend held out a hand to stop him, eyes narrowed in concentration. "Hold it. Who else knows this?"

"Just Brenner. And me." Gavin's eyes flicked nervously between Townsend and Jake. "And you, now."

"Get Brenner and bring him here. And keep your mouth shut," Townsend instructed, falling back into his chair and reaching immediately for his whiskey.

"What immunity theory?" Jake asked, setting his own glass back onto the desk in front of him. "Who have you been communicating with?"

"The ham radio has proved useful," Townsend said, evasively.

"If there's some way of getting immunity, the community needs to know," Jake asserted.

"We don't know anything for sure just yet. And it serves to have the community, shall we say... uncertain. It provides a level of—for want of a better word—control."

What the hell does that *mean?*

Gavin returned with Brenner, and Jake couldn't hold back.

"It's *not* okay to hit a woman," he blasted at Brenner, not flinching at the other man's glare.

"Bigger fish to fry, son," Townsend warned. "Brenner, who else knows about the immunity theory?"

"It's not a theory, boss. The group in NYC confirmed it. Anyone still alive has a natural immunity to Sy-V. The immunity mostly appears to be in clusters, as though it's some kind of environmental factor that's protected us."

"Who else knows?" Townsend growled.

"No one. Just us."

"Good. I want it kept that way. Now, I need you to do something for me. Find Jefferies and bring him in. He's breached orders and needs to face the consequences."

Brenner left, and Townsend turned to Jake. "This town is divided, and I need to know you're with me. You wanted to know about your grandmother? Jefferies went rogue." He paused, slugging back the rest of his whiskey.

Jake's stomach dropped. Time distorted, sound and action losing synchroneity. He watched Townsend's mouth forming entire sentences, but his brain struggled to make sense of what he was hearing.

"... accused them of using up resources... acted of his own volition... disposed of the bodies..."

Jake shoved his chair back so hard that when he stood, it toppled.

"What're you saying?" His voice was tinny, far away. Drowned out by the blood thumping in his ears.

"I'm sorry, son. He'll be punished accordingly."

"What the fuck are you saying?" Jake yelled.

"Jefferies killed your grandmother."

CHAPTER FOURTEEN

Mac needed the world to stop. Just, stop. The horrifying scenes from the hospital continued to flicker against her closed eyelids, causing them to twitch. She rolled restlessly in the bed, wishing she'd taken Kat up on the offer to keep her company.

Tiredness had seeped into her bones. She'd sat on the tiles while in the shower; her body was spent. She had nothing left. She'd dropped, listless, onto the bed—afraid to close her eyes, but unable to help herself.

She *knew* her father was among those piles of decomposing bodies, and she was bereft. The realization she'd hoped he'd one day redeem himself—own up to and apologize for being a shitty father—was bitter. Because now he never would.

Mackenzie shuddered, running her hands up and down her arms. She was afraid the stench from the hospital was embedded in her pores.

Dex snuffled from the floor at the foot of the bed, and she pulled back the sheet and called for him to join her under the covers. His warmth and bulk were comforting, and she buried her face in his fur.

Jake would have a fit at seeing the dog in the bed.

Jake.

What a shitty time to realize you weren't "falling" in love. You were *in* love. Head over heels, in fact. Right when he was breaking her freaking heart. She could not, *would not*, let Jake dictate her life. His bullshit savior-complex was untenable.

And the fact he couldn't see through Townsend? Made her want to punch him. Hard. It had taken all her self-control—and Chloe's hand on her arm—to stop her screaming at his willful blindness. Walking away from him in that alley was one of the hardest things she'd ever done. Because she hadn't lost him, she'd let him go.

MAC SLEPT FITFULLY, waking early to let Dex outside. Splashing water on her face in the bathroom, she shied away from the mirror; her blotchy complexion and puffy eyes evidence of her grief.

Grief for her father. For Jake. For the loss of the world as she'd known it.

A heart-rending howl had her running from the bathroom and following the sounds of anguish to the kitchen, where she found Rachel and Caroline comforting Chloe.

"What? What is it?" Mac cried, holding onto the kitchen counter for support. "What's happened?"

Rachel held Chloe, who was doubled over, arms wrapped around her middle as she sobbed. Caroline stood to the side, somber.

"It's Grams," Caroline said. "Jefferies killed her. And everyone at the travel lodge." She held her hand over her heart as her eyes brimmed. "I'm so sorry to be the one to deliver the news."

Falling to her knees in front of Chloe, Mackenzie reached for her, her arms encompassing Rachel's. They stayed like that until Mackenzie's knees were aching, and still they didn't move. At last, Chloe's sobs ceased, and she shrugged from the tangle of Rachel and Mackenzie's arms, pulling away and gasping in air as though she'd been underwater.

Caroline made coffee and ushered them to the kitchen table where they sat, stunned.

Mackenzie's face was wet from silent tears, and her heart was bloody and raw.

How much more could they take?

"Why?" Rachel asked. "It doesn't make sense."

"Nothing makes sense," Mackenzie replied dully. She held the coffee mug between both hands, hoping to absorb some of the heat and drive away the chill that shrouded her.

"Tell me again," Chloe demanded.

"I only know what Buddy told Jim. Townsend has accused Jefferies of going against orders and killing everyone at the travel lodge. He's put a bounty on Jefferies' head and they're searching for him now. Apparently, earlier today, Jefferies told some men that Townsend was going to make him a scapegoat, and he was going to ground."

"But *why*? And how did he... do it?" Chloe whispered.

"They're saying Jefferies lost it when the old people kept asking questions and demanding to get out. But I don't know any of the details. I'm sorry."

"So we don't know where her... her body is?" Chloe whispered.

"I'm sorry, Chlo. No." Caroline pulled her hair from its disheveled bun and retied it, eyeing them with a weary expression. "I need to get home to the kids, but I'll send word if I hear anything."

They jumped as the front door crashed into the wall as it was opened violently. Loud, masculine voices had them scrambling from their chairs.

"Jake?" Chloe called, confused.

"This is the militia," yelled a voice. "Everyone inside, get down on the floor with your hands on your heads. Do not try to run, we have the house surrounded."

The women froze.

Tom Brenner barreled into the kitchen.

"Down on the floor!" he shouted, brandishing a rifle.

Immediately Mackenzie and the other three dropped, her cheekbone slamming onto the travertine tiles in her haste. Another two men rushed the room in a volley of shouted commands, and instinctively, she raised her hands over her head.

"Check the rest of the house," Tom instructed.

Mackenzie could feel the men walking around the room, but she kept her head down. Her breathing was erratic and spots danced in front of her eyes. She blinked rapidly, trying to clear her vision.

Someone's coffee mug had tipped over, and a steady stream of coffee spilled, pooling before her. Dex was barking from the backyard. The refrigerator's motor kicked on.

Black boots stopped beside her. "Are you Mackenzie Lyons?"

Her voice caught in her throat.

The boot nudged into her side. "Answer me!"

"Yes."

"Get up. You're under arrest for treason."

Her mind refused to latch onto his words.

"Up!" This time, the boot was forceful.

Mac scrambled to her knees, palms slipping in the spilled coffee. Rachel protested and then gasped in pain as the butt of a rifle was jammed into her shoulder.

"Which one of you is Caroline Boston?"

"She's that one," Tom answered for them, tipping his chin at Caroline's prone form.

"Right. You, up," he commanded.

Mackenzie and Caroline stood, shaking hands clasped in unity.

"You're both under arrest for treason. Get your hands behind your backs."

"John, what's going on?" Caroline asked.

John. Right. John Kelly. Mackenzie vaguely recalled him from her childhood. Was he an accountant? Lawyer? He had a receding hairline and a ginger beard that was peppered with white.

"You're under arrest for terrorist activities and for conspiring against the council. We're taking you to town hall to be sentenced." John's voice was monotone.

"John—"

"Shut it, lady," the other man cut her off.

"What do you think you're doing?" Chloe cried, scrambling to her feet. "You're not taking them anywhere. Get out of my house!"

Dex's barking had become frenzied.

Tom rounded on Chloe, his rifle raised.

"Rachel! Get her out of here. Find Jake!" Mackenzie screamed.

Rachel stepped in front of Chloe, facing Tom with her hands raised. Without a word, she began moving backward, forcing Chloe toward the back door. When Chloe began to shout, Rachel spun and locked her elbow around Chloe's throat, shoving her outside where they both took off running.

Mackenzie's chest released marginally. Chlo and Rach were safe.

"Tom! What's going on?" Quinn strode into the kitchen, followed by the man who'd been scouting the house.

"Boss's orders. We have to bring them in."

Mackenzie felt a sharp tug as a plastic tie restrained her wrists behind her.

"Just hang on a minute," Quinn barked. "You—"

Kat burst into the kitchen, skidding to a halt at the scene before her.

"Fuck. I thought,"—she paused for breath—"I could get here before them." She panted, eyes latching desperately onto Mackenzie. "Everyone's talking about the arrest warrant. And that motorcycle gang, they're at the bridge demanding entry."

At that, the militia men stilled.

"We need to get back to town hall. Now," Tom ordered.

"What? No!" Kat launched herself at Tom, with Quinn intercepting her. Two guns swung her way until Quinn growled, a barely veiled threat.

"Let me go!" Kat screamed, as Quinn hauled her out the back door, whispering urgently into her ear.

Before Quinn could object again, Mackenzie and Caroline were roughly hustled from the house and bundled into an SUV. Caroline was sobbing, pleading with John. But Mackenzie was numb. Nothing touched her. Sound was muted and time had a hazy quality to it.

What had she expected, coming back to Sanford? This town wasn't her home. And Jake wasn't for her. She'd known that all along. She was tired of the struggle. The struggle to adapt to this new life, the struggle to fit with Jake. Love shouldn't be this hard.

Townsend wanted to throw her out of his town? Okay. She'd go back to the city, bunker down in her apartment. The girls weren't going to like it, and her heart wrenched a little. But she'd been gone for years. They'd be okay without her.

MAC BLINKED SLOWLY. Had Maggie just slapped her?

"Ow. Maggie!"

"Snap out of it, girlie. We need you," Maggie said.

Mackenzie looked around. She was inside town hall standing between Caroline and Maggie, and they were pushed back into a corner and penned in by the backs of armed guards.

"Why are you here?" Mackenzie asked Maggie.

"Same as you. Townsend needs to prove a point, and we're it."

"What point?" cried Caroline. "This is ridiculous."

"That he's the boss. And anyone against him gets thrown to the wolves."

That made Mackenzie think of Dex, and tears clogged her throat. She knew Chloe would look after the dog, but she'd become attached to him.

Voices reverberated off the high ceilings as more residents entered the hall. Mackenzie hadn't realized the town still had so many people—there must've been close to three hundred. They were anxious, agitated.

Only a few spared a glance at the women held prisoner. They were too preoccupied trying to get answers from Townsend's men.

"We can hear the motorcycles—"

"What if they breach the bridge and get into town—"

Where was Jake? Chloe, Rachel, and Kat weren't among the crowd of people. Were they looking for him? Did he know she'd been taken? Did he care?

She wanted to slump to the ground, but Maggie's sharp elbow was in her side and Caroline was holding her other arm.

A hush fell over the room, and Mackenzie heard the self-important footsteps of Townsend as he entered. She couldn't see him over the crowd of people until he ascended the podium, gazing benevolently at those gathered before him.

"Thank you all for coming," he began, raising placating hands as several voices shouted from the crowd. "I know you're concerned, but your fear is unfounded. I will keep our town safe."

Townsend didn't need a microphone; he was a gifted orator with an invested audience. He was measured and calm, a balm against the rising tide of apprehension.

"There are those among us who wish to disrupt the peace and order we have established, and we cannot accept that. We are living through extraordinary circumstances, which require extraordinary actions. We cannot allow certain individuals to risk our safety."

Mackenzie felt the heavy weight of stares as several in the crowd turned to her.

"And so, my fellow townspeople, we must deal with the traitors."

———

JAKE WAS SITTING on Gram's stoop, where he'd watched the sun rise, the sky lightening from black to charcoal to gray. His ass and feet were numb, which was a nice distraction from the shredded, pulpy mess of his heart.

He wasn't brave enough to face Chloe. To tell her Grams was dead, that she'd died on his watch. Because it *was* his watch; with their parents overseas, it was his duty to protect his family, and he'd failed.

Mackenzie didn't get it. She'd never had a family. She didn't understand the overwhelming need to protect what you loved. And now Grams... his throat swallowed convulsively, bile threatening.

Why hadn't he gone to see Grams as soon as he'd returned from Chicago? He knew the answer, of course. Mackenzie. He'd been so beguiled by their fledgling love, he'd neglected his responsibility. Resentment began a low burn in his belly. He'd forfeited his grandmother, for a relationship that was now nothing but ash.

In the early dawn hours, he'd cried for the loss of Grams, but now he steeled himself. Now he needed to face his sister. To be there for her through this senseless tragedy. He knew there was a manhunt for Jefferies, but he honestly didn't give a damn. The fury of his grandmother's murder was directed at himself. Jefferies may have pulled the trigger, but he was but an arm on the beast. The beast Townsend had created.

Disillusionment threatened to swamp his resolve. He'd always prided himself on being on the "good" side. He didn't believe in shades of gray. But who was he kidding? Townsend wasn't gray, he was black. And Jake had been following him willfully.

"Jake!" Chloe and Rachel careened around the corner, red faced and out of breath.

He stood, feet stinging with pins and needles. They knew. "Chlo. I'm so sorry."

"What?" She looked at him with confusion, panting. "Grams."

"Oh." Her face fell, tears welling.

"It's not that," Rachel said. "It's Mac. Townsend has had her arrested!"

He stared at her dumbly, not comprehending.

"Jake! We have to get to town hall." Rachel clutched his arm, her nails digging through his jacket sleeve. "I'm sorry... I'm sorry about—about Grams. I know... look. We can't think about that now. We have to get Mackenzie back."

THE STREETS WERE quiet as they approached town hall, and once they entered, Jake understood why. Every remaining resident of the town was here.

Townsend had the stage, and Jake had to concentrate to hear him over his own labored breathing and the throb of his gunshot wound. The girls had their hands on their knees beside him, catching their breath.

"In this new world, we have to make unsavory compromises," Townsend was declaring from his position at the front of the crowd. "We are not making allies of the men at our gates. But to satiate them, to protect our town from their invasion, we will bargain with them. These traitors will be traded for the very thing their dissent was threatening, the stability and safety of our town."

Jake's knees buckled when he saw Mackenzie, Caroline and Maggie dragged onto the podium, bound and gagged. Galvanized, he pushed at the backs of those in front of him, struggling to move through the crowd, intent on reaching Mackenzie.

"Hold up there, Jake. Where do you think you're going?" a quiet voice said in his ear.

Trent and Gavin had flanked him, halting his movement.

"We can't let this happen, you know that," Jake gasped.

"The only thing we know is that Townsend asked us to restrain you until the formalities are complete," said Trent. "So move on back with us, and let the boss do what needs to be done."

"You can't do this!" Jake screamed as Trent and Gavin hauled him to the recesses of the hall. Several heads turned his way, but no one spoke up. "You can't barter with human lives!"

"You don't get it, do you?" Trent said, conversationally. "These people are scared shitless. They'll willingly trade someone else, so long as it's not them."

"Townsend is doing this for the greater good," Gavin added.

"Were you ever on Maggie's side?" Jake said, holding his wounded side. It felt like a hot poker was stabbing him mercilessly.

"We're on the surviving side, Jake. Which is where you should be."

"Hold up!" Rachel's strident voice reached him, and he jerked his head toward the front. "Why are you doing this? There has to be another way."

"What about whiskey?" That was James, who stood beside Rachel. "Offer them whiskey in return for leaving us alone."

"I'm not giving these degenerates our whiskey." Townsend laughed.

"You can't give them our *people*!" Chloe screamed. She turned to those around her. "If you let this happen, you're all complicit in what happens to them!"

As he struggled against Trent and Gavin, Jake could see

the crowd murmuring. The rapt attention they'd focused on Townsend was dissipating.

"This is what dissension looks like!" Townsend bellowed. "I won't let our community be divided. We stand united. And unless you want that motorcycle gang to invade our town, this is what's happening!"

Mackenzie, Caroline, and Maggie were dragged to an offstage exit, thrashing and yelling against their makeshift gags. Jake saw red. His elbow snapped upward, slamming into the side of Gavin's face, who stumbled backward. Gasping through his own pain, Jake spun to face Trent.

Trent dropped his hold on Jake. And raised his pistol.

The loud, reverberating boom of a gunshot had them freezing. Donny, Maggie's son, stood on the top step of the stage, a bloom of red spreading across his chest before he fell. The crowd at the front of the hall began screaming, pushing back into those behind them until a wall of people surged toward where Jake stood.

"Stop!" Trent shouted. "Back up!" He fired his AR-15 into the ceiling, which only added to the chaos.

Using their distraction, Jake ran for the back door. Gavin attempted to stop him, but Jake slammed his fist into Gavin's face, noting with satisfaction the crunch of nasal cartilage.

He didn't have a plan; he just knew he needed to get to the bridge before they handed Mackenzie over to the gang. Sprinting through the foyer, he burst outside, swinging left, and then right.

"Jake!" It was Jim, waving frantically at him from the street corner. "I have a truck!"

Jake heaved himself into the passenger side as Jim gunned the engine.

"Jesse knows where Chloe stashed the weapons they found. We're meeting him at her place," Jim said.

"We don't have time! We need to get to the bridge," Jake screamed. Sweat streamed into his eyes, and he swiped at the sting of it.

"We can't do anything without weapons," Jim replied grimly. "Hang on." He mounted the curb and drove the vehicle through a front yard and down a side lane, leaving toppled trashcans in their wake.

Jesse was waiting, laden down with several rifles.

"Do they have ammo?" Jim called as Jesse slid into the backseat.

"In the backpack," Jesse confirmed.

"Go. Go!" Every molecule in Jake strained to reach Mackenzie. He was white-knuckled. Desperate. The truck roared as Jim punched through the gears, single-minded in his focus.

Jesse leaned forward between the front seats, passing Jake a rifle.

"Is it loaded?"

"Yes."

"Good." Jake wouldn't hesitate to shoot to kill. Again.

THEY WERE TOO LATE.

Jake canvased the area around the bridge frantically, but there was no sign of the women.

Buddy, shaken, was standing guard at the blockade, unable to take his eyes off the road leading out of town. Quinn had his back to them, and it was only when Jake vaulted from the vehicle and ran to him he realized Kat was cradled against Quinn's front, sobbing uncontrollably.

"What happened? Where did they go?" Jake cried,

grabbing Quinn's shoulder. Jesse and Jim flanked him, guns raised as they searched the horizon.

"I'm sorry. I'm so sorry," Quinn muttered, not meeting his gaze. "There were too many of them. They were all on bikes, except for three in a van. That's what they used to take the women," he grimaced. "Kat and I came straight here, thinking we could ambush the gang, or get intel. I don't know, really. But Jesus, Jake. There were twenty of them. Fully armed. They were their own army."

"How long ago did they leave?" Jim demanded, already swinging around and heading back to the truck.

"Five minutes, maybe?" Buddy said, and then, ashen-faced, fell to his knees, retching into the dirt. "Sorry. I'm sorry." He wiped his mouth on his sleeve. "They shouldn't have done that. Townsend... he, he shouldn't have done that."

"Where were they going? Back to Dutton?" Jesse asked.

"Get in the truck," Jim growled. "We don't have time to stand around."

"We need to know where they're going," Jake countered. "Quinn, did they say anything that would help us?"

"Prestige Plaza." Kat hiccuped. "The gang are based at the Prestige Plaza in Dutton." She tugged at Quinn's hand. "Come on, let's go."

"Not a chance, kitten," Quinn said. "You're not going anywhere." He caught Kat about her waist, holding her back. "You need a plan, Jake. You can't take them on without one."

Jake knew he was right, but it didn't matter. Plan or no plan, they needed to get the women back. Fast. Who knew what was happening to them right now?

Terror grappled, threatening to obliterate rational thought. If anything happened to Mackenzie...

Who was he kidding? It had happened. *Was* happening. And he needed to get to her.

"Quinn, take Kat home," he instructed.

"No, man. I'm coming with you."

"No, you're not. You need to take Kat and find Chloe and Rachel. Protect them."

Jake knew Quinn was torn, and honestly? He needed Quinn's help to get the women back. But Jake also needed to know that someone was looking out for Chloe, Kat, and Rachel.

He'd lost faith in Townsend and trust in Sanford.

Resolutely, he nodded at Quinn. "Look after them."

"I will."

"Get in the fucking truck!" Jim yelled, already behind the wheel and revving the engine.

Jake and Jesse ran, sliding into their seats as the truck was already moving.

"Wait! I want to come," Buddy yelled.

"You sure?" Jake called out the window. "We won't be welcome back in Sanford, you know that, right?"

Buddy paused, and then nodded, climbing in beside Jesse. "Let's go."

CHAPTER FIFTEEN

Mackenzie, Caroline and Maggie had been shoved into a white minivan. The kind a soccer mom would drive, with snack wrappers pushed down between the seats, and a set of child's fingerprints marring the window.

Sitting bound and gagged in the back seat, Mackenzie had the insane urge to laugh. She'd been trafficked to men tattooed in mayhem, and all she could smell was rotten banana.

When the driver of the van pulled up at Dutton's one and only luxury hotel, the Prestige Plaza, she closed her eyes against the utter surrealism. She'd been expecting a grungy warehouse. Or a derelict apartment block. But at the end of the world, it seemed the meek had not inherited the Earth. Instead, the scum were rising, and making themselves comfortable between premium Egyptian cotton sheets.

The door slid open, and Caroline shrank back against Mackenzie, a muffled scream coming from beneath her gag.

"Shut up, bitch," said a biker, pulling Caroline from the van.

But there was no venom behind his words. The men on motorcycles who had escorted them were relaxed and joking with one another, pleased at a job well done. There was an air of excited expectation that had Mackenzie's skin crawling.

Mackenzie and Maggie were dragged from the van, blinking at the row of motorcycles parked beneath the grand awning of the hotel. Instead of a bellhop, a woman greeted the returned marauders. Clad in tight, ripped jeans, she had lurid tattoos covering every inch of skin bared by her midriff tank top. The lush hair that spilled down her back was as black as the makeup rimming her eyes. Eyes that were gleeful.

"Boys! What have you brought me?" she drawled, stopping short of the women and assessing them. "Only three?" She raised one eyebrow.

"Come on, Gemma. This is a good haul, and you know it," said the seedy man who had been giving orders. He strode to Gemma and snaked an arm around her waist, lowering his head to suck lasciviously on her neck.

She pushed at him impatiently. "How many people are still in the town?"

"Who cares? It's just another ass-end-of-the-world town," he replied.

"No, it's not," Gemma snapped. "Sanford has a whiskey distillery, and I want it."

They turned away, their voices lost to Mackenzie.

Her family was in Sanford. Chloe and Rachel and Kat. And Jake. How much danger were they in? Whatever negotiations Townsend thought he'd pulled off meant nothing to these people.

"Take them to one of the empty suites," Gemma tossed over her shoulder. "The one at the end of the corridor hasn't been used yet. And hands off the merchandise. Understood?"

There was grumbling as the women were escorted inside.

"Gemma has West pussy-whipped. I didn't sign up to be bossed around by no woman," said the man holding a gun to Mackenzie's back. "Gem might've gotten us out, but I'm about fed up taking orders from her."

"I told you before, Leon, what she don't know won't hurt her." The man behind Caroline leered, groping at her ass. "This one bit me when I was adjusting her gag, and I'm looking forward to breaking her in."

"Mickey, I don't know that's a good idea. You know what Gemma did to Nick."

"Nick was stupid enough to get caught. I ain't gettin' caught."

They entered a spacious suite, pristine with its perfectly angled sofa cushions and tautly stretched bed linen. The man holding Maggie released her bound wrists and turned to Mickey.

"West wants me back downstairs. If I were you, I wouldn't be touching anything until he's paraded them around. Hard to hide bruising when they're naked."

Grappling with the makeshift gag, Maggie yanked it free. "I'm fifty-three. No one's parading me around naked!" she yelled.

"Some of us have been in the clink for years. We're not picky," Mickey said.

"Prison?" asked Mackenzie. Leon had untied her gag and hands and she rubbed at her raw wrists, wincing.

"We'd still be there if Gemma hadn't come to get West when the shit hit the fan," said Leon. He shook his head, frowning. "Still don't mean she gets to call the shots now."

"Leon, you good to look after the women? I'm taking Mickey downstairs with me," said the other man. "I don't have the patience for Gem losing hers over him fucking what isn't his."

"We brought them in!" objected Mickey. "We should at least get a crack at them before they go into rotation."

Mackenzie's mind blanked on what "rotation" could mean. She sank to the floor, holding her knees to her chest and rocking gently. Gently. Just keep rocking, and nothing would touch her.

She was cold and sweaty. And thirsty. So thirsty.

The carpet in the suite was nice. The expensive kind. Probably wool. Mackenzie started stroking it. She could lie down right here and just go to sleep. And maybe when she woke up, she'd be back in Chloe's guest bedroom with Kat spooning her.

A boot nudged her, and she groaned. It was the same spot she'd been kicked back in Chloe's kitchen.

"Get into the bathroom and clean up. You look like shit," Leon instructed.

Maggie reached down to haul her to her feet, and the three of them, walking as a huddled mass, entered a bathroom that was larger than Mackenzie's bedroom back in Chicago.

When Caroline tried to close the door, Leon thrust it back into her face. "Nope, no closed doors. The last woman we had wiped her own shit through her hair, trying to make herself disgusting enough that we wouldn't touch her. Crazy bitch."

Mackenzie rushed to the vanity and gagged into the marble sink. With shaky hands, she turned on the faucet, splashing water onto her clammy face and then cupping her hands to gulp at it.

"That's it, honey. Feel better?" Maggie soothed, rubbing her back.

"Why are you so calm?" Caroline hissed.

Mackenzie took a deep breath. The water had steeled her resolve and cleared her head. Raising it, she caught Caroline's frantic eyes in the mirror.

"We need to get the fuck out of here," she whispered fiercely. "We are not going to be some commodity that gets paraded around naked and then *used*," she spat.

Where had this sudden strength come from? Knowing she had nothing to lose? Because nothing could be worse than staying here as *merchandise*.

"Why is it so much worse that it's a woman who's doing this to us?" Mac asked, recalling the satisfied smirk Gemma had worn. The thought made her spit into the sink, her saliva acidic.

"Hurry the fuck up in there," Leon called. "You've got two minutes."

They took turns washing their faces and using the toilet. The scent of expensive hotel soap only highlighted the stench of their fear-drenched bodies.

When they emerged, Leon directed them to a plush sectional sofa and threw them cookies from the minibar.

"West is gonna wait until tonight, when all the boys get back in from looting. So you ladies just relax, get some sleep. You won't get much later." He grinned.

A pit opened up inside Mackenzie, dark and deep.

Leon leaned back against the headboard, his boots smearing muck across the bed covering. He'd turned on the enormous flat-screen television and was flicking through the hotel's R-rated movie selections.

"Leon, what's going to happen to us?" Mackenzie asked, leaning forward to catch his eye. They needed information, and maybe if they could establish some kind of connection with him, they could get him to help them.

"Same as what happens to all the women," he muttered, not taking his attention from the heaving breasts on the screen. Thank god it was muted.

Caroline nudged her with a what-are-you-doing expression.

"They can't all be monsters. We need to use his name, let him know our names," she whispered. "Make him see us as something other than merchandise." Mackenzie turned back to him. "Leon, I'm Mackenzie. And this is Maggie and Caroline. "Do you have a sister? Mother? Because—"

"Don't bother," he interrupted. "I ain't gonna be your friend. The only friend I have is me, and that's who I'm looking out for. Me." His eyes flashed to hers, and then back to the porn. "The best I can offer you is some advice. Don't fight and try not to get beaten on. The more bruises you have, the more likely the next man will add to them, until you're too beaten up and they shoot you. Got it?" He turned up the volume.

"I'm never going to see my kids again." Caroline stuffed a fist in her mouth, tears spilling down her face.

"Someone will come for us," Mackenzie said fiercely.

"Who? Jake?" Maggie asked wearily. "Where's that boy of yours, Mackenzie? Because I didn't see him anywhere today. Maybe he's feeling guilty and couldn't show his face."

"Why would Jake be feeling guilty?" Mackenzie hissed.

"How do you think Townsend knew about that meeting in the distillery? Jake was the one defending that asshole, and he was the one having closed-door meetings with the mayor."

"What? Jake would *never* put us in danger! It could have been Trent or Gavin. Did you see them today?"

"Oh, honey." Maggie sighed. "I'm not saying Jake meant for this to happen. That fool of a boy probably thought he was helping, telling Townsend our plans to keep the peace in Sanford."

"What was it he said? That Townsend's rules might seem severe, but they were for our protection?" said Caroline.

Mackenzie felt gut punched. She collapsed back into the sofa cushions, her chin falling to her chest.

Had Jake caused this?

"Why just us?" Caroline said. "We weren't the only ones."

"Who knows? We're expendable? He had to use someone to show the town what consequences looked like," Maggie answered.

"Those gunshots as they were taking us away from town hall. What do you think they were?" Mackenzie asked, raising her head with new hope. "Someone was trying to stop Townsend."

"Maybe. I know Donny would've raised a fuss. But that boy of mine isn't stupid enough to single-handedly wage war against this gang."

"Jake will come," Mackenzie said stubbornly. "And Jim. Chloe and the girls will come up with a rescue plan. We're not alone."

"Look around, girlie. We're alone. I know you don't want to believe Jake had anything to do with this, but he did. We're here because of Jake."

———

DESPERATION CLAWED AT JAKE, making it hard to breathe. He was sitting in the passenger seat of Jim's truck a half block from the hotel with Jesse and Buddy in the back.

"I don't know if I can wait until nightfall," Jake admitted tightly, eyes stinging from the intensity of his watch on the front doors of the Prestige Plaza. "Anything could be happening to them and—"

"Fuck it, Jake! Shut up!" Jim slammed his hands onto the steering wheel.

"We can't sit here and do nothing!"

They'd had this argument several times already.

"We can't help them if we're dead, man," Jesse reasoned. "And this place is crawling with bikers. We've seen at least twenty coming and going, and there were twenty in the group who took them from Sanford."

"They could be the same twenty!" Jake said, jaw tight. Frustrated.

"Or there could be forty," Buddy ventured, holding up his hands at Jake's furious look. "I'm just saying. Either way, they outnumber us."

They fell into silence, watching as a high-end Mercedes drove onto the sidewalk in front of the hotel. Two men exited, bickering.

Jake jumped from the vehicle, setting his teeth against a stab of pain from his side. Using the cover of parked cars, he crept closer to the hotel, followed by Jim, Jesse and Buddy.

"Who fucking cares? This fancy piece of shit couldn't fit all the boxes. We should've taken that truck," grumbled the passenger of the Mercedes.

"Just help me unload, dickhead," said the driver.

The arguing men popped the trunk and began unloading crates of liquor and boxes branded with a cigarette logo, and another two men came out of the hotel to help them with their haul.

"Thought you were hitting up the hospital? Gemma wanted drugs," one of them commented.

"Have you been near that hospital? It reeks. So many dead bodies you can't even pull into the emergency bay. No thanks."

They disappeared inside.

"Why do you think they're unloading at the front, and not driving around back to the loading bay?" Jake asked, more to himself than anything.

"Think we should split up? Two of us go check out the back?" Jesse said.

"I think so." Jake looked at the older man. "Jim?"

"Yeah, okay. I'll wait here with Buddy. Just don't fucking get caught."

Jake knew they needed to be smart about this. They were outmanned and outgunned. Unquestionably. But they had the element of surprise. These assholes weren't expecting them.

Jesse nodded, and the two of them ran to a recessed shopfront, eyes scanning the streets.

"I say we make a run for it now, while we can't see anyone," Jesse said.

"Just because we can't see them doesn't mean they're not around. Or watching from the windows," Jake cautioned. "I say we go a block left and approach from behind, rather than come up the side."

Jesse nodded, and they steadily moved forward, sticking to shadows created by the afternoon sun. Sweating beneath his jacket, Jake's shirt stuck to his back uncomfortably, even as his hands reddened in the cold. He fisted them.

Every second was an agony of not knowing. Was Mackenzie okay?

He muttered a curse, and Jesse glanced at him, concerned. "You okay?"

"Stupid fucking question."

"Right. Sorry."

The back of the Prestige Plaza was nowhere near as glitzy as the front, featuring a cement loading dock, a row of dumpsters, and several industrial-looking roller doors.

"Shit!" Jake ducked behind a parked car, dragging Jesse down with him. "Did you see that? A guy came out of that door over there."

They raised their heads to look through the passenger window of the car, tracking the movements of the person who'd just emerged.

"It's a kid," Jesse murmured.

Jake realized he was right. The kid couldn't have been more than seventeen, with the gangly awkwardness of a teenager. He pulled a Zippo from his pocket and lit a cigarette, slumping back against the wall as he inhaled deeply.

"Is he armed?" Jake asked.

"Not that I can see," Jesse replied. "What're you thinking?"

"I'm thinking we jump him, see what information we can get from him."

"Risky." Jesse raised his eyebrow. "You sure?"

"Got a better plan?"

"Okay. How are we going to do this, then?"

"We need to act fast. He'll have that cigarette finished in a couple of minutes."

"Let's do this," Jesse said. "Just try not to let me get shot."

"I'll do my best." Jake felt predatory. Feral.

He darted away on swift, soundless feet, crouching in a shadow until he saw Jesse amble toward the kid, shouting a greeting. The kid jumped, dropped his cigarette. But instead of confronting Jesse, he turned and began running to the door he'd come from.

"Fuck!" Jake swore, pushing his legs into a sprint.

In his periphery, he saw Jesse closing in on the kid, but Jake was closer. He stretched, throwing himself into a tackle as the kid's hands grappled with the door handle. They crashed to the ground, Jake's knees taking the brunt of the fall and his wound re-opening with a bloody gush.

"Please don't hurt me!" The kid was sobbing, his arms held protectively over his head.

Jesse extended a hand to help Jake up, and then pulled the kid up, too.

"Shut up!" Jesse shook him. "Is there anyone else around?"

The acrid stench of urine hit Jake, and he realized the kid had pissed himself.

"I'm sorry I came out here. I know I'm meant to stay in the kitchen," the kid cried, snot dripping from his chin. "Please don't hurt me."

"Jesus, let's get him away from here," Jake grumbled, pressing against his wound to check it had stopped bleeding.

"You're not taking me back inside?" the kid asked.

"What? Why—oh. You think we're part of the gang? Fuck no," Jake spat.

They walked two blocks back from the hotel before stopping in an empty side alley.

The kid was groveling, pleading for his life, and Jake's patience snapped.

225

"Would you shut the fuck up!" he yelled. "How about you tell us everything you know, and then we'll decide if we're going to off you or not, okay?"

"Jake, keep it down, man," Jesse warned.

"Fuck off, Jesse. We're not here to babysit. This little dipshit is going to help us because, if he doesn't, I'm going to rip his fucking head off. Now, why don't you get Jim and Buddy, while Dipshit and I have a little conversation?"

"My name is Zed," the kid mumbled.

"I don't give a fuck what your name is," Jake responded, watching as Jesse disappeared out of the alley before turning to Zed. "Three women were brought to the hotel earlier today. What do you know about that?"

"I got nothing to do with it, I promise!"

Jake restrained from slamming his fist into the kid's face. Barely.

"Tell me what you know," he gritted out. "Or I swear to god I'll shoot you right now."

"It's Gemma. We worked at the Prestige together, before. Well, she was in management, and I was just in the kitchen, but—" He checked himself at Jake's fierce expression. "She went to get her boyfriend out of prison and came back with a whole bunch of them.

"Some of them used to be in a motorcycle gang and they went to the clubhouse first, took all the bikes. They're bad, real bad. I just keep my head down and make sure they get fed. Gemma's got them all out looting for supplies. She's stocking up. And sometimes they find women and bring them back, but I swear, I don't touch them!"

The sound that came from Jake's mouth was animalistic.

Zed shrank back, his whole body shaking.

"How do I get them out?" Jake forced the words

through his teeth. His jaw was locked tight, aching with the strain of holding himself back.

"Well, there's... I mean, they have a lot of guns. And someone guards the room they're in."

"What room? Where are they kept?"

"One of the suites on level five. But they won't be there much longer. Soon as it gets dark, the men will all start coming back in, and Gemma's running a lottery tonight. The men..." He bit his lip and looked away from Jake.

"The men *what?*"

"The men who bring in the best supplies go into the lottery to win a night with one of the women," Zed whispered.

The shadows on the street were already lengthening. It would be night within the next hour.

Jake could feel the ticking of time with each beat of his heart. "How do I get inside?"

CHAPTER SIXTEEN

"Should we be worried about catching Sy-V from these people?" Caroline whispered.

"That might be a blessing," mumbled Maggie. "I'd rather die than stay here as their toy."

"Didn't you listen to Jesse?" Mackenzie said. "We're probably immune."

"Which means so are they," Caroline said. "Unfortunately."

The afternoon had slipped away as the women sat on the sofa, crying, whispering together, slipping into fitful jags of sleep before jerking awake. The serrated edge of terror was a constant grind against Mackenzie's nerves until she wanted to scream.

She'd given up defending Jake. Maggie was convinced he was responsible for betraying them. Instead, the women had taken turns watching Leon, hoping he'd fall asleep or get distracted enough for them to overpower him.

But then Mickey had returned, furious that Gemma wasn't allowing the men who'd brought the women in to enter the lottery.

"I don't care what else gets brought in today, nothin' is going to trump these three. She shoulda let us all have a turn with them first. The *least* she could do is include us in the lottery," he grumbled.

"What time does West want them downstairs?" Leon asked, picking at his teeth and glancing at the women.

Mackenzie stilled, the emptiness of her stomach forgotten.

"An hour," Mickey replied, glancing at his watch.

"We bothering to put them through the shower?"

"Nah. I've got a better idea on how to fill the time." Mickey grinned, his tobacco-stained teeth flashing. "This one over here owes me an apology."

He stood, thrusting his thumbs through the front belt loops of his filthy jeans, eyes locked on Caroline.

"Okay! Okay, please," Mackenzie called out. "Caroline can apologize, she's really sorry for biting you." She turned desperately to Caroline, who was mute in panic. "Caroline! Say sorry," she pleaded.

Caroline was shaking her head in distress, her fist back in her mouth and strings of saliva streaking her chin.

"She's scared, she's just scared! She's not saying she's not sorry," Mackenzie babbled as Mickey walked to stand before them, rocking back on his heels with a smirk.

"I like the way you beg. It's real pretty," he said, his attention now on Mackenzie. She shook in revulsion as he perused her body, his eyes sliding over her as though she were already naked. "But I like to settle my scores. And you're a pretty one, so you're going to take a pounding later tonight. I'll give you a break now."

Horror had Mackenzie's chest squeezing painfully tight, and she tore at her jacket pocket to find her inhaler. Gasping for shallow breaths, her hand shook so hard that

Maggie held the inhaler to her mouth as she sucked back frantically.

Mickey reached down and grabbed Caroline by the upper arms, pulling her to her feet. She was floppy and unresponsive, immediately collapsing onto the floor.

"Fuck, woman!" Mickey cursed.

"Stop. Take me instead," Maggie yelled, falling to her knees and covering Caroline's body with her own. She looked up at Mickey. "I'll take her place."

"I don't want you, old woman," Mickey sneered with derision. "Get out of my way." He kicked, his boot connecting with the side of Maggie's head. She cried out and fell to the side, allowing Mickey to drag Caroline by her hair into the middle of the room.

"Ever had a dick up your ass?" Mickey grunted, pushing Caroline onto her stomach and straddling her thighs as he unbuckled his belt.

The room came into sharp focus for Mackenzie, the cottony haze from lack of oxygen dissipating into dreadful clarity.

Leon had moved closer, riveted by the scene before him with one hand already shoved down the front of his pants. His gun lay, forgotten, on the nightstand.

Mackenzie didn't think. She had the weapon in her hand before she'd decided to move. She noted absently her shakes had gone, her hands were steady. Mackenzie didn't even worry she wouldn't know where the safety was or how to take it off. It was easy. It was right there, and gave a satisfying click. And she raised the gun right behind Leon's head, and she pulled the trigger. Easy.

The blast of sound was shocking, and she faltered at the kickback. Mickey was screaming something, and wrestling with the jeans around his ankles. He had a gun in his back pocket and she knew she needed to kill him. Now. Because once he had it in his hands, they were going to wish they were dead.

And so she did. She raised the gun again, feeling the pull in her shoulders, and squeezed the trigger.

Mickey fell backwards, his lifeless body flopping awkwardly to the floor.

Seconds ticked by.

Mackenzie finally lowered the gun, letting it hang loosely from her fingers. The metallic scent of blood was overwhelming and her ears were ringing in the sudden silence.

Maggie and Caroline, both still on the floor, stared at her. Stunned.

No one moved.

Outside, a motorcycle roared by.

"Fuck. Fuck-fuck-fuckity-fuck," Mackenzie whispered, stepping backward to sit on the edge of the bed. "I killed them."

"You did good, girlie." Maggie stumbled to her feet, holding her head and wincing.

"Let's get the fuck out of here," Caroline said, reaching for Mickey's gun.

She was wet and sticky, wiping bloody hands futilely against her equally bloody jeans.

Mackenzie nodded, resolutely not looking at the bodies of Leon or Mickey. "We have less than an hour before we're taken downstairs. We need to move quick."

Caroline heaved to her feet and ran to the bathroom, where Mackenzie could hear her vomiting. She came out with a clean face and hands, and lips tight with determination.

They were getting the hell out of here.

It was almost too easy, softly opening the door and finding an empty corridor.

"Left or right?" Maggie asked.

"Right. There were stairs next to the elevator," Mackenzie replied, Leon's gun heavy in her hand.

The corridor stretched before them, dotted with room doors that threatened to open and expose them at any moment.

Mackenzie ran forward, reaching the elevator first and unable to stifle a scream when she saw the floor numbers lighting up as it ascended. "Hurry!"

Caroline was supporting a lurching Maggie, and Mackenzie dashed back to help, practically dragging them to the fire escape doorway.

The fourth floor lit up on the elevator.

The fire door was heavy, and for a moment, Mackenzie panicked that it was locked. When it grudgingly opened, she pushed Caroline and Maggie through, following so hard on their heels both of them stumbled.

The door was swinging closed, the strut mechanism slowing its movement until Mackenzie yanked on the handle. It hadn't latched properly when she heard the terrifying *ding* of the elevator reaching their level.

Oh god, oh god, oh god.

The three of them froze, soundless, expecting the door to burst open.

Nothing.

"Quick, quick!" Mackenzie hustled them, ducking beneath Maggie's other shoulder. But they couldn't fit three abreast down the stairwell and she paused, unsure if she should lead the way, or protect their rear.

A flash of doubt had her focus wavering. What did she

think she was doing? She was going to get them all killed. Or worse.

"Girlie! Get moving!" Maggie hissed, pushing her forward. "Don't lose it now, we need you."

It was enough to clear her indecision. She leaped forward, gun raised. The slap of their feet descending the stairs was unbearably loud. Level four. Level three. Level two. They paused.

"Let's stop on level one and see if there's a service elevator," Mackenzie said. "If we keep going down these stairs, we'll end up in the lobby, right?"

"Exactly where we *don't* want to be," agreed Caroline.

They rushed the last level of stairs, listening at the fire door for any sound beyond.

"I think I should go out," Mackenzie stated. "I've got the gun and, if I get caught, they'll only have me and not all of us."

"What? No!" Caroline protested.

"Just let me find where the service elevator is and make sure there's no one around," Mackenzie insisted. And then, not waiting for their reply, she pushed the door open cautiously and slipped through. It snicked closed, and she was alone.

Adrenaline spiked her throbbing heart, and she scanned left and right, searching for a telltale exit sign. Nothing. She ran to the very end of the corridor, terrified at every moment of discovery. It finished with a wall of glass overlooking the street outside. No service elevator.

Mackenzie remembered a nightmare from her childhood, where she was trapped in an endless maze with no hope of escape, and despair threatened to swamp her.

Retracing her steps, she reached for the fire door when

she noticed an unobtrusive door beside it, with a small Service sign.

"Oh god!" she gasped, pulling it open to reveal a second set of elevators. "Oh god, thank you!"

She flung open the fire door to a cowering Caroline and Maggie, who followed her without question to the service elevator.

"Kitchen?" Her finger hovered over the control panel of buttons.

"Laundry," Maggie said. "They'll be using the kitchen, but I'll wager they haven't set foot in the laundry."

Mackenzie's stomach dropped along with the elevator. What if there was no exit from the laundry? She hated that there was only one way to find out.

———

"CAN WE TRUST HIM?" Jim said, rubbing his hand roughly against his whiskered cheeks.

Jake was crouched between Buddy and Jesse, with Jim taking up the rear, waiting behind the row of dumpsters at the back of the hotel for Zed's signal.

"We don't have a choice," Jake snapped.

"Are you still bleeding?" Jesse asked, eyeing Jake's side.

"It's fine. You patched it up, and it's stopped bleeding. Quit thinking about me and get your mind on what's about to go down."

Jake was tense and coiled. Ready.

Zed was going to take them in through the kitchen and escort them to the suite upstairs, promising to act as a decoy if needed. In return, he wanted to leave with them.

As much as Jake wanted to go in with guns blazing and kill every single last one of the bikers, stealth was the only way he knew he could get Mac out safely. And failure was not an option.

When Zed's arm stuck through the kitchen door, waving an empty garbage bag, they sprang to life, running for the back entry.

"They haven't brought the women down yet, but everyone's heading to the ballroom to hear Gemma announce the lottery," Zed said, motioning them into the stainless-steel industrial space. "We can take the service elevator."

Jake handed Zed their only spare weapon, a small hand pistol. "Know how to use this?"

Zed nodded, and Jim glared first at Jake, then at the kid.

"Don't make us regret giving that to you," Jesse muttered.

The five of them crowded in front of the doors to the elevator, going over Zed's directions for the fifth floor. Jake needed them to shut up and do the job. His skin was crawling with suppressed anticipation. He needed Mackenzie back in his arms.

"Ah, shit." Zed inhaled, eyes trained on the lit-up floor numbers. "There's someone coming down!"

"What? Fuck! I just pushed the button to make it stop," Buddy cried.

"What do we do?" Zed asked, wide-eyed.

"I'm not getting shot in the back as I run away," Jake declared, widening his stance and raising his AR-15. Shoulder to shoulder, the others did the same.

"No hesitation. Shoot to kill," he instructed, voice firm.

The *ding* of the elevator arriving was innocuously cheery.

Jake's finger twitched on the trigger as the door began sliding open.

Inhale. Fire on the exhale.

He breathed deep, blood thundered in his ears.

"Jake!"

"Stop!" Jake's shout was hoarse. Ravaged. He staggered backward.

"Caroline!" Jim surged forward, knocking Maggie as he clutched his wife. "Oh god, Caro!"

Mackenzie blinked at Jake, steady hands pointing a Glock at his chest.

"Whoa. Mac, it's okay." He raised his hands, reaching for her. "Come on, baby. Come out here to me."

Slowly, she lowered the pistol before launching herself into his arms. Her shoulders shook with sobs and he held her tight, tighter. It was hard to breathe around his heart in his throat.

"She's hurt! We need help!" Jim roared, oblivious to the noise he was making. Jake looked up to see him patting Caroline feverishly, looking for the source of the blood.

Jesus Christ. Caroline was covered in it. How was she still standing?

He pried Mackenzie's reluctant body from his, setting her away so he could see her properly.

"Are you hurt?" Terror bled through his question.

"I'm fine. She's fine. We need to go!" Mackenzie's eyes were wild, her breathing choppy.

"Do you have your inhaler?" he asked, prepared to carry her out if necessary.

"I'm fine," she repeated impatiently. "How do we get out of here?"

Her urgency finally registered through his euphoria. They weren't safe yet.

"This way," Zed said, starting forward.

As a tight group, they ran for the exit, Jesse and Buddy carrying Maggie between them. Bursting through the door into the night, Jim took the lead, directing them to where they'd left the truck.

"Go, go!" Jim urged, almost stumbling as he looked over his shoulder at the hotel.

At any moment, Jake expected the night to erupt in gunfire.

He tugged on Mackenzie's hand, urging her to run faster.

And then they were there, the truck parked inconveniently beneath the bright spotlight of a street lamp. Jesse and Buddy helped Maggie into the bed of the truck and jumped in after her, while Jim pushed Caroline into the front passenger seat.

"Um, I can still come, right?" Zed's hand was on Jake's arm, grasping. "Please say you'll take me with you."

"Get in the truck, kid," he replied gruffly.

JIM DROVE to the outskirts of Dutton, putting distance between them and the gang, and outrunning the glow from the streetlamps. The craving to disappear into the darkness was deep in Jake, and he suspected Jim felt the same.

"What happened back there? How did you get away?" Jake asked. "And if that's not your blood, Caroline, whose is it?"

"I... it's—"

"It's a long story," Mackenzie interrupted. "Let's not go over it now."

The truck slowed, and then stopped, idling on an asphalt road that had petered to gravel. Jim asked, "Where to?"

Jake looked at Zed. "Any ideas?"

"Sanford. We're going back to Sanford!" Caroline cried. "My kids!"

"Honey, we can't go back," Jim said somberly. "Not now. We'll get the kids, but we can't go back now."

"Oh god," Mackenzie leaned forward. "Gemma wants the whiskey from the distillery. They're definitely going back to Sanford."

Caroline's anguished sobs filled the truck, and Mackenzie burrowed her head against Jake's chest. He pulled at her until she was sitting across his lap, her hammering heart beating against his.

The truck shifted as Jesse jumped from the back, making his way to Jim's window. "That farmhouse isn't far from here, the one we went to after we got away from them last time." He looked at Jake. "It's only about a mile away, right?"

"Yeah, good idea. It's far enough away to avoid detection, and they've already looted out this way. Hopefully, there's no reason for them to come back."

"Do you think they'll look for us?" Mackenzie asked, lifting her tear-stained face to him.

"Maybe. But they don't know we were there with a truck. They'll think you're on foot and shouldn't search too far from the hotel."

"We need to get Maggie somewhere I can look at her. I think she has a concussion," Jesse said. "Jake, can you direct Jim?"

Jake nodded, and they started off again, slower this time because Jim wasn't risking using the truck's head-lights to show the way. He was light-headed with relief when the red-roofed farmhouse materialized out of the darkness.

"Think anyone's home?" Jim asked, cutting the ignition.

"Not sure. We didn't think so," Jake answered, searching the front of the house for any sign of habitation.

Jesse appeared again at Jim's window.

"Wait here and I'll scout it," he said, running off on light feet.

Jim turned to look at Zed, who'd made himself small and unobtrusive in the back seat. "Hope this stray is as helpful as that one."

Jake had a good feeling about Zed, but knew the kid would have to earn their trust. In the meantime, Jim would keep a sharp eye on him.

"It's clear," Jesse called, jogging back.

"We'll be along in a bit," Jake called, as the others made their way inside.

He sat in the backseat with Mackenzie in silence, watching the glow of a flashlight come from inside the house.

"Jake, I—"

"Wait. I need to apologize. I've been stupid. So fucking stupid." Jake turned Mackenzie until she was straddling him and he could cup her face with his hands, his thumbs running over her cheeks. "I'm so sorry, babe. For everything."

"It's not your fault... is it?" Her pained confusion slayed him.

"You were right. You didn't need my protection, you needed my support. And what's worse, I trusted Townsend over you," he admitted.

"You... you told Townsend about the meeting at the distillery?" She stiffened, her hands dropping from his forearms.

"What? No! Of course not! Why would you think that?" Now he was confused. "Jesus, Mac. Why would you think that? I might not have agreed with what they said at the meeting, but I would never have betrayed everyone. Betrayed *you*."

"How did he know about it, then?"

"Trent and Gavin. Assholes," he spat.

"Oh." She softened again, her thighs molding over his and her face clearing. "So, Sanford. We can't go back?"

"Not at the moment, no."

"I wish we had Dex." Her shoulders slumped. "You could probably go back, though," she whispered. "If you snuck in, Townsend might still trust you."

"Mac! I'm not going anywhere without you, ever again. And you can't think I'd support Townsend after this?"

"Before, you were on his side."

"Before, I was stupid. Now, I'm on your side."

He brought his lips to hers, so close he didn't know who was inhaling and who was exhaling.

"You still love me?" she breathed.

"Always."

"Even though I don't have deodorant and I smell?"

"Yes, babe."

"And now that we have no toothpaste?"

"Yes, babe."

"You know I love you, right?"

"About time you admitted it." He grinned, slanting smiling lips over hers. She opened for him, their tongues tangling and their souls realigning.

Because, this? Was everything. Nothing else mattered.

EPILOGUE

"Oh, god!" Mackenzie whimpered.

"Not god. Use my name, Mac," Jake chastised.

"Jake," she moaned into his mouth, tightening her legs around his hips as he thrust again, her ass sliding on the laundry table.

His big hands grasped her thighs and pulled her back onto him, his cock driving deep.

"So good, so good," she chanted, leaning back on her hands and tilting her pelvis forward. She wanted more. She wanted *everything*.

She and Jake had spent the last three nights since they'd been at the farmhouse muffling their hunger for each other, aware of their proximity to the others. But today, hiding out in the laundry room, Mackenzie couldn't contain the utter divinity of their bodies moving together.

When Jake leaned over and bit into her neck, sucking hard enough to bruise, she screamed.

His teeth scraped down her skin, mouth latching onto her exposed breast, tongue flicking and lips sucking. His hands rose to cup her, pushing her breasts together and groaning as he lavished attention between them.

The tug and pull on her nipples was an exquisite frustration; she needed that friction lower, and Jake had slowed to a gentle rocking of his hips, which was *beyond* maddening.

"Jake!" She yanked at his hair, hard. "Enough. You need to fuck me. Now."

"So bossy." He smirked, raising his head to nip at her pouting lips.

She growled, and he laughed.

"Okay, babe. Okay."

He pressed her thighs wider and pushed deeper, holding tight to her hips and fucking deliciously deep. Mackenzie squirmed, wedging her hand between their bodies so she could circle her clit. Fast. Faster.

On the precipice, Mackenzie stilled to watch the pure masculine beauty of Jake's features. His eyes were closed, his concentration complete as he pounded his devotion into her.

"I'm close, Mac," he groaned, throwing his head back.

"Let go," she urged, watching.

"Not until you do."

His eyes opened, tethering her to this moment. To him. Caught in his gaze, she climaxed with unmitigated intensity.

They rested, forehead to forehead, panting. The power had gone out the day before, and not come back on. Mackenzie shivered, her bare skin breaking out in goosebumps. Without electricity for heating, they'd need firewood. Winter was coming.

"Buddy and Jim are going to chop wood tomorrow,"

Jake said, reading her mind. "You still okay with Jesse and I going across to the barn to bury Lee?"

She nodded.

Jake had committed to his promise of backing off on the overbearing protective bullshit, and she appreciated the new transparency to their relationship.

"Maggie's going to show Zed and I how to set up a greenhouse. We're going to grow vegetables with seeds we found in the back shed," she said. "Zed's got some ideas on how to pump water from the stream, too."

"He's a good kid," Jake acknowledged. "Has he said much about his family?"

"He doesn't want to talk about it."

The sadness was pervasive, mourning Grams, losing contact with Chloe, Rachel and Kat, and coming to terms with their ordeal at the Prestige Plaza. She still had flashbacks of shooting Leon and Mickey, which left her shaky. It was hard to wrap her head around the fact she'd killed another human. *Two* humans. When that happened, Jake wrapped his arms around her and rocked, not saying a word.

It helped that Jake and Jim had been giving them all lessons on using each of the different guns they had, although they were still too wary to fire them, in case the sound gave them away. Occasionally, in the distance, they'd hear motorcycles, but so far, no one had disturbed them.

Knowing their friends and family in Sanford weren't safe was a burden they had to bear, harder for Caroline than anyone. She was withdrawn and listless, pining for her children. It broke Mackenzie's heart and was driving Jim to despair.

Maggie, on the other hand, was driven by a burning need to destroy the Prestige Plaza and all its inhabitants, followed swiftly by Townsend. She'd taken the news of Donny's murder hard and spent her waking hours plotting vengeance. They debated constantly over the best course of action; infiltrate Sanford and overthrow the council, or get their people out and abandon the town, making a new home for themselves.

Because while the knowledge of their immunity to Sy-V was a relief, it didn't mitigate their current circumstances.

The reality of the world they now inhabited.

And so they planned. And waited. And survived. Together.

THE END

STAY IN TOUCH!

Want to keep up-to-date on what's happening in Jacqueline's world? Sign up to her email newsletter! You'll receive behind-the-scenes photos, romance memes, book reviews and other awesome stuff. (Jacqueline is well aware "awesome stuff" is a broad term).

Sign up! https://bit.ly/2W1y31C

Or, you can jump over to her Facebook group - Love at The End of The World for giveaways, memes and more!

ABOUT

Jacqueline picked up her first Mills & Boon novel when she was fourteen, and fell head over heels in love with the romance of a happily-ever-after. Sweet Valley High just couldn't compete after she got hooked on dashing heroes and plucky heroines.

She has a Bachelor Degree in Print Journalism but, having always been tempted to embellish the facts of a story, decided she was more suited to writing works of fiction. She writes in between wrangling two daughters and her very own tall, handsome husband. *wink wink*

For more on Jacqueline, you can find her at:
www.jacquelinehayley.com
Instagram @jacquelinehayleyromance
Facebook /jacquelinehayleyromance

ALSO BY JACQUELINE HAYLEY

THE AFTER SERIES

Prequel (novella)

The Beginning of the End

Book 2

After Yesterday

Coming soon...

Book 3

After Tomorrow

Book 4

After The End

JACQUELINE HAYLEY

PANDEMIC

THE BEGINNING
of the end

PREQUEL TO THE AFTER SERIES

THE BEGINNING OF THE END

It's the beginning of the end...

Seventeen-year old Cassie is home alone planning her first ever house party, unaware the deadly Sy-V virus has begun to ravage humanity. But when most of her classmates fail to show for the party, she can't contact her parents, and her best friend becomes sick, in the blink of an eye her entire world changes.

Stephen has lived next door to Cassie forever, only as the virus tears their friends and family apart, the boy-next-door suddenly becomes a hero burning brightly in the devastating dark of their new world. But no way could she fall in love. Not at this moment. With this boy. Right?

This novella is a prequel to The After Series, which begins with *After Today*.

AFTER
yesterday

JACQUELINE HAYLEY

Surviving the virus was one thing, surviving humanity *after* is another.

Rachel Davenport has always liked things ordered and neat, so when the Sy-V virus decimated the world around her, she was left reeling. With winter closing in and danger everywhere she turns, the last thing she needs is the unexpected arrival of her former high school sweetheart—a man who left her without so much as a goodbye.

When James O'Connor crossed the country to declare his love for Rachel, the girl he left behind eight years ago, he knew he'd have a fight on his hands. But the girl he left has become a woman he struggles to recognize. As the apocalypse forces him to balance his morality against Rachel's determination, can he cross the chasm growing between them?

As humanity crumbles around them and survival becomes everything, James and Rachel must choose between what is smart, and what is right.

The stakes are higher than ever... can love survive a second chance?

Printed in Great Britain
by Amazon

87872139R00149